LORDS OF
THE STORM

DOCTOR WHO – THE MISSING ADVENTURES

Also available:

LORDS OF THE STORM

David A. McIntee

DOCTOR WHO

THE MISSING ADVENTURES

First published in Great Britain in 1995 by
Doctor Who Books
an imprint of Virgin Publishing Ltd
332 Ladbroke Grove
London W10 5AH

ISBN 0 426 20460 3

Cover illustration by Alister Pearson

Typeset by Galleon Typesetting, Ipswich
Printed and bound in Great Britain by
Mackays of Chatham PLC

Introduction

Free! Free at last! Of historicals, that is. Not that I don't
like doing them, but I seriously needed a change. Speaking of which, since *Sanctuary* was a more emotionally
based book, with a grim ending, I reckon it's definitely
time for a different tone. Therefore, this is more your
old-fashioned space opera with shootouts, spaceships and
lots of corridors. Since nobody really writes space opera
these days, I suppose that makes it historical – or at least
nostalgic – after a fashion.

But, enough of that. Thanks are due to the regular cast
at Virgin, and Alister Pearson for the cover with its
excellent likenesses, but especially Terrance Dicks, whose
idea for a Scottish-named Sontaran was better than mine.
(The shame, the shame . . .) Also, to avoid confusion, I'd
just like to make it perfectly clear that this storyline was
submitted at least six months before *Shakedown* was even
a glint in Terrance's eye.

Now, go strap yourselves in; I'm going to make the
jump to lightspeed . . .

For Paul, Martin, Keith and John, for what it's
worth after what I've done to them. Now that
Shakedown is a sequel to this, guys, do you think
I could sue Dreamwatch for plagiarism –
retrospectively, as it were?

Prelude

The Lords of the Storm are also approaching.
Their war vehicles are nearing the land . . .

The computer-enhanced starbow shrank and faded from the forward viewer as the laws of physics reasserted themselves once the Goban-class-III gunship was back in realspace. It was a disorientating experience, but the refreshing energy burn Lieutenant Loxx had taken made the warp-jump pass more easily for him. The steady repetition of the distress signal from somewhere out in the diamond-scattered blackness was a point of focus and purpose, however, and one which demanded concentration.

The faintly misty ribbon of stars that was draped across the infinite darkness like a fur stole slipped past to the left as Loxx switched over to the sublight drive and wheeled his ungainly gunship around in search of the source of the signal which had alerted his squadron.

Rescuing the personnel of the cruiser in distress meant little to either himself or the cruiser's crew, but destroying the aggressors who had surrounded it was quite a different matter. There would be great glory in punishing the enemy for this outrage, he thought with relish. None of these reflections distracted him from punching up the displays of his passive sensors. Such a battle as had been reported would be putting out enough energy for him to track across half the quadrant without giving away his position by sending out active sensor transmissions.

The reaction came almost instantaneously, three red

1

enemy arrowheads dancing around the green oval of the harassed cruiser. With a quick glance to check that everything on the weapons panel was fully functional, Loxx armed torpedoes and banked towards the engagement site.

Several brighter specks of light flickered ahead in the fringes of the Lagoon Nebula; flashes of focused solar radiation being directed at the tumbling cruiser by the three diamond-form enemy corvettes which were clustered around it. As yet there was no sign of a fighter escort, and the corvettes exhibited no behaviour to indicate that they had detected the gunship squadron. 'Transfer aft shield power to boost forward deflectors until we're through their line,' Loxx broadcast to his wingmen. 'Fire when ready.'

Loxx liked this sort of stand-off surprise attack. When the corvette detected his squadron, it would launch its fighters to intercept them. But this would be too late to save the corvette from torpedoes which were already running. That way, he and his squadron could enjoy the thrill of direct combat instead of running a gauntlet to get a closer torpedo shot.

The sensor-lock warning light flashed the instant Loxx's torpedoes left their launch pads; the corvettes had detected the torpedo launch and locked on, but they were too late. The needle-like shapes of enemy fighters spread out across the gunboat's approach vector, bursting forth from the corvettes like spores from a puffball. The gunship vibrated as the first missiles impacted on the forward deflector shields, but Loxx was unconcerned; his speed had taken him to within the enemy's safety range. The enemy missiles' safety systems ensured that they didn't arm until they had travelled far enough that they wouldn't just lock on to the ship which launched them instead of on to their target. In any case, the double shield strength would take far more punishment than these mere pinpricks.

As he sped past the fighters, the corvette ahead suddenly

2

shuddered, too slow to evade the torpedoes. The glow at the heart of the ship dimmed as the torpedo impacts disrupted its power supply. Someone on the cruiser had great clarity of purpose, Loxx noticed, as the larger ship's gunners took advantage of the corvette's distress to open fire with a full broadside. The corvette shuddered momentarily, then flew apart into millions of fragments as the cruiser's broadside sheared through the corvette's faceted hull and sent a spreading cloud of twinkling crystalline filaments fading into the nebula's lucent dust cloud.

The fighters wheeled and spun with remarkable unity of formation in an attempt to cut off the gunships, but Loxx quickly dropped into a position to flank them on the port side, evening out his shields just in case a fighter was quick enough to outflank him. He doubted this would happen, though; the gunship was slower, but the fighters would sacrifice speed to remain in strategic formation. As Loxx expected, the fighters spun as one, to take the nearest fighter out of his line of fire. In doing so, however, they left a gap open which afforded a clear shot at the fourth ship in the line.

Loosing his missile, which had no range safeguards, Loxx swung wide as the enemy fighter vanished with a brief flicker of ignited atmosphere. The formation closed ranks, but the minuscule amount of time this took enabled the other gunships to swarm around them in unpredictable patterns, missiles streaking like meteors to extinguish the tiny sparks of life in the fighters.

Loxx allowed himself a brief smile. This was far more exhilarating even than the delicious energy burn which so exquisitely refreshed him in quieter moments. The visible panic with which the enemy reacted to their lightning-fast attack was exquisite, reminding Loxx of the joy of victory at previous battles.

Evidently recognizing the danger, one of the two remaining corvettes rolled away from the cruiser, bringing its main batteries to bear on the swarm of gunships. Loxx reduced his velocity, to give more time for sustained fire upon the corvette, whose main batteries would be too unwieldy to track effectively and lock upon him at even half speed.

Keeping his target reticule locked satisfyingly upon the mirrored facet of the corvette's bridge, Loxx launched a torpedo from each of the six forward launchers. Streamers of focused solar radiation stabbed out through the darkness, consistently slashing through the point where the gunship had just been, but never just where it now was. The entire hull of the corvette shuddered as the multiple impacts hammered into its bridge.

The ship's colour abruptly altered as a crack lanced out through the crystalline hull, refracting the starlight slightly differently to the rest of the ship. Loxx could hardly believe his luck, half-expecting the crack to vanish like an illusion, even as he switched his weapons power to the main cannons and opened fire on this new weak-point in the multifaceted enemy hull.

The inpouring of energy was too much for the now-flawed hull to bear, and it came apart in a painfully slow ballet of spinning fragments. The atmosphere ignited an instant later, and Loxx was momentarily blinded by the flare, though he felt his vessel shudder as pieces of debris skimmed past the shields.

The last corvette was backing off from the cruiser when Loxx's vision cleared, though it was keeping up a steady stream of fire into the cratered hull. He transferred power back to the torpedo-arming circuits and targeted the corvette, but too late.

For a moment, as its drive unit flared into life, Loxx thought the corvette was about to make the jump into warp. Instead, it leapt forward, directly into the slowly tumbling cruiser.

The too-few tiny flashes of launching escape pods that dotted the cruiser's hull were almost instantly swallowed up by the far greater blast of energy that was released upon impact, as the two ships were reduced to their component molecules in the explosion that ensued.

4

Loxx had to admire the enemy's courage for that act, though of course the loss of so many of his comrades encouraged his resolve to kill twice as many of the enemy in the next engagement. The last couple of fighters flashed out of existence, and Loxx saw that there were only two fewer green 'friendly' markers on his sensor display than there had been when his squadron had launched.

He knew that there would probably be a few enemy survivors floating around outside, but wasn't interested in them. If he saw one, a single shot would dispose of it, and he knew the other pilots would feel the same way. He doubted that any of the cruiser's escape pods would have survived, but knew it was his duty to look.

Setting the gunship on to a spiral search pattern at minimum speed, he switched his communications system to the emergency beacon frequency. Several escape pods were transmitting, and he locked on to the nearest, preparing to dock with it. It was a shame that these few had been denied their glorious death, but Loxx knew they would be reassured by the thought that they would have another chance. Each of them would prefer to die in a closer and more personal combat.

No doubt, therefore, they would all redouble their contribution to the war effort.

Prologue

AD **2370**

The sulphurous mass of the gas giant Indra was calm
against the glittering expanse of stars, its rings of rocky
particles canted to reflect the sun with all the striations of
a slice of ancient redwood. Though half of the storm-
streaked giant was in theoretical night, sufficient solar
energy was retained in its magnetosphere to make the
night side glow faintly of its own accord.

This did little to lighten the infernal hue of the third
moon, the peaks of its orange mountains frosted with the
white of frozen sulphur dioxide. It passed over Indra's
clouds like some crusted globule of clotted blood, the
pale peaks flaring intermittently with massive electrical
discharges. Writhing fingers of energy sparkled over the
mountain-tops before being quickly sucked back into the
collection aerials that were securely fixed there.

Lower, past the horizon of this airless moon, the five
million or so amps of electrical charge that Indra blasted
out were channelled down into the storage cells built
into the rocky foundations under the heavily radiation-
shielded complex of squat buildings and passages which
cowered against the darkened cliffs.

Armoured viewports lined the outer wall of one
passage halfway between the light-speckled slab of the
living quarters and the domed central control. Bas-
relief friezes of the ancient gods decorated the spotless
inner wall, as in so many of the complex's passageways.

Chandra kept half an eye on the landscape as he strolled along this corridor, feeling a decade younger — and slimmer — in the one-sixth Earth gravity of the small moon.

It was like looking out on a jagged sea, lit by the fiery glow of a sluggish river of molten rock which flowed past the base of the cliff, hundreds of yards below the lowest level of the complex. No comparison with Dante's inferno had ever really occurred to him, though he had heard several people comment on this, but he had always considered it particularly apt that the first crew to discover the satellite had named it Agni, after the god of fire.

The thick radiation door separating the wide passageway from the work complex itself slid aside with a heavy metallic clanking, and Chandra dismissed the local landscape from his mind. It was easy enough to do, as he had seen it every day for the last eight years, except while on leave.

Ahead, the corridor widened still further, branching off here and there to lead the staff to the various sections on this level. Chandra went only as far as the nearest lift, however, which was empty so early in the day. He looked up at the camera and microphone set into the ceiling. 'Level three, central control.' The lift started into motion, humming smoothly upwards for a few seconds before opening on to the split-level central control for the station.

None of the colourful murals and friezes which decorated the rest of the complex had been placed in this spotlessly white and silver chamber, lest they distract the attention from the various indicators and read-outs which were a constant source of multicoloured reflections in the central work pit.

The morning shift of overalled technicians was already casting watchful eyes over the instruments that monitored the energy transferred through the station. Chandra secretly suspected that the station would operate with a fraction of the staff, but since there was room for all here, who was he to deprive men of work?

It was really nature which did the most important job, of course. Agni's position in the densest part of the synchrotron radiation belt in Indra's vast magnetosphere formed one terminal of a magnetic flux tube: a conduit for vast electrical discharges, which could be used and directed.

Every day for eight years, Chandra had sat here with his tea, ordering occasional maintenance and making reports in triplicate back to the sixth moon. Still, at least it would be the harvest season soon, and the station would brighten considerably with the arrival of the airavata harvesters. There had been excellent breeding conditions in Indra's atmosphere, Chandra had noticed, so the spoils should bring the colony a good return from the spacer corporations.

All that was still a few weeks off, though, and the banalities of normal work were closer at hand as he lowered his rounded frame into the seat in his office on the circular catwalk which rimmed the work pit. 'Anything interesting?' he asked the world at large.

'Not really,' Noonian, his lanky and unkempt-looking engineering chief replied, settling down with a strong coffee. He was rarely to be found in his own office on this upper level. 'Sadruddin's wife still hasn't wakened from her coma.'

'I meant on the station, not on the holo-soaps.'

Noonian grinned through his beard. 'Even less interesting. The flux tube is still discharging within normal limits. We had a short-out in the Vaisyas' snack vendor on level four, so we're requesting supplies to be passed down from the Kshatriyas' dispensers.'

'Make sure the Kshatriyas know there'll be no maintenance for them if they don't agree. We can't go to Sudra dispensers.'

'Definitely not. Oh, and the cat still hasn't got rid of any of the mice in hydroponics. Personally, I think the mice have made some kind of deal with it.'

'We should make it a better offer. Are you still –' He was cut off by a call from one of the consoles in the work pit. 'What is it?'

'Supervisor!' The operator, whom Chandra thought looked still adolescent, waved at the console. 'Look at these readings from the navigational beacons; some kind of interference in our Doppler-shift readings has just started.'

'Microscopic gravitational lensing, perhaps,' Chandra said thoughtfully, scratching his jowl.

'Or maybe the hyperspace egress of a cloaked ship,' Noonian suggested.

'The first Spinward harvester ship's not due for a couple of months.'

'Hyperspace egress,' the young technician reported finally. 'Estimated mass at least fifty thousand metric tonnes, course unknown.'

'Begin full scan for gravitational lensing effects closer in,' Chandra ordered, 'then contact Raghi and ask if there's a ship due in.'

Major Karne watched the moon grow larger in the central viewing tank, but kept his thoughts to himself. Commander Loxx didn't bother to wonder what those thoughts might be. 'Take the ship out of Clear,' Karne commanded him.

Unconcerned at the difference in instrumentation between his old gunboat and this destroyer, Loxx was adjusting the controls even as the last syllables left Karne's lips. His superior's features – the rotten-wood shade of the Jingo clan – were inscrutable, Loxx felt, but at least he seemed to know what he was doing when it came to mounting surprise attacks. Perhaps that was why they had worked so well together for the last ten years. The prediction Loxx had made so long ago about the destroyed cruiser's lone survivor had been proved right. Karne had indeed redoubled his efforts – he seemed to be interested in everything.

This, Loxx thought, should be a quick and clean victory, just the way things ought to be.

Screens all over central control flashed into life, displaying scrolling analyses of sensor information, or computer-enhanced images of the source of the alarm. Ignoring the pictures, which as yet showed only stars, the supervisor skimmed through one sensor log on the nearest monitor. 'Unidentified ship materializing at fifty thousand miles.'

'She's arming forward weapons array,' someone called out in a shocked tone.

Chandra leapt to his feet, hurrying down into the centre of the room. 'Raise the meteor shield!'

'It won't keep out their energy blasts,' Noonian said softly, so that only Chandra could hear. He took another sip of coffee, as if the emergency didn't bother him.

Chandra scratched his head, fingers running through the thinning hair. 'Maybe not, but unless they get lucky and hit the generators, they can't come in for a landing while it's still up. It only needs to hold long enough for us to get a message back to Raghi.'

The bulbous grey ship shuddered into visibility, a mass of clotted metal like some monstrous tuber. 'Forward meson cannons armed,' the weapons officer reported.

Major Karne didn't answer immediately, instead watching as the rocky moon grew larger on the forward screen. He had always liked to launch an attack from as close in to the target as possible; it was both more satisfying to see the enemy's pain close at hand, and less likely to give the victim time to respond. 'Range to target?'

'Fifty thousand miles. They have raised a meteor deflection barrier.'

'Prudent of them, I'm sure. Scan for defensive weaponry.'

'Low-power masers only.'

'Lock forward cannons on maser batteries.' Karne

10

couldn't help but feel a thrill at the approach of the decisive moment. 'Fire when ready.' He relished the words.

'Lock masers and fire,' Chandra ordered, knowing that it wasn't going to be enough.

An older man with greying hair and a red uniform played his hands across the defence console. 'Firing. Their shields are holding.'

'Divert storage cell power to the meteor shield.'

'Rerouting power supply,' Noonian called out.

'They've locked on to our masers; be quick with those shields.'

'Fifty per cent increase in shield power achieved.'

'They're fi–' A tremendous blast of sound suddenly exploded around the control crew. The lighting flickered, while the sparks from exploding junction-boxes made up for the sudden dimness as the supervisor watched the walls shudder under the impact. A couple of technicians were catapulted over the railing from the upper level as the instrumentation there tore itself apart. A distant booming howl echoed through the corridors. 'Damage report!'

The officer who had been manning the defence grid's console picked himself up with a hacking cough. 'Maser batteries three and four destroyed. One and two operational, but power down 65 per cent.'

There was another thunderous report, and thin streamers of dust from the ceiling formed insubstantial pillars here and there around the room. 'Transfer emergency power to the masers,' Chandra gasped out through the choking dust turned to an infernal cloud by the emergency lights. 'Return fire!'

'We haven't got any masers any more!'

'They'll try to break through the shield, then. Transfer everything except life support to bolster the meteor shield, then open up the armoury and have the Kshatriyas move into defensive positions.'

11

'I have Raghi Control,' the communications officer announced.

Chandra wasn't foolish enough to think that contacting home would save the staff, but Raghi might be the next target, so he had to warn them. 'Put them through to my desk.'

The armoury contained only thunderflashes and a variety of stun-guns, designed to paralyse or stun through judicious use of sound waves, since energy weapons might disrupt the delicate electronic systems around them, and no one in his right mind would risk compromising the station's structural integrity with explosives or projectile devices. Few of the station staff were Kshatriyas, the warrior class, and so most of them held their sonic stunners awkwardly in sweaty palms.

A large group of nervous personnel, led by a sergeant in a rumpled red Kshatriya uniform, took up positions by the inner doors of the hangar level. Squeezing themselves behind any available pillars or furniture at the relatively spacious junction, they all started now and again as screeching vibrations from the station's strained power systems made the floor quiver.

'Hangar level secure, but –' The sergeant trailed off in surprise as a figure in gun-metal armour coalesced out of thin air and turned to face him. The faint buzzing of stun-guns that filled the corridor didn't even distract the invader, who blew the sergeant out of his way with a rapid stream of high-energy particles from the weapon he held in one hand.

The other civilian defenders all turned and ran, but the invader gunned down another two of them even before a new pair of armoured intruders materialized at the far end of the passage, cutting them off.

The remaining Kshatriyas died in an instant, their red-uniformed bodies toppling like discarded marionettes. The invaders ignored the irradiated corpses, leaving them where they fell, as they clustered the terrified civilians around the inner pressure door to the hangar. The first invader who had arrived pressed a button on a small box that was attached to his wide belt. *'Van ghor-saan nu; klam gral tonn.'*

Deep in the rock behind the station's buildings, a virtually bottomless shaft enclosed the network of huge crystalline columns of the storage cells that held the charge drawn down by the collection aerials. Shining metal struts supported the columns, gleaming in a strangely oily fashion. The light was dim, and pulsed with the faint static discharge of escaping photons as a number of mixed Kshatriyas and technicians dragged heavy storage boxes across the main doorway.

Three more invaders formed behind this embryonic defensive position, and shot the armed defenders in the back before they even knew what was happening.

One of them touched the box hooked on to his belt. *'Gen ghor-saan nu; stang tonn.'*

Fifteen million miles from Agni, a white-flecked world the colour of petroleum green wheeled across the plane of the ecliptic. Ripples in the clouds were the tell-tale scars cut into the atmosphere by jagged peaks below, proving that this was no ivory-smooth billiard ball.

Not far south of the equator was a crescent barrier of the highest peaks, separating a number of lakes from the azure sea. Inland, the mountain range tailed off from a domed observatory on the clifftop, along a gentle but long slope southward to a densely forested lakeshore. To the west, a smaller building was nestled among the trees further along the shore, while a sprawling jumble of pale buildings faded into the distance on the far side of the lake. The dizzying spires of the most fashionable architectural styles mingled with the archaically beautiful gilt domes and arches of tradition, while plainer and more utilitarian buildings clustered around them like worshippers at the feet of their gods.

13

In the centre of the mirrored cobalt lake, a long expanse of marble and sandstone sat placidly on the calm waters, its arched and vaulted windows making it look not unlike a motionless liner. There was a mass of the dark green of well-tended trees at the west end of the complex, rising from a cloistered square, while the flat rooftops were bedecked with neat and tidy garden plots.

On the north shore of the lake, straddling the river that wound through the mountains to the sea, a series of pillars supported a great dome, beyond which rose a number of parabolic dishes ranged around the perimeter of the spaceport.

A small and ageing, general-purpose planet-hopper swept downward towards the spaceport, its pilot never ceasing to admire the view of the countryside all around. Nur eased off on the ion drive, and switched to reaction control jets to gently guide her vimana across to the government enclosure on the east bank.

Her lustrous hair was bunched up in a jewelled net, which couldn't disguise the fact that it was clearly very long. She was quite slim and had a rather delicate jaw, traits that betrayed the family relationship to the man beside her. Her father shared her slight build, but there was a faint network of lines across his face, and his slightly greying hair was short and side-parted.

He watched her with a faint smile, glad at the moment that a vote had prevented the adoption of the purdah into their new world, since he'd never seen anyone with as flawless a gift for flight as his daughter. He certainly wouldn't want to be flown by anyone less than the best. Of course, at other times, her stubborn flightiness was a pain, but what could he do?

The flattened trapezoid's tripod landing gear settled on to the concrete with only the tiniest sensation of touch-down. Raja Ambika Karan Pratapsinh, Preceptor of the province of Kuru, slipped out of the copilot's harness as Nur shut down the ship's flight systems, leaving only a

14

hollow silence in the absence of the gentle hums and buzzes of flight.

Ambika hadn't assisted with the flight, of course, despite his choice of seat, and admitted to himself that he would have preferred to enjoy the more comfortable surroundings of the well-equipped passenger compartment. But he was proud of his daughter, and knew that she enjoyed his appreciation of her skills, so he always sat with her on the flight deck. He stood, straightening the maroon silk coat that wasn't too dissimilar to a Kshatriya uniform, and reflecting that his prime minister would be quietly disapproving at the wrinkles left in it by the harness. Those wrinkles didn't seem to matter so much in Nur's crumpled jumpsuit and flight jacket, even though the latter was silk as well. He had given her that himself; to offset the less pure material of the jumpsuit. Through the sloping viewport that enclosed the flight deck, he could already make out a small electric car coming over from the terminal for him.

He caught Nur's eyes following his gaze, and she smiled knowingly. He shrugged. 'The Spinward ship has probably come early. There's no need for you to cut short your holiday as well; why don't you go back and enjoy the rest of the week?'

'Because it was a very boring island.' Ambika winced, relieved that his erstwhile hosts weren't around to hear that. If Nur was going to be Rani after him, he'd have to teach her to think first and speak later. Her straightforwardness was a pleasantly refreshing trait, though, for someone used to diplomatic circles. 'Besides, I brought along a cargo of orchids for the roof garden, and I'll have to collect the payment.'

Ambika descended to the main hold at the rear of the flight deck, his daughter following. 'It's not as if you need it.'

She gave a vague facial shrug. 'The orchid grower does.'

'Yes, I'm sure.' Ambika was so visibly making the

15

effort to restrain an urge to grimace that Nur decided it was best not to mention how badly he was doing.

'Look, I always bathe after being near anyone who digs in the dirt, all right?' She unsealed the airlock and thumped the control that lowered the ramp. The prime minister was looking up at Ambika with a look of profound disapproval while a Kshatriya held the car door open for the Raja. 'Don't worry, there's nothing important going on these days.'

Space traffic control was housed in an angular sandstone complex not unlike a cut diamond which was on a hill on the opposite side of the river from the spaceport proper. The walls sloped outward a short distance, creating a shaded cloister before tilting up towards what would have been a pointed tip, had the architects not seen fit to slice it off and replace it with a roof garden of dishes and lance-like antennae.

Inside, the staff of Raghi Control stared at their wall's mosaic of screens in stunned shock. Despite the warm afternoon sunlight that filtered into their communications centre, every one of them was gripped by an unshakable chill.

On the screen, Chandra's normally stout and sturdy features looked haggard and nervous as he kept glancing away, punching up views of the other sections of the station on the internal monitors. They couldn't see what he was watching, but the tinny sounds of chaos from the station intercom were audible in the background.

'I can't even see through the interference and get some measure of what they're up to. We're as secure here as we're likely to get,' he reported, 'but probably not for long. Have they landed anywhere on Raghi?'

'Not as far as we can tell,' the ground-control supervisor replied. 'There seems to be just the one ship. Who are they?'

'That's something, I suppose. I believe we can hold them for a while . . .' Chandra's attention had been usurped by something off-screen. Already, screams were echoing more loudly over the communications system, to the accompaniment of a bizarre warbling that was somehow instantly recognizable as some kind of weapon firing rapidly.

'Who –' The screens exploded into static with an electronic howl.

The garden had been so peaceful before the invasion of insistent bees that he still wanted to remain there. The constant noise was overpowering, though; so much so that he could still hear it now that the garden was gone.

It wasn't bees, Captain Sharma's still-muggy brain finally realized, but the intercom in his cabin aboard the *Nandi*. With a conscious effort to come fully awake, he sat up and pressed the relevant button on the small console set into his bedside table. 'You can stop paging, Parvi, I'm awake. What is it?' He rubbed at his tousled mop of black hair as if trying to start the circulation going.

'A message from Raghi, sir. All communications from Agni have ceased, and their last transmission sounded like a distress signal.'

This banished the last vestiges of sleep from Sharma's mind. 'What kind of distress?' he asked, struggling into his Kshatriya uniform. It seemed he would have to forgo trimming the neatly kept beard that he felt helped define his angular features.

'Apparently they're under some form of attack.'

'Acknowledge the message and tell Raghi we're on our way, then try to contact Agni – I think the current supervisor is called Chandra – and find out what's going on.' He depressed another switch. 'Nirad; new course, two-nine-five mark zero-zero-one.'

The leading edges of her arced forward section, slim rear wing and ventral engines reflecting the pastel inferno of

17

Indra and Agni, the *Nandi* fell inward on a long parabola from her patrol course towards Agni.

Commander Loxx watched with distaste as two of his troopers herded yet another group of whimpering technicians out from the operations complex at gunpoint. The humans marched disconsolately, with their hands on their heads.

Loxx thought it was a crass display of base cowardice. The very concept of surrender was an insult to his warrior's nature, even though it appeared that the survivors might actually prove useful. He did, after all, have some standards.

He strode into central control, and felt a warm glow of pride as he saw his troopers already tending to the damaged consoles. A small group of humans huddled by some kind of food dispenser like frightened prey.

Loxx removed his helmet, and activated his communicator, ignoring the reactions of the humans to his pure and finely ochre-patterned Clan Gunar features. 'Loxx to Major Karne.'

'Karne here. Is the station secure?'

'Secured, sir, with a captive labour force. The commanders here did manage to send a message for assistance. A cruiser is en route from patrolling the system's rim.'

'Understood, Commander. Process the humans as instructed.'

'Yes, sir.'

The armoured viewport that stretched around the bridge of the *Nandi* was the centre of attention for the ship's command crew, or at least the port side of it was. Fifty miles beyond it, the rooftops and collection aerials on Agni crept past like cooled slag crusting atop the embers of a furnace.

Jahangir, his wizened and leathery face sheathed in a white mane, let them watch. There wasn't much for them to do right now, and he was sure they

18

were professional enough to look after their posts even while sightseeing. After all, as the ship's medical and psychological officer, he would know if any of them were unable to do so.

Like most of Raghi's medical practitioners, he had been born into what was originally a Brahmin priestly lineage. He sometimes wondered if that was why he was so adept at ministering to psychological needs; it wasn't too dissimilar to spiritual needs, as far as he was concerned. On the other hand, since he wasn't a born leader, he didn't feel so adept at taking Captain Sharma's place while Sharma took a landing party across to the Agni station.

From the raised command podium, he had seen the running lights of Sharma's shuttle as it dropped away from the ventral hangar to swoop down to the energy station a good ten minutes ago. Surely the shuttle should have settled in the hangar bay by now?

The gently tilted sandstone walls of Raghi's space traffic-control centre seemed suffused with soft afternoon light, but this only threw the crackling monitors for Agni into sharply needling relief. 'What news?' asked Ambika. There were, of course, people who handled these situations, but as a leader he felt it was his responsibility to show that he was not afraid to lead by example. Within reason – he wouldn't go shopping in the Sudra quarter of the city, for example.

Without warning, the monitors tuned to receive signals from Agni flashed into life. A uniformed Kshatriya loomed into one of them, tapping the lens. 'Captain Sharma of the *Nandi* reporting. Are you receiving, Raghi Control?'

'This is the Preceptor, Captain. We read you.' On screen, Sharma's eyes widened momentarily, then he composed himself.

'The *Nandi* achieved parking orbit a few minutes ago, Excellency,' Sharma answered, looking tired. 'We saw no

19

sign of life, but that two maser batteries had been destroyed.'

Ambika nodded silently, his angular features arranged into a thoughtful expression. 'And are you conducting a full sensor sweep?'

'There's no sign of any other vessel. I think that Chandra may have been confused by some sort of meteor shower.'

'That hardly seems likely; we've all seen those before.'

'I think he realizes that. At any rate, I've brought a vimana across to the station to conduct a proper search.' He shifted out of sight, so that the watchers could see the wreckage that was scattered across the control room. In the background, a few men were patching up pieces of equipment. 'There has been some loss of life – there was a breach on the hangar level – but Chandra and most of the others are all right. They were sheltering in the underground storage levels, and there has been no damage to the energy collection and transfer systems. If it's all right with you, Excellency, I would like to remain a while and help with the repairs before bringing Chandra back for debriefing.'

Ambika mulled it over; Chandra was going to have to answer for this, as he should have kept the meteor shield up, but he didn't want to risk any breakdown in the station's vital performance thanks to a delay in repairs. 'Very well, do what you must. The inquest into these events and Chandra's competence will have to wait until Agni is fully operational.'

'*Raja Ki Jai Ho.*' Sharma saluted. He broke the connection.

Sharma straightened and looked over the communications desk to where Chandra was standing with the armoured form of Commander Loxx. Loxx pressed a stud on the largest box on his equipment belt. '*Gen-tran vo, Karne tor. Bronn saag na-keng.*' He stepped over to Sharma, who waited patiently for his new orders, and pressed a

20

different button. 'Your work is satisfactory, human,' he hissed, this time in perfect Hindi. 'Prepare a duty roster that will give each of your crew time on this moon, then ready your shuttle to return to your ship.'

Something was wrong, Sharma knew, but he couldn't quite work out what. It was best just to obey, he decided. 'Yes, sir. *Ki Jai Ho*.'

One

Either very far away, or very close, depending on one's attitude to relativity, a ginger-headed sallow youth in an English school uniform squatted by a humming and blinking electronic mushroom in a clinically white chamber, rooting through an unfolded toolbox.

A hand on the end of the sleeve of a red-trimmed white cricketing jersey emerged from under the hexagonal apparatus. 'Finkle-groober.'

'Finkle-groober,' Turlough repeated in what he hoped was an affirmative tone. He hadn't stayed with the Doctor after he was freed from the Black Guardian's influence just to fetch and carry; there were people who did these things, or at least there were at home. He picked out a probe with a confusing series of joints, and pressed it into the hand. It disappeared under the complex console, and a staccato series of beeps and burbling whistles started emanating from somewhere under the cylindrical nest of pastel filaments that oscillated at the heart of the console.

Turlough wasn't entirely surprised at the Doctor's sudden obsession with maintenance; he probably wanted to busy himself away from thinking too much about Tegan's departure, and worrying about whether it was a consequence of his own behaviour. Turlough could understand that discomfort all too easily. Although the Doctor's mind might be sufficiently occupied, his own was stagnating just sitting here beside the toolbox, and he was more than ready for a change. Somehow, he thought reluctantly, the TARDIS just wasn't the same without Tegan. Quieter, he'd be willing to admit; but there was something refreshingly stimulating about a good argument between friends. He hoped they were friends in the end, though it hardly mattered now.

'Is all this really necessary?' he asked finally. 'I mean, it's not as if anything is actually wrong, is it?'

The noises stopped, and the Doctor slid himself out from under the console. He didn't look much more than a few years older than Turlough himself, with side-parted blond hair, friendly blue eyes, and disarmingly boyish features which were usually formed into a laid-back expression of pleasant interest. Right now, however, he looked up at Turlough with a wearied look of impatience. 'Not at the moment, no.' He pulled himself out from under the console, brushing absently at the jersey and candy-striped trousers. 'I don't know about you, but I rather think I would feel safer after doing a complete check. What with the Daleks' time corridor, I still haven't had the chance to make sure that the spatial distribution caused by the Gravis and his drones has left no permanent damage.'

Deciding to try for a placating mood, Turlough nodded agreeably. 'I'm all for feeling safe, but isn't it rather dangerous to interfere with vital systems while we're still in flight?'

The Doctor gave him a long look, then sighed resignedly, and stabbed at a few controls. 'All right, Turlough. I'll see if I can find a suitable local place to stop.' The three monitors set into alternate panels on the console sprang into life, displaying a schematic of an eight-planet system around a third magnitude star.

'Where are we?'

'Some way out from Earth. The Unukalhai system, Earthdate 2371.'

'Never heard of it.'

'Alpha Serpens Caput.'

Turlough did a quick mental calculation; his people were a spacefaring race – though he himself had been trapped on Earth until relatively recently – so he might

23

have seen or heard something about this region. 'That's in Tzun space,' he exclaimed after a moment. 'Nobody in their right mind goes there voluntarily!'

'Not any more. They were wiped out by the Veltrochni in the 2170s. That's odd . . . There's an Earth-type ecosphere on the sixth moon of Unukalhai IV.'

'A gas giant,' Turlough read from the monitor. It certainly didn't seem the sort of place to look for an Earthlike biosphere; the moons of such bodies were usually either frozen deserts or volcanic infernos.

'A large one, at that. More or less a brown dwarf, in fact. Still, if it's close enough, I don't see any harm in taking a look.'

'Look, Doctor, there's an entry in the data bank for Unukalhai.'

'Really?' The Doctor rarely used the data bank, preferring, Turlough suspected, to try and keep an air of personal knowledgeability rather than be seen to rely on any *aides-mémoire*. Being a mere mortal, Turlough was willing to take any help he could get, even from the computer's memory. Shrugging on his pale beige frock coat, and checking that a celery stick was securely attached to the lapel, the Doctor moved round to look reluctantly over Turlough's shoulder. 'Unukalhai IV: mass, angular momentum . . . Ah. Sixth moon terraformed by Earth's Colonial Office circa 2247. Well, that explains the biosphere.'

'Wouldn't it be more prudent to do this work there? Just in case.' He tried to sound offhand, but suspected it wouldn't come out that way. Somehow the TARDIS seemed to be a machine built just to prove the truth of what Tegan had referred to as Murphy's Law.

The Doctor smiled. 'Why not? If it's been terraformed, there won't be much risk of natural disaster or native pathogens.' He turned back to the console, manipulating the controls with renewed eagerness. 'We can just find a quiet corner and' – he patted the console gently – 'give the old girl a proper overhaul.'

24

'Of course, Doctor.' There had to be a first time, Turlough hoped.

Nur stared across the marble tabletop at her father, her dark eyes almost pleading. 'You know I hate these things.' Though the two of them were alone at breakfast, she could never quite rid herself of the feeling of being watched by the life-size dancers and hunters painted on to the walls. Of course, she should be used to it after having lived her whole life here, but she preferred the inconvenience of feeling watched; it reminded her that she was who she was and not the at-ease-anywhere diplomat her father had hoped for. She needed that reassurance at times like this.

'My dear, you know equally well that such engagements are expected of you. As my daughter, the people like to know that you are taking an interest in their lives.'

'Fine, then I'll fly the tour routes. Isn't that meeting the people?'

'Nur –'

'It's not as if we're royalty; you're a regional administrator of a colony, and I'm a charter pilot, not a diplomat.' It seemed that she was doomed to have this conversation every few months, when her father's aides suggested that a civic engagement was in order. She had nothing against giving everyone a morale-boosting visit, but was perfectly well aware that she wasn't trained to deliver such a thing. All that ever happened was that she blundered through the day trailing after her father like a toddler while her ship sat gathering dust.

This time, though, the prospect was worse. 'Besides, you know I loathe hospitals. You always feel that Rudra is waiting round the next corner.'

'Preferably in his healing aspect rather than plague.' Ambika sighed. 'I know you dislike these demands on your time, but old habits die hard, and the population has grown accustomed to these visits. They expect them.' He looked away briefly. 'I didn't expect you to have to take

25

up these duties, but with your mother gone . . . It's only one afternoon, and you said yourself that your ship was overdue its latest service. I can have it done while you're visiting the centre. Besides, like it or not, as the permit-holder for a government vimana on preferential routes, you are technically a provincial government representative. The law states that any new state-funded facility must be inspected by a provincial representative before its operational licence can be granted, and you do qualify.'

'Not to inspect a medical facility; they could have put in portable outside-broadcast units in place of crash-carts, and I wouldn't know the difference.'

Ambika waved her protest away. 'All that has already been dealt with in a variety of separate visits – the facility is for Kshatriya use, after all. This is purely a formality, for the sake of appearances.'

Nur didn't doubt that, though she felt his meaning was deliberately vague. 'Theirs, or ours?'

'Look, the administrator of the centre is a friend of mine, a Brahmin named Jahangir. He was the *Nandi*'s chief medical officer until that disturbance a few months ago, and now that there are no more injured on Agni he's getting the promotion he deserves. I would prefer it if he also got the respect he deserves.'

'People might expect PR visits, but they know me well enough by now to expect me to have other ideas.' She knew it was no good; in the three years since her mother died, she'd never yet got out of going on one of these visits. Unfortunately, her father was right about the people's expectations and, without their fulfilment, Ambika might find himself stripped of his position come the next referendum. The prospect of losing the free maintenance and toll-free landing permits always sealed the decision for her. 'Atcha . . . A full service? Done by the time we get back?'

'But, of course.' Ambika set down the glass of orange juice he'd been sipping along with his breakfast. 'I know you value your independence, but you must follow your dharma as well. I am proudest when you can balance them both.' Nur flushed slightly. 'Arjun has all the details of your itinerary, but it is very simple: go there, look around, shake a few hands, then come back.'

'You didn't say to be interested.'

Ambika gave a resigned smile. 'Even I can't ask the impossible.'

The distant calls of birds drifted across the lake, mingling with the gentle chugging of boats on the water. The occasional dying howl of a flight landing at the spaceport did little to interrupt the faint hubbub of faraway chattering from the city on the western shore.

The spreading branches of an orange blossom at the corner of a slightly raised promenade along the shoreline offered a pleasant shade from the golden sunlight, and it was on the fringes of this cool shade that a yellow light began to form. Heralded by a strangely ethereal elephantine trumpeting, the light was joined by a rapidly solidifying patch of blue.

Unlike the glowing azure of the sky, or the mirror-finished cobalt of the water, this blue was a timeworn and faded shade of paintwork, peeling from the wood of this strange hut. A sign above the double door proclaimed POLICE PUBLIC CALL BOX.

The wooden doors rattled open, and the Doctor stepped out on to the sand-blown stone walkway, unrolling his Panama hat and jamming it on to his head as he looked around keenly. Turlough followed a little more cautiously, but everything seemed quiet enough, and he just caught himself reflecting that Tegan would have liked this place. The air outside the TARDIS was warm and thick with the scent of exotic flowers, tinted with a freshness blowing in from the lake.

'It's so much like the Meridian Palace at home.' Turlough couldn't help feeling an involuntary shiver as a twinge of bittersweet childhood feelings swept over him. The similarities ended with the impressive curve that

27

arced across a quarter of the sky here, of course; his own world had three rather small moons, not a huge and ghostly companion planet. 'This sunlight's strange.' He concentrated on the present. 'A gas giant would have to be quite far out from the sun to make a stable system, but it's as bright as a day on Earth here.'

'Hmm.' The Doctor squinted up at the gas giant. 'This moon was terraformed anyway, so I imagine the sunlight has been similarly artificially enhanced.'

'In-station fusion satellite?'

'Why waste valuable resources building an expensive and short-lived thing like that, when there's so much energy there for the taking?' The Doctor nodded towards the gas giant. 'Either another moon, or a space station, positioned right in the synchrotron radiation belt would draw off a continuous current of several million amps down a magnetic flux tube. An inexhaustible energy supply which they could use for any purpose, including artificial sunlight.'

'Are humans so far advanced so quickly?'

'Theoretically yes, but in practice it's hard to tell with humans; the Romans had the level of technology required to build the gramophone and the steam engine, but they just never actually did it. But they do say that necessity is the mother of invention.' The Time Lord strolled off along the promenade, hands in pockets.

The local populace didn't give them a second glance, Turlough noticed, which meant they probably hadn't noticed the TARDIS materialize in its shaded corner. They all looked human enough, though with deeper skin tones than most of the other boys at Brendon. Turlough had lived on Earth long enough to recognize most of the varieties of humanity, however, and suspected that these people were from the Near East, or perhaps India.

They turned on to a broad avenue lined with market stalls mostly selling fruit or seafood. Here there were even more people going about their business. There were a few members of other human races scattered here and there, though they mostly wore Corporate or Colonial Office spacer uniforms or coveralls as opposed to the local brightly coloured silks.

The Doctor tilted his hat to a more jaunty angle as he paused both to take bearings and let Turlough catch up. 'What we need is a nice little villa or cottage to hole up in while we give the TARDIS her check-up. Of course, the operator isn't really supposed to carry out servicing himself, but I don't really relish the prospect of being tied down into the Presidential throne with red tape just for the sake of a few minor adjustments that should really be covered by the service contract.'

Turlough pondered this for a moment. Why was it that the Doctor had to keep on changing things? 'I thought we would be staying inside the TARDIS.'

'Well, we could, but I like to go native a little. You know, get into the swing of things locally. There's no sense in going to all the trouble of finding a nice planet if you're not going to go out there and experience it to the full, is there?'

'I suppose not.'

'Besides, we need somewhere to keep the TARDIS; we can't just pop in and out of it on a street corner.' He stopped to look pointedly at Turlough. 'People would stare.'

All right, Turlough thought, I give up. 'How do we find a place to stay, then?'

The Doctor sighed. 'We ask at an estate agent.' He turned the next corner on impulse. 'Of course, on most colonies you just ask a public information terminal for the nearest unoccupied residence.'

Turlough looked back at the corner they had turned. 'Like that one, you mean?'

The Doctor turned on his heel and grinned. 'The very thing.' There had been quite a few shop fronts there, and there were many in this street as well, all neat and tidy despite the dust and bustle, with sparklingly clean windows and signage. They were also all very much alike, and he had the feeling that it would be very easy to get lost in this city. Fortunately, the access booth should be able to help them; he could but hope, anyway. The Doctor had moved on ahead, and was keying through the on-screen index by the time Turlough reached him.

'What language is that?'

'Hindi, I think. The TARDIS's telepathic circuits aren't as effective on written language as spoken. Computer, where can I find accommodation?'

'Do you require hotel accommodation or a full residence?' the toneless voice asked.

Turlough tapped the Doctor on the shoulder. 'Don't you think a more private residence might be best?'

'We don't really need that sort of luxury . . .'

'We also don't need everyone in the building having a look at the TARDIS.' It wasn't that he didn't trust anyone, he told himself, but you could never tell.

'Yes, I suppose that's a point.' The Doctor turned back to the computer terminal. 'Some sort of villa, I think.'

'Seventeen property dealers have villas for sale or rent.'

'Ah.' The Doctor looked apologetically at Turlough, who groaned inwardly. It was going to be a long wait if they had to go through every list, translating as they went.

Two

The dawn chorus came as an irritating surprise to Turlough, the birdsong drifting in through the open window by his bed from the trees in the secluded mezzanine garden. He had vaguely hoped that either no birds would have been imported from Earth, or that the gently increasing light with no direct solar source would confuse the creatures into silence. Evidently they had adapted to their new home with aplomb.

Perhaps he was being too negative; he wondered if maybe he would be better off giving thanks that for once he'd had a peaceful night without being shot at or locked up. He wished he'd never heard the saying about the calm before the storm – or the cliché about things being too quiet. He reluctantly psyched himself up to get busy in the kitchen. Having seen what the Doctor's restaurant had ended up like, he certainly didn't want to encourage the Time Lord's culinary ambitions – which meant he'd have to arrange breakfast himself.

The thought of the Doctor made him hesitate, wondering where he had gone. A moment's listening enabled him to identify a vaguely tuneless whistling among the garden's birdsong. Obviously the Doctor had gone out to the TARDIS to make an early start, which was so typical of him. Turlough occasionally wondered if Time Lords ever actually slept, since the Doctor was always busy at something.

As if the mere thought was a summons, the Doctor breezed casually into the villa, having abandoned his frock coat and found a short-sleeved version of his question-mark shirt. 'Ah, there you are. Good.' Turlough opened his mouth to speak, but the Doctor simply handed him a pitcher of fruit juice and pressed on regardless. 'Everything seems more or less fine, but there are a few bits and pieces that could do with replacement circuits, and there should be electronic supply houses somewhere in the colony.'

'Anything particularly urgent?'

'I thought that while we were in dry dock, so to speak, it's about time I saw to the chameleon circuit . . .'

'Ah, nothing particularly urgent.'

A couple of birds, kalkalachi by the look of them, were flitting across the treetops around the foot of the lake's guardian mountain as Nur's car passed between two domed marble pavilions. Beyond this softly glowing gate, a web of low buildings linked several larger pavilions, while the air circulated coolly between sandy pillars.

The car drew up before a shaded verandah which fronted a long entrance building built in a strangely pleasing mix of traditionally cool white marble and modern polychromatic glass, which was looking very smoky and refreshingly shady on such a sunny day. Quite a crowd was gathered under the awning, Nur noted with dismay. She had nothing against the medical staff or outpatients who were gathered, even though they were of social groupings that were more prone to spiritual pollutions, but the sight of a cluster of people her own age – and not a few younger still – wearing camera masks made her want to stay hidden in the car.

Tonight, she thought, half of Raghi will see how uncomfortable I look in a sari. She wondered if she should gain a measure of revenge by delicately informing the press that their garish camera masks, with their insectile compound lenses, were just a shoddy civilian exploitation of the lookdown-shootdown equipment worn by fighter pilots. She'd never worn one herself, of course, but pilots were pilots, whatever colours they wore.

Arjun, her mother's wiry and balding driver and bodyguard – inherited along with these duties after the shuttle crash – opened the door. Since his back was to the crowd, he allowed himself a conspiratorial grin for her. The fresh sea scent that wafted in relaxed her somewhat, and she got out stiffly, having to turn sideways in the seat first, thanks to the restrictive dress. She couldn't allow herself to lose her concentration for even an instant to return Arjun's look, since her carefully practised diplomatic smile tended to become rather fixed and glassy if she wasn't careful.

A tall and still muscular man, despite the white-haired onset of later years, stepped out to meet her, a blandly experienced diplomatic smile vaguely softening his chiselled features. Despite his age, his eyes glittered with suppressed excitement of some kind. 'Namaste. I am Jahangir, administrator and chief consultant. I promise I will try not to bore you too much.' He smiled falteringly, and she got the impression that he was as uncomfortable as she was.

Relieved that someone around here seemed normal, if rather distant, she smiled back and allowed him to lead her in through the smoky doors. Arjun closed the door and followed impassively after her, though she knew he would be amusing himself by thinking of ways to tease her about her discomfort later. The gathered staff and patients parted as Jahangir led the way through the automatic doors. 'This is, of course, simply the visitors' and outpatients' entrance,' he said, without really looking at her. She supposed he was proud of his new charge. Jahangir walked along beside her, pointing out the main features of the reception hall in a bland tone, scarcely looking at her though his manner was polite enough. Idly wondering with part of her mind how the overhaul was going, Nur nodded whenever it seemed appropriate. Jahangir probably wouldn't notice how much attention she was paying anyway, since he seemed very withdrawn.

33

It must be the weight of responsibilities of the medical service, she thought.

In the pyramidal building across the river from the spaceport, Karan's cubbyhole was right on the edge of the waist, which meant that one wall bulged outwards, a long thin tinted window running the length of the room. Luckily he was barely over five feet tall, which was probably why he'd been put in this office. On the other hand, the fact that he was almost as wide as he was tall didn't help matters. He often felt like a round peg in a square hole, quite literally. His job was sedentary enough – and a useful scapegoat for his physique. But when nothing much was happening in his assigned sector, Karan liked to look out there, calmed by the view of the trees and lakeshore below.

He glanced back at the bank of screens now and again, just often enough and just long enough to make sure that he would notice if anything did come towards Indra from the inner part of the system. He doubted that anything ever would come that way; the inner planets were just uninhabitable rocks in which even the less fussy mining corporations had declined any interest.

His deep-set eyes flicked across the screens again, but every pixel there had a catalogue number attached, proving they were just rocks, and known ones at that. He turned back to the window, then looked round again. Something was crossing the face of Indra on one of the monitors. It must be quite close to the navigational beacon in question, he realized, since it was clearly discernible as a black speck on the face of the planet.

Adjusting the focus, he sharpened the image, programming the buoy to track it. Its course suggested it wouldn't come any closer to the buoy, but he could live in hope. Perhaps if there was a closer viewpoint. He snapped his fingers unconsciously; the *Nandi* was still out there, as she had been for the past month.

Leaning forward, he punched the communications button. 'Vijay, get me Captain Sharma of the *Nandi*.'

Nur felt as if her back was itching from the pressure of the eyes upon her. This inspection tour had to be conducted if the centre was to get its licence to practise, but she had no idea what she was supposed to look for. Of course, in reality the papers were all signed and she was just here for a bit of public relations, but she still thought it would have looked more reasonable to send someone who knew about these things. She just didn't have the power to refuse outright, though, as the family as a whole was stronger than any of its members.

That was the story of her life, she thought.

The entourage was currently entering a well-lit room with a low ceiling. Stacks of specimen slides were ranged against the walls, while a trio of electron microscopes dominated the far end of the room. Their smaller optical cousins were scattered throughout. Jahangir frowned slightly. 'This is a research lab, or will be once it's all fully stocked.'

Nur stepped aside and peered through the nearest microscope's eyepiece. Jahangir took half a step towards her, then restrained himself. All Nur could see was a mass of semi-opaque blobs with little crystalline blisters attached. She straightened, wondering how anyone would want to work with such uninteresting substances. 'It seems fine to me. I'm sure the lab will do a lot of useful work.'

Jahangir hesitated, then nodded hastily. 'I am certain of it. If you follow me, I will show you the operating theatres; we have invested a great deal in the very latest equipment.'

A gentle chiming announced Sharma's appearance on the communications screen in Karan's office. '*Namaste*, Captain,' Karan acknowledged. 'I apologize for disturbing your duties, but our tracking monitors are picking up some sort of metallic mass approaching the defence grid from in-system. Does it register on any of your scanners?'

'Metallic mass?' Sharma looked as if he were about to say something which excited him, but then the animation faded from his sharply chiselled face. 'We read it,' he said slowly, then stiffened slightly. 'We read it as a chunk of meteoric iron. It's probably a trans-solar asteroid tossed out of orbit by a particularly strong prominence or flare.' He gave a strained smile that immediately made Karan feel guilty about disturbing his work. 'If you log it as usual, we'll have it named after you.'

Despite his long service in space monitoring, Karan had never had any body named after him, and couldn't help but feel a little proud. His fears shrivelled away in the light of the literally rewarding reassurance. He tried to look unflustered and professional. 'As you say, Captain, and thank you for your assistance.'

Sharma nodded, and faded from the screen.

Jahangir hovered nervously behind Nur as she and the entourage of gawpers returned to the T-junction behind main reception, this time from the opposite side to the one which they had originally taken. Fortunately there was a clock on the wall, so she could surreptitiously check the time without risking seeming rude by glancing at her watch.

To her surprise, it was already approaching two in the afternoon. To make up for the guilty delight she felt, she forced herself to look more interested in the nearest set of double doors. She walked over, reaching for the handle. 'I'm afraid that room contains only files and medical records,' Jahangir put in hastily, interposing himself between her and the door.

She stepped back, a little startled, then recovered herself. If she absolutely had to end the visit here and get back to her ship, then she wasn't complaining. 'Ah, patient confidentiality? I understand.'

'If you would like to view the gardens . . .' Jahangir smiled nervously, as if he had been caught in some misdemeanour. He probably thought interrupting her was a capital offence, she decided.

'I'd like to but –' she put on a long-suffering expression that was as much practised as experienced – 'I do have another engagement today, and I might have already spent more time here at your fascinating centre than I really should.'

Jahangir nodded graciously. 'I'm sure it will be less glorious once your presence has gone.' Nur smiled weakly; she hated all this nonsense. Anybody would think she was royalty or something. At times like this, she felt as trapped in an unwelcome world as she imagined the lowly Harijans must feel in their station. As if reading her mind, Arjun opened the car door for her.

Mumbling a vague farewell as Jahangir blessed her for making the visit, Nur waved to the staff and patients and ducked into the car. As soon as the door was closed, she let the forced smile drop. 'Arjun, I am never doing this again; you can tell my father that. Leave this sort of thing to royalty, or someone familiar with the building statutes.'

Arjun just smiled and shook his eagle-nosed head as he started the car. She knew it was a silly suggestion anyway; the colony was a republic, after all. Someone had to be a figurehead for national morale now and again; so who else would do it than the family of the highest elected official? They had barely gone a few hundred yards when Arjun pulled into the roadside.

For a moment, Nur had the awful suspicion that some sort of addition to the visit was in order – something that would definitely delay getting back to check up on the *Garuda*'s overhaul. Instead, as they pulled into a shady curve in the winding road, a larger vehicle which had been coming up towards them passed by. As it passed, Nur saw that it was an ambulance, with the black pools of the windows reflecting a shadowy afternoon sky.

It was odd that an ambulance should be rushing up to a day clinic, Nur thought; it wasn't as if the place was built to deal with emergencies. She told herself to stop being so stupid. It was probably just chartered to bring in someone in a hover chair. Anybody would think that Jahangir's jumpiness was contagious.

That would be one for the books, she thought with a grin as they started off again; paranoia discovered to be a virus.

'She's gone,' an orderly reported.

Jahangir nodded sagely, glad that the preceptor's daughter was out of the way. 'The media people?'

'At a buffet in the courtyard.'

'Good. Make sure none of them go wandering. Have the gate guards send the new donors in.' Jahangir walked out on to the carefully swept parking area beyond the artful stained glass of the automatic doors.

A stretch-bodied ambulance was already gliding along the tree-lined grove, the bright morning light reflecting from its mirrored windows like flashbulbs frozen in mid-detonation. The faint rush of its tyres on the road ceased as it drew up in front of the doors, the silence of its electrolytic drive leaving Jahangir wondering vaguely whether the engine was still running or not.

Several orderlies followed Jahangir out into the heat, their stiff bearing looking a little out of place while dressed in their white smocks. Opening the doors, each pair of orderlies drew out a wheeled stretcher on which a white-draped patient twisted and strained against restraining straps.

Jahangir cast an experienced eye over the first patient, a youngish man. The patients' eyes rolled crazily in their sockets, as if trying to punctuate the incoherent grunts that escaped his lips. Jahangir's heart ached to see people this way, which was one reason why he had become a doctor. Suffering was something he couldn't abide. He just wished that he hadn't been responsible for it. 'Are the others the same?' At least he didn't actually have to touch the bodily matter of the patients; that would have been the last straw for him.

'Yes, sir,' one of the orderlies replied. 'Another three rejects.'

Jahangir sighed resignedly. There always had to be someone different from the rest. 'Very well. Take them through to the isolation wing and administer the usual treatment. I'll come over to write the reports shortly.' He stepped back to allow the orderlies past, turning to watch the shrinking dust trail left by Nur's car. If only he could have said something . . . but he was glad that he hadn't.

Because then he would have had to kill her.

A dull pounding was fading just above his eyes, which glistened like newly hatched chicks in their nests of surrounding lines. He wished he could ease it by not worrying. Instead, he went inside to look for some painkillers.

Three

The streets of the lakeside city weren't quite as crowded as Turlough had expected, though there were indeed shoppers and traders all over the place. He was more surprised by the lack of vehicles on the ground; quite a few people were riding by on bicycles, but powered vehicles seemed restricted to the occasional delivery truck. Air traffic provided a constant buzz, however, with quietly humming vehicles skimming the rooftops every few moments.

Now and again, a pair of red-uniformed guards would check the doors of one boarded-up shop front or another. The streets were an odd mixture of gleaming shop fronts and wheeled carts piled high with oddments. The odd fast-food stall wouldn't be so surprising, but Turlough thought it more than a little strange to see wheelbarrows full of data crystals, and spare parts for spacesuit life-support packs being peddled outside glittering department stores full of fine rugs and the latest fashions.

'I'd have expected taller buildings in such an advanced city,' Turlough said, as much to relieve the boredom of walking around as anything else.

The Doctor looked around. 'Quite the opposite, surely? Besides, this is all culturally traditional style; that probably explains why the palace out on the lake looks so much like the Pichola lake palace at Udaipur. Humans seem to feel most comfortable with familiar things.'

Turlough couldn't disagree there, though he had the nasty suspicion that it was about the only thing you could rely on where humans were concerned. He'd been keeping an eye on the passers-by just in case, since the one thing he'd learnt was that you never knew what a human was likely to do next. They were peaceful enough now, but he was painfully aware that they could turn on the new arrivals at any moment, for no particular reason. Then again, maybe it just seemed that way because of the type of people he'd met.

It was still better to be on the safe side. He shifted the carton of electronic spares he was carrying to a more comfortable position, wondering why he hadn't handed the burden back to the Doctor once the Time Lord's hands were free when he had finished paying for them and put away his credit chip. 'Will these be compatible with the TARDIS's technology?'

'Oh, absolutely. It'll all be a bit of a lash-up, but I don't see why not.' The Doctor suddenly stopped, swivelling on his heels. 'Do you smell that?'

Turlough looked around. 'I can smell a lot of things. What particular "that" did you have in mind?'

'It's coming from this way.' Beaming broadly, the Doctor crossed the street. 'Mawaki-kachori; unmistakable.' Turlough followed carefully, wondering if this was some sort of bizarre alien lifeform. The Doctor seemed breezily unconcerned. 'Fruit and nut pastry with honey,' he explained. 'We can't miss this just to mess around with some circuitry.'

Feeling cold was unusual. With the long daylight hours and constantly controlled climate, no one ever expected to quiver involuntarily like a plucked string. The unexpected terrified Chattar; he had always been comfortable knowing how every part of his life fitted into the scheme of things.

He didn't know how the racking chills that made him shake could possibly fit into his life. It was so bad now that he couldn't even eat. Excusing himself from the low table around which his brother and their sons sat, he left while pre-prandial drinks were still being consumed. He

41

collapsed on to his bed, clenching his fists in the hope of taking his mind off it.

His wife Seeta must have heard him leave the dining area, and came in to look down at him with eyes that he thought mirrored his own subdued panic. 'Let me bring a doctor,' she pleaded. 'This is just getting worse.'

As if he didn't know. He shook his head, sending droplets of cooled sweat across the sheets. 'It's nothing. It'll pass.' He didn't know for sure, of course, because he didn't know what was wrong. If an expert told him it was serious, he'd have to believe them, and that would end his hopes that it was nothing. 'These things happen.'

'The other wives say there's a plague. Every other household has had a case.'

'Then the doctors here will be busy.' Couldn't she see that she was scaring him, or did she just enjoy it? He regretted the thought immediately; he knew her better than that.

'I'll go elsewhere, then.'

Chattar was about to forbid it, but then thought better of it. It would make her feel better, and he could keep fighting his fears, as no doctor from among the Vaisyas or Kshatriyas would bother with a Sudra patient. At least, he hoped not.

The sunlight was so strong that every shadow cast under the trees was both clearly defined and inky black. A verdant halo surrounded the pools of darkness. The sergeant winced as he heard his cohorts lumbering through the undergrowth in a chorus of crashes and rustles.

He wondered whose idea it was to use the trees for a stealthy — if he had a sense of humour he would have laughed at the irony, regardless of the noise it would make — approach to the private residence ahead. Surely a surprise attack was something you did by beaming straight into the location of the target and getting on with it?

The major, of course, was a spacer, not a dirtside

trooper. He sometimes wondered whether the Army Space Corps ever gave a moment's thought to the part played by ground troops. Of course not: all they cared about was getting their precious merit awards. Still, at least they didn't have as much fun.

True, tramping around this offensively hot and overgrown planet with a couple of rookies who thought stealth had something to do with black paint was not inspiring. However, at least there would be a brief thrill of combat at the end of it, and that made it all worthwhile. Well, slightly, anyway; the humans just didn't have the stamina for a really good fight.

Reaching a gap in the foliage, where a short slope of tangled roots led down to a baking road surface, the sergeant raised a hand to call a halt. The crashing to either side of him subsided. 'Right, lads,' he hissed, 'the target comes along this road every day at exactly the same time, according to our sources. A couple of short bursts to the nose of his vehicle should stop it, then we grab him, stun him, and take him back. Clear?'

'Clear,' the others echoed.

'Good.' He gestured towards the trooper to his left. 'Nothing's coming yet, so you get across that road, and we'll hit him from both sides.' He paused, recalling that the others might not know which vehicle was which, and could jeopardize everything if they started shooting at the wrong passer-by. 'Whatever happens, hold your fire until I start shooting.'

Pandit had left work for lunch at his tennis club; it was an informal meeting place in the hills for representatives from most of the pharmaceutical companies, and they all frequently pretended to their superiors that they were actually socializing with members of other industries. That had started lest their superiors think they were swapping secrets, but now it had become a habit. He doubted that those superiors really believed them any more anyway.

43

Tossing his racquet into the passenger seat of his car, he started up the electrolytic motor, ready to head back to the research labs. The drive was a short one, but always pleasant. The greenery on the hillsides was always worth watching, while the onboard trip computer actually controlled the car.

The car had just rounded a corner into a tree-lined vale, when it lurched with a sharp crack. A second blast of sound sent a cloud of smoke billowing from the front of the car, which slewed round towards the trees. Startled into alertness, Pandit grabbed the steering wheel and hit the manual override control. The steering wheel immediately yanked itself out of his grip as the nose of the car ploughed into a peepul tree.

Pandit's forehead bounced off the dashboard with a dizzying impact. He instinctively raised a hand to his head, and it came away slick with blood. Before his hand could reach the door handle, a shaft of daylight punched its way in through the ceiling, which was parting with a metallically tortured wail.

For a moment, Pandit thought he was having a delusion brought on by concussion, as a thick triple-digited gauntlet reached in through the gap. He turned to dive out of the car, then froze. A pair of empty eye-sockets was staring at him from the midst of a curved metallic head. Another pair of gauntleted hands punched through the window, and tore the door free from the car, tossing it carelessly aside.

The grey apparition loomed closer; some sort of device was in its hand. The last thing Pandit thought, before a flashing light drained his mind away into the darkness, was that he hoped his bowels would hold.

Turlough decided that the mawaki-kachori was edible, if not his sort of thing. It had been invented by humans, of course, which was a handicap from the start as far as he was concerned. The Doctor, on the other hand, had licked his fingers clean as soon as his serving

44

was gone. 'Haven't tasted it since the Mutiny,' he said confidentially.

They had stopped for the food in a small community meeting place, where a few vendors of refreshments had set up their stalls, as had a couple of newsagents. A wailing voice was already intruding on Turlough's consciousness, and it took him a few seconds to locate a woman who was looking around in visible agitation.

He would have admitted to a certain curiosity as to what was wrong, but his experience of these things had led him to the conclusion that they were best left alone. He looked to see whether the Doctor had noticed, and saw that he had. He looked to be in two minds about whether to step in or not. 'Shouldn't we be going?'

'I suppose so . . .'

By now the woman had reached the small public information booth, and Turlough could make out tear-streaks on her face. 'I just want to know where I can find a doctor for my husband,' she was saying. 'The ones for the Sudra quarter are all busy, and I think he's dying.'

'I'm sorry, there's no one available,' the voice from the booth said. Turlough could almost hear the Doctor's mind reaching its decision, and heard the resigned sigh he gave. He supposed it was for the best, since it would be a pity if someone died, but he didn't have to like it.

The Doctor had already stepped across to the booth and doffed his hat. 'Perhaps we can help,' he suggested. 'I'm the Doctor, this is Turlough, and we couldn't help overhearing that you're in some difficulty . . .'

'You're a doctor?' Her tone around the words was like the fingers of a drowning man around a straw. She smiled hesitantly through her distress. 'It's my husband, he's sick —'

'Well, you lead us to him, and I'll see what I can do.'

Turlough lifted the carton of electronics spares with a rueful smile, and followed as the woman led the Doctor out of the meeting area, tugging at his arm all the way.

* * *

45

The silent Arjun held the warning ribbon aside to allow Nur to reach her father. Ambika was curiously examining a tennis racquet beside a crashed groundcar with one door missing. Another taped-off enclosure a few yards into the undergrowth contained a couple of Kshatriyas scanning the car's door.

Ambika turned at her approach, tossing the racquet back on to the passenger seat. 'Nur, what brings you here?'

'We were on our way back from the inspection you wanted.' She looked the car over with concern. Crime wasn't something she was familiar with, and she would definitely prefer to keep it that way. 'What happened here?'

'I wish I knew. A Kshatriya skimmer called in a report of an abandoned car spotted on a routine fly-past. When a squad arrived, they found this.' He gestured towards the torn roof and scorched front wing.

'Then what brings you here?' Surely the regional governor had more important concerns, she thought. Besides, she'd hate to think the perpetrators might harm him if they were still around.

'This scorch mark indicates some sort of energy weapon – not exactly common possessions. If someone's been importing them illegally, I want to know about it.'

Nur nodded. There was always someone willing to cause trouble for anyone in a position of power. 'Of course.'

'How did the inspection go?'

'Guess. It looks all right to me, but then so does the old water purification plant, and that's been condemned. There was one thing though . . . An ambulance.'

'It is a hospital, Nur.'

'Yes, but not for emergency cases. Besides . . .' She couldn't quite vocalize how uneasy it had made her feel. 'It was all blacked out. I don't know, it was just a bit strange.'

Ambika considered this, then shrugged. 'It's probably just the latest design fashion. Don't worry about it. The

Garuda's service will be completed by now, so go and check her over.' He smiled. 'If anyone has to worry about anything, it'll be me about this kidnapping.'

Jahangir paced around the man who stood catatonically in his consulting room. He was tempted to say that this was hurting himself more than the man, but didn't bother; the man wouldn't take any notice, and he certainly wouldn't convince himself. 'What is your name?'

'Pandit Lal,' the man said dreamily.

'Where do you work?'

'BRW Laboratories, in the biochemicals division.'

'How long have you worked there?'

'Sixteen years.'

'What is your field of expertise?'

'Polymerase chain reactions.'

Jahangir wished he could tell him to run, or even kill him. He turned to the three armoured figures that waited by the door. 'This is the one. You may take him up when ready.'

The Doctor had rolled up his hat and tucked it away in a pocket somewhere. 'Pulse is a little fast,' he commented, releasing Chattar's wrist. 'I couldn't place the cause, though. He's definitely not running a temperature.' Turlough watched curiously as he moved the shivering man's head from side to side. At least this was just an illness. He hoped.

'That's odd . . .' The Doctor poked at Chattar's cheek with his index finger. 'I've never seen anything like this before.'

Turlough crouched down beside him. 'What's so unusual?'

'Feel for yourself.' He directed Turlough's hand towards Chattar's face. Turlough almost jumped when his finger made contact; the cheek wasn't soft and fleshy, but relatively hard, as if it had been frozen and wasn't thoroughly thawed yet.

47

Turlough hadn't seen anything like it either, though perhaps he might have if he hadn't been trapped on Earth for half of his education. It did sort of engage his curiosity, though, and he could almost forget the possibility of infection from what might be some new plague.

The Doctor moved back to the bedroom door, where the rest of the family were watching. Seeta gave him a questioning look, and the Doctor returned it with an apologetic one. 'Too early to tell, and not really my field, I'm afraid. Has he been ill recently; before this, I mean?'

'He had a cold a couple of weeks ago, but it only lasted a few days —'

'There's an ambulance out here,' Turlough interrupted.

'I haven't called one.' Seeta and the Doctor joined him at the window. Outside, a long ambulance with blacked-out windows had drawn up silently. Two white-garbed orderlies were already bringing a wheeled stretcher towards the door.

Turlough shrugged. 'Perhaps the person in that information booth had a change of heart.'

'Possibly,' the Doctor said doubtfully. As he spoke, a squat flying vehicle with several red-uniformed men inside settled into the street. 'Local police?'

'Kshatriyas,' Seeta corrected him. 'The military are in charge of civil security as well.'

'I hate to say this, but those ambulance orderlies probably know more about this sort of thing than I do. It might be for the best to let them get him to a hospital.'

Chattar groaned, and arched, but couldn't get any recognizable words out. 'I suppose so,' Seeta agreed quietly. She turned to the rest of the family, who were blocking the door. 'Let them through.'

Waves of nausea washed away the peaceful darkness, and Pandit Lal squinted at the harsh white lights under which he woke. He quickly realized that his light-headedness wasn't just due to the after-effects of unconsciousness, but that he was indeed lighter. There was a musty smell in the air, like something dead that had lain in the desert too long. Pandit coughed and tried to sit up, but an immensely strong hand pushed him down.

The smell grew stronger as the owner of the hand moved round to lean over him. 'Not yet, human. But your eagerness to get to work is most gratifying.'

Pandit's natural response to the grotesque face and oily breath was the urge to scream. Instead, to his immense puzzlement, he found himself nodding. 'Yes, sir,' he heard himself say. His voice held none of the astonishment he felt.

The ambulance had left, with Chattar securely strapped to the stretcher. Seeta, however, was not pleased at being left behind, and sobbed loudly on the steps outside her front door. 'Look,' one of the Kshatriyas, a burly man with a piggish nose, said, 'we understand your concern, but it's best not to risk further infection. This is standard procedure in these cases.'

The Doctor looked round quickly. 'Cases? You mean there have been others like him?'

The taller Kshatriya looked warningly at her compatriot, who smiled weakly. 'Cases of sudden illness occasionally happen. As to whether they're the same . . .'

'Doesn't it concern you just a little? I've never seen anything quite like that, and if it's a new pathogen your species might have no immunity.'

'Why *should* you have seen anything like it?' the female Kshatriya demanded. 'Are you a doctor?'

'Yes, as a matter of fact I am.'

'Then you ought to appreciate the good sense in not leaving others open to infection.'

'Ah, then why aren't you quarantining us? Or is it just that you know it isn't infectious?'

The female Kshatriya narrowed her eyes, visibly losing patience. 'I see you're offworlders. I could "quarantine" you very easily.'

'I'm sure you could. Since we've been in contact with

49

the victim and his family it would be likely that we're infected, too — if there's really an infection at work. I think it would be better if you just took us to your leader.'

'What?'

'Whoever's in charge of this city. If this thing spreads, you're going to need all the help you can get.'

'The Preceptor doesn't see anyone without an appointment.'

'Then let's go and make one.'

The Kshatriyas looked at each other. 'There's a long waiting list.'

'Ah. Then perhaps the Kshatriya sabha would care to examine paragraph 14,511 of the Colonial Office statutes? The parts governing the risks of the introduction of non-indigenous pathogens? Words to the effect that any warning of such introduction by a doctor has to be taken seriously.'

'The sabha is not in session today.' The woman looked at her partner indecisively. 'Very well. We will take you to the palace and apply for an emergency submission, but I can't guarantee that the preceptor will be available.' She turned back to the flier they had arrived in.

'You could go into variety with a memory act like that,' Turlough said quietly. At least dying on stage was preferable to the risk of the real thing.

'What memory? I made it up on the assumption that nobody could remember such extensive legislation.'

Four

The communal square was relatively secluded, and a central pool gave a hint of welcome coolness and moisture to the air. A series of shaded arches surrounded the edge of the square, every third arch masking the door to a home. A larger arch on one side was technically blocked off by a large wrought-iron gate, though this had stood ajar for as long as the residents could recall.

A small knot of children dashed around the gate, racing each other towards the door of their home. A bright-eyed man and a round-faced woman followed, both looking rather weary. They didn't get the chance to follow their offspring to the door, however, as a thick arm swept out from the nearest alcove, snapping the father on to the baked flagstones.

The children yelped in terror as their mother dropped the small hamper she held, and stepped towards the fallen man. Her own scream never got past her throat, as a squat and burly form in armour as dark as the shadows which had cloaked it lunged out and clapped a hand over her mouth. An identical figure raised a small device to her face. It buzzed faintly as it lit up with the harsh glare of an electrical discharge, and she slumped without a sound.

The children shook their father frantically, reluctantly unable to take their eyes from the creatures, which must surely be demons of some kind. Their fears of the supernatural nature of the assailants increased sharply as both demons, and their mother, faded into thin air like dreams departing from a waking mind.

* * *

Once the Kshatriya flier had landed in an enclosed landing pad, the tall female captain had led the Doctor and Turlough through an open enclosure lavishly decorated with remarkably lifelike mosaics of all manner of peacocks and out into a shaded corner of a walled square. A low table of inlaid wood stood on a terrace over a marble-rimmed lotus pool, where a man waited in a cane chair, sipping some bright liquid. He was wearing a carefully tailored silk suit and looked to be in his early forties, but something about his calm demeanour made Turlough suspect that he must be a good decade or so older than that.

A younger woman sat beside him in a rather incongruous flight suit which strangely appeared to be made of silk. She was attractive enough, for a human, though her nose was perhaps a little too prominent to be beautiful. Still, she was only human, after all, so what else was to be expected?

He looked at the captain. 'Are these the ones?'

'Yes, Excellence.'

The Doctor stepped up on to the terrace, putting his palms together and bowing slightly, with a disarming smile. '*Namaste*.'

Ambika nodded slightly by way of acknowledgement. 'Please sit down. You'll accept some refreshments, I trust? Nimbu pani, perhaps?'

'That would be delightful.'

Ambika gestured to the captain to depart, and started pouring the same bright green liquid into two glasses from a frosted pitcher. Turlough took a cautious sip, and found it pleasantly refreshing. It didn't have the faint oily air of alcohol, and seemed to be some sort of fruit squash. 'I think you'll find it pleasing enough.'

'Delicious,' the Doctor enthused. 'Your captain there said you were rather busy.'

'My daughter and I have so little time together each day that you could term it that way.' Turlough looked over at the girl in the flight suit, wondering just what rank

52

she held. She looked back with a bland half-smile. 'I must admit to a certain surprise that you were admitted at all; though, of course, I'm delighted to chat.'

'I'm afraid I had to impress on her the urgency of seeing someone in authority.'

'About our medical service, I understand. The captain tells me you're a doctor.'

'Among other things. Your medical service seems rather impersonal. More importantly, though, there seems to be disagreement over whether there have been any other cases of the same illness. That does rather tend to make me wonder.'

Ambika shook his head. 'There are many causes for the same symptoms; as a doctor, I'm sure you're aware of that.'

'Nevertheless, any unusual illness on what is after all a relatively new world . . .'

'This was a dead moon, right down to the bacteriological level, before our grandfathers set up their atmosphere processors. Every lifeform here from the single-cell up was brought from Earth. There are no indigenous pathogens.'

'It must have been a huge undertaking,' Turlough interrupted, unable to control his surprise. 'To create this whole ecosystem . . .'

Ambika smiled beneficently. 'Hardly create. All this is but a copy of our original home. It was a massive operation, though; our records tell us that it took forty million people nearly a quarter of a century to terraform this moon. The population has grown somewhat since then, of course.'

The Doctor looked suitably impressed. 'Only the largest corporations could have funded that.'

Ambika laughed. 'Not actually. Raghi is completely independent of any of the corporations; this was a purely cultural effort funded by public donation. We do have a certain amount of trade, of course; we sell airavata to Spinward, for example, but they have no influence over us.'

'You can never be sure about that; perhaps they're Taoists.' The Doctor looked squarely back at him. 'About this illness; if you need any help –'

'Doctor,' Ambika snapped, 'I have already told you that there is no cause for concern. There have been no other cases.' He sighed in the grim way that reminded Turlough so much of his headmaster, and the youth could sense the first threat coming. 'All visitors from Colonial Office or Alliance worlds are welcome here, so long as they don't violate any of our laws. I would consider any attempt to start a panic such a violation.'

Nur's head snapped round towards her father. 'I don't think they want to start a panic,' she said. 'They're just concerned, that's all.'

'Do I tell you how to fly your ship? I'd appreciate the same restraint from you with regard to how I do my job.'

Nur reeled back as if he'd slapped her, her eyes wide. Turlough gave her a wry look. The Doctor drained his nimbu pani and stood up. 'I think it'd be best if we left now, Turlough. Obviously the authorities have the situation under control.' He never took his eyes away from Ambika's.

Ambika rose also. 'The captain will show you the way out. Enjoy your visit.'

It took all of Turlough's self-restraint not to scoff out loud.

Major Karne emerged from what used to be Chandra's office, irritated at being called in the middle of some important calculations. He sometimes wondered if he would ever be free to finish his job, or whether Loxx would hound him for the rest of time. If only Loxx knew what he knew, he thought. 'Yes, Commander?'

Loxx led a group of troopers through a control centre tinted amber by the light of the setting Indra; a human shuffled along at the centre of the group. Karne thought it was a female, though it was hard to tell, since their own race had no males or females *per se*. 'Phoolan Indrani,

54

virologist,' he announced, indicating the human.

'Send her to Pandit and assign her to cell modification. There have been far too many rejections in the first caste.'

'Yes sir. Shall I send for our next conscript?'

'By all means. Perish the thought that we could fall behind schedule. The general would negate us all.'

Nur went down to the fountain in the courtyard garden, and sat on a miniature stone elephant, tossing pebbles into the water. Her father's curtness just hadn't been like him at all. He had always adhered to the principle that guests should be honoured.

She glanced back at the table, and saw him look away quickly. Evidently he had been watching her, which meant that he was probably feeling twinges of guilt. That would be more like him; the unpleasant responsibilities of a regional governor meant that he was as much a prisoner of his station in life as was a tanner or any other Harijan. Perhaps she should remind him of his own insistence that everyone sometimes has to do things they don't like. Better not, she decided; he wasn't in the mood for that sort of comment.

The gaunt form of Arjun emerged from a shadowy doorway, then moved quickly to the table. Nur got up and went to see what he wanted; from the troubled expression he wore, it was obviously something important. Another case of this disease, perhaps. Arjun bowed slightly to Ambika, with his palms pressed together. 'My apologies for the interruption, Excellence. There has been another abduction. Phoolan Indrani's husband reported her missing a few minutes ago.' Arjun shifted uncomfortably. 'He says two aliens took her.'

Nur felt her heart sink, knowing what her father would think. Hardly surprising, since she feared it too. 'Not the two offworlders who were just here?'

'No, apparently these weren't human at all.'

'Nevertheless, they did seem intent on stirring up

trouble . . . Have someone keep an eye on them, just in case. Is this Indrani the virologist?' Ambika asked. Arjun nodded, and Ambika immediately stood up. 'Have the area sealed off and send a detachment round to search for evidence as to the nature or identity of the kidnappers. Perhaps this has something to do with these disease cases after all.'

'Cases?' Nur asked. 'You did lie . . .'

'I don't want public panic.' Turning away from her, Ambika accompanied Arjun back into the shade. Nur watched in shock as he left; what else had he lied about to avoid panic? A thought struck her, remembering her trip to Gul Mahal. That strange ambulance she had seen: could it have been the same one as the Doctor told them about? Perhaps it was being used to kidnap people, using the crime to cover up the disease.

If none of her own people would do anything about it, then she'd do something herself. The thought was probably in vain, she knew; her whole upbringing had told her that a single life was too powerless to make a difference. On the other hand, she certainly didn't fancy leaving it all to two offworlders; that might embarrass her father far too much. She knew he wouldn't approve of her involving herself, but she didn't really care as she was determined to be her own woman.

Nur waited a few moments until she was certain that Arjun and her father were definitely gone, then hurried across the courtyard to the main hall. An annexe off to one side held Arjun's office. As well as being the family's driver, he was also head of security for them, and she'd been living in the palace long enough to know that Arjun's office was full of surveillance and communications equipment.

Today, she was most interested in the latter. Her pass key got her into the office, which was dim apart from the softly winking lights of the LEDs and flickering monitors. One of the monitors was maintained on a direct link to the Kshatriya headquarters on the mainland, since they were responsible for security. Since a Kshatriya had brought the Doctor and his friend in from the home of the ill Sudra, perhaps she had been in attendance at other cases. At the very least, there might have been some sort of Kshatriya presence at these events, and that meant everything would be kept on record. The Kshatriyas were very meticulous in that regard.

She logged into the communications system, and a junior officer in a smart uniform appeared on screen. 'How can I help you?'

'I'd like to be put through to the records office data system.'

'All our records are classified. What is your security clearance?'

'Pratapsinh violet zero two.' The clearance was quite high, though it was actually granted to her for the sake of flying through normally restricted airspace and having higher technology for her ship. She didn't feel any particular need to inform the officer of that; a clearance was a clearance as far as she was concerned.

'Putting you through.' The image dissolved into a swirl of pixels which soon formed into a menu screen. Opting to search by keyword rather than search through endless databases, she froze. What keyword would she put in? She didn't have a name for the disease, the offworlders wouldn't be linked to any other cases, and there must be several hundred Chattars in Kuru. A surname might have helped, she realized belatedly. She screwed her face up as if trying to physically squeeze the right word out from her mind. Kidnapping, she decided finally. If there was a connection, then perhaps this Chattar would be listed as a kidnap victim. It was a ridiculously long shot, but someone once said that every probability curve had to have a far end, and even a million to one chance was better odds than the state lottery.

She typed in a request for reported kidnaps in the past few days, and the response was instantaneous. There were quite a few names, though she wasn't sure whether to bother scrolling through all of them; all she was interested in were names beginning with 'C'. There was no 'Chattar'. Skipping through the rest briefly, to take her mind off the disappointment, she noticed a Pandit Lal, research biochemist, and recalled that that was the man whose car her father had been checking.

She wasn't interested in prying into private details, but she couldn't help noticing in the 'Occupation' section that every single one was a scientist or engineer of some kind, mostly biologists and chemists, but a few physicists and mechanics as well. In total there seemed to have been dozens in the last few days. If this had been going on for longer, the tally could conceivably run into hundreds.

Five

Ambika was awakened from a light doze in front of the news channel by a steady beeping from the screen's pager. 'Yes, what is it?' He hadn't intended to fall asleep, but it had been a long couple of days, and he'd hardly slept for two or three nights.

'The administrator of the Gul Mahal facility is here to see you, Excellence,' Arjun's voice said. 'He says he has a solution to a problem you share.'

Ambika found the phrase curious, but then Jahangir had always been slippery like that. 'Send him in.' He switched off the news channel, and was just placing a pair of cups of fresh Mysore coffee on the desk as Jahangir came in. The Brahmin doctor looked exceptionally tired, and Ambika wondered just how hard he had been pushing himself over the unfortunate victims of this strange illness. He wondered if it would cheer him up to have the condition officially named Jahangir's syndrome, or something of the sort.

'Sit down and have a coffee,' he recommended. 'Then tell me what it is that brought you all the way back here.'

Jahangir sat with an expression of relief that was almost painful, and sipped at a coffee. 'It's about the possibility you raised, of this condition spreading; or of someone releasing it by' – he smiled faintly – 'misadventure.'

'Go on.'

'We don't know whether this illness is spread by contact or air. It seems reasonable, therefore, to isolate sufferers as completely as possible.'

It didn't take a 30-year medical man to work that one

59

out, Ambika thought. 'What did you have in mind?'

Jahangir hesitated, as if resolving some internal struggle. 'While I was treating the injured on Agni a couple of months ago, I had the chance to work with their facilities. It seems to me that they are adequate for the research into this illness. I believe it would be safest all round to move the sufferers to Agni, and place the station in quarantine. That way there can be no risk of the infection spreading from those we've already taken into care.'

It certainly seemed logical, Ambika thought. No bacterium could cross space, he hoped. 'What about the station's crew and families?'

'I've already discussed this with the . . . people in charge. They agree to it on, ah, humanitarian grounds.'

Ambika mulled it over as he drained his own coffee. Distance between disease and the population was definitely a good thing, he was sure. 'All right. I'll have Agni quarantined. Do you want a vimana put at your disposal?'

'The *Nandi*'s shuttles will do. Captain Sharma has already granted us their use.'

'Good.' Ambika wasn't concerned about people jumping the gun or anticipating his instruction; this was use of initiative and teamwork, after all. 'I'll see to the details immediately.'

'The other project,' Jahangir prompted hesitantly.

'Going according to schedule. The Sudra population will be completed by tomorrow. We'll begin on the Vaisyas immediately; I already have some men working on the filtration plant for the Vaisya reservoir to allow the compound through.'

'My chemists will be ready.'

Nur had slipped out into the hall when she heard someone in her father's study. When the visitor left, she was not too surprised to see that it was Jahangir. It just confirmed her growing suspicions. He looked worn out, yet walked proudly nonetheless, giving the impression

60

that some sort of support was physically holding him up. He didn't show any sign of noticing her, and Arjun opened the hall door to let him out.

A visit from the head of the medical centre she'd visited earlier seemed strange, since her father had been so dismissive of the Doctor's worries. Had he changed his mind? Ambika stepped out into the lattice-walled square, breathing the fresh air deeply, and nodded when he saw her standing there. 'Busy?'

She shook her head. 'Not really. Wasn't that Jahangir, from Gul Mahal?'

'Of course, I hadn't realized you'd have met him today. Yes, he had a few ideas for a new . . . isolation ward.'

Nur didn't believe in coincidence that much. 'So, you're having second thoughts about the Doctor's worries?'

'Perhaps it would be better to say I sought a second opinion, from a doctor with a wide range of experience.'

Nur knew what he really meant by that; it was an attitude she'd encountered many times while looking for charters. 'You mean he's older.'

Ambika looked pained. 'He was also chief medical officer on the *Nandi* until recently. I think that shipboard experience gives him a wider perspective on possible alien pathogens.'

'The Doctor is an offworlder; perhaps he's seen a lot of such things as well.' He certainly had that slightly saddened air of one who's seen too much suffering, regardless of his obvious youth.

Ambika smiled slowly and slyly. 'Ah, I see. I'm sure he means well, but I think Jahangir knows his job. There's no danger in these few instances of ill-health. Trust me; offworlders don't take care of their health as we do, so it's only to be expected that they are more open to pollution.'

There were only two receptionists on duty when Jahangir returned to the Gul Mahal medical centre, and neither of them paid him any attention beyond a casual greeting. He couldn't recall the last time he had slept, and longed to let himself drift away on the couch in his office. Instead, however, he walked straight past his office door, and unlocked the door to the room which he had earlier thought Nur was going to enter.

The room was circular and empty apart from a tripod-mounted device that looked like an ancient movie camera. Locking the door behind him, he pressed a sequence of buttons on the device, and stepped in front of it. After a few seconds, a creeping pins-and-needles sensation spread out from his chest, finally reaching his fingers and toes. As the feeling grew stronger, the sterility of the medical centre washed away to the cold starscape of Agni's sky, and when the sensation faded, Jahangir found himself standing in the observation dome on the roof of the topmost part of the Agni complex. Ignoring the small shrubs and pot plants dotted around, he left the dome.

Jahangir's first instinct was to stop to help the collapsed workers dotted around the corridors between the observation dome and central control. His legs refused to stop, and insisted on carrying him down and into the control amphitheatre.

Major Karne emerged from Chandra's office on the raised level of central control, and looked down expressionlessly. Loxx and Captain Sharma accompanied him, Loxx being equally inscrutable, while Sharma looked somewhat dazed. Jahangir wondered if that was how he himself looked to others. 'Don't expect me to read your mind,' Karne said finally. 'Have you succeeded with your task?'

'I've done what I could, sir. This station has been declared a quarantine zone, so the regional governors themselves will issue instructions prohibiting visits here.'

'A fine irony.' Karne turned to Sharma. 'Nevertheless, it might be prudent to take precautions. Your crew will be fully conditioned by now, so return to your ship and remain on station, just in case. One of our lieutenants will go with you.'

'Yes, sir,' Sharma said, a little sluggishly.

Nur paced the smooth floor of the hallway nervously, in two minds about her father's attempt to reassure her. His dismissal of the Doctor had been so unlike his normal easy-going self, and she was sure that he was hiding something about Jahangir's visit. It was more of a feeling than anything else, but such deceit with her was so rare for him that it always stood out.

She wasn't particularly concerned by the thought of him not wanting to tell her something that was none of her business, but for him to cover up a subject by evasion rather than simply saying that she didn't need to know . . . She felt insulted by it, and also worried that he might be in some kind of trouble.

Unfortunately, she couldn't really confide in just anyone; she was the regional governor's daughter, after all. This offworld Doctor, though . . . He wouldn't know enough about her station to be intimidated, he seemed trustworthy in a relaxed and open sort of way, and he already shared some of these concerns. She didn't seem to have a lot of choice, so she returned to Arjun's office.

Arjun seemed to be on duty 24 hours a day, and today was no exception, as he too had returned to his customary post. 'What can I do for you, Nur?'

She pointed at the desktop terminal in his cluttered security office. 'A data search. Can you find out where the two offworlders are staying?' She wished she'd done that first.

Arjun grinned lopsidedly. 'We've got over six hundred offworlders on surface here in Kuru alone.' The smile softened. 'I assume you mean this Doctor and Turlough.' He reached up to the touch-sensitive screen to key in his request. 'You know that private details in the datanet are confidential.'

'You're the one with clearance.'

'Unless it's revoked for doing things like this. They've hired a villa: 17 Niwas Ghat. You can probably see it from the west wall of the garden.'

'Thanks, Arjun.'

'Don't mention it. Please.'

'I won't tell if you won't. Have someone bring a skimmer round.' She left the security office and made her way down to one of the island's own ghats, a flat expanse of sandstone that terminated in a series of steps down into the water of the lake. A small hovercraft was already waiting by the time she got there, a Kshatriya manning the simple controls.

She stepped in and sat down. 'Take me across to Niwas Ghat.'

The man nodded, and set the vehicle in motion. The journey took only a couple of minutes, and she was soon stepping on to the much larger lakeside ghat. Some bathers and washerwomen were busy there. There was no need, and this artificially created watercourse was not holy in any way, but the daily ritual was an ideal social gathering, so the customs had been kept. The hovercraft headed back to the island palace as Nur threaded her way through the chatting people and up a few steps to the road that ran along to the private villas, each of which had private access to a fenced-off section of the ghat.

A brief walk brought her to the walled-in garden of an airy villa. As she entered the garden, Nur could see that a tall blue box, about the size of an information booth, was positioned on the lawn. Ignoring it, she went up to the villa's front door, and rang the bell-pull that was beside it. A distant tinkling came from somewhere inside. There was no reaction, so she rang again after a few moments, thinking that it would be just her luck if they weren't actually in.

'Can I help you?' The voice from behind startled her, though it was friendly enough. It was the Doctor. Turlough stood beside him, and nodded in greeting.

'Well, you could start by not sneaking up on me like that.'

'Ah, sorry. I was doing some work in the, er, shed. I saw you through the . . . windows.'

Nur looked across at the blue box. It did indeed have windows, but they were frosted, and none too clean either. What did it matter, anyway? she asked herself. 'I shouldn't have snapped, but you gave me quite a shock.'

'Purely unintentional. Am I to take it that this visit means His Excellency has changed his mind?'

'I'm afraid not.' She thought carefully, not wanting to give the offworlder the wrong impression about her father, whatever she feared privately. 'I just –'

'Noticed that he lied to us about whether there had been other cases, and worried about what he might be getting himself into?'

Nur stepped back slightly. 'How did you –'

'He isn't very good at lying, and you seemed surprised when he denied any knowledge of previous cases.' The Doctor smiled reassuringly. 'I've had experience of this sort of thing before.'

Well, she told herself, you did think the Doctor shared your concerns about this. Why be so troubled that you were right? She didn't want to make her father look bad, however – he did have a lot to worry about. She took a deep breath. 'He's not very good at lies, because he's not used to telling them.'

Turlough smiled wryly. 'I thought he was a politician?'

'Unwillingly. Officials here are selected at random by a computer program; it gives a fairer demographic spread and means power-seekers have no more chance than anyone else. He was a liner captain before getting picked for this job. Personally, I don't envy him it, and there are times I'd give anything just to be that liner captain's daughter.' She shrugged. 'There are responsibilities I'm not suited for.'

Turlough looked surprised. 'Surely you can't be against having a steady government post?' He gave her an encouraging look. 'To afford that palace, your father must be well paid.'

'Yes, I can. You know how politics is full of bribery and corruption?'

'So I'm told,' the Doctor said with a straight face.

'Well I couldn't find any.' She gave an exaggeratedly sweet grin. 'Use of the palace is the only stipend, and it's as much a place of employment as anything else.'

'Nice work if you can get it.'

Karan returned to his office from lunch to find a signal light blinking at him from his console. He didn't need to look to know which buoy it was from. Obviously the meteoroid had moved on into the next sector and was registering on that buoy's sensors.

He was just about to cancel the signal when an idea struck him. If the body was going to be named after him, he ought to at least familiarize himself with it. If nothing else, it would make an interesting topic to tell the family about. He dropped into his seat, and called up the buoy's telemetry, excited at the prospect of seeing his discovery.

The telemetry screen cleared, then displayed a time-coded starfield, with the russet curve of Indra to one side. At first Karan couldn't make out what the signal was telling him about, but then a black spot began to creep in from the edge of Indra, like a blemish on its face.

It was far too distant for its shape to be clearly discernible, but Karan tried anyway, getting the computer to tweak the image into sharpness as best he could. It didn't have that much effect, but it did give the uneasy impression that there was something distinctly odd about the blemish. Its edges were still fuzzy, but it seemed almost regular in shape – rectangular, or perhaps cylindrical.

There were records of such forms in nature, but nonetheless he couldn't help wondering if Sharma had been right with his declaration that this was a meteoroid of some kind. Why would Sharma have lied, though? He thought of checking with the captain again, but decided otherwise; the object would come within range of another buoy in a few hours, so perhaps he would get a better view of it from that.

He downloaded the telemetry into a private file, and called up a navigational program. He had two sets of telemetry data already, so perhaps he could backtrack to its point of origin, and see if it had passed by any other buoys, perhaps during his off-shifts.

Setting a coffee-maker to work, he settled in for a long and hard afternoon.

The Doctor and Turlough listened intently as Nur told them about Jahangir's visit, and the nature of the abductees. They sat round a table on the patio, sipping cool fruit juices. Nur had politely declined, of course. She was sure they meant well, but one could never be too careful when it came to accepting food from offworlders, since they would have neither known nor cared about the station of the vendor from whom they had bought it.

'You're sure your father said he was seeking this Jahangir's opinion on these cases?' the Doctor asked.

'Yes. Jahangir's an old friend of his; I'm told he delivered me. Well, supervised anyway. He'll have avoided soiling his hands.'

'Interesting. When was the first case?'

'The first one I heard of was about six or seven weeks ago. Nobody noticed much at first, because there was an outbreak of the cold among the Sudras.'

'Only them?'

'All the old castes have separate sections of the city.'

'How very convenient,' the Doctor said dryly.

Turlough raised an eyebrow. 'Seems reasonable to me. Things are just the same at home. It makes for cosier groupings.'

'This new illness,' the Doctor said. 'Which castes have been affected?'

'I don't know.' She could guess, though, now that she came to think of it.

'Yes,' the Doctor said, agreeing with her unspoken

67

comment. 'All right; why should Jahangir have a wider experience than someone who's travelled a lot?'

Nur shook her head. 'That's just ageism. What's that got to do with it? Father says he's trained in space medicine for his tours in the Alliance fleet. He helped out with the trouble on Agni recently, just before his appointment to Gul Mahal.'

The Doctor looked at her askance. 'How recently was this trouble on your moon?'

'About two months ago.'

'Well, why didn't you say that in the first place?' The Doctor shook his head despairingly. 'There's trouble on your moon, and two weeks after at least one of the crew returns, there's a spate of strange illnesses, and a series of kidnapped scientists?'

'Perhaps someone's building a collection,' Turlough suggested.

Nur ignored him, feeling a faint chill. 'You mean, he might have brought something back with him?' She tried not to sound too unnerved, but doubted she was succeeding; some alien disease to which humans might have no resistance was just too horrible to think about. That was the sort of threat you couldn't just flee from, because you'd never know if you were carrying it with you.

'Perhaps; perhaps not. But it does seem possible.'

'I suppose it could explain why Father's so put out, if his friend is even indirectly responsible.'

'Then you could probably do with some advice, not to mention information. Turlough, could you find your way back to the house we were at, where Chattar was ill?'

'I imagine so. Is there any particular reason?'

'I'd like you to go and see the families of this Pandit Lal and Phoolan Indrani. Find out what skills they have that might be particularly valuable, especially in terms of medical work.'

'Wouldn't it be better to confront Ambika with what we know?' Turlough's tone was very reluctant.

'No, I don't think it would. That's the sort of thing that

68

could get us locked up again. This might well be important, Turlough.' The Doctor paused to think, then raised a hand to forestall Turlough's inevitable protest. 'Just find out if any of them have been to Agni.'

'And what will you be doing?'

'It might be wise to take a look at Agni itself. If there has been some sort of outbreak there, we'll need to know what it is and how it started to spread.'

'You'll take the TARDIS?'

'Ah, I think it would be best not to. We don't want to give the local engineers any funny ideas. Besides, the TARDIS has never been that good at short hops, even when the coordinate override was still connected up.' He turned to Nur with a disarming smile. 'I don't suppose you know where I could get transport up to Agni?'

'Well, I really shouldn't give lifts to men on their own, but as a doctor I suppose I could trust you enough to take you there myself.'

'Not just any doctor,' Turlough corrected her. 'He's also President of Gallifrey.'

Nur almost laughed. Some people would say anything to make themselves look important, and she expected Turlough to claim he was the prime minister or something, but she was forestalled by the Doctor's rather embarrassed look. A trickster wouldn't look so caught out at the claim, and she wondered if this was true. She hoped so in a way, since at least it would prove that it wasn't just her who wanted a degree of freedom from those sort of responsibilities. She'd never heard of Gallifrey, but there were so many colonies these days . . . 'Is that true?'

'It's largely an honorary position, and the planet more or less governs itself,' the Doctor said uncomfortably. 'And I didn't ask for it, either. Now, I suggest we get on with our work.'

'No time like the present.' She saw that Turlough was looking not unlike an abandoned puppy. He was obviously just the Doctor's servant. 'Sorry, kid, but duty calls.' And for once she was going to answer it.

Six

Out-snobbed, Turlough thought as he hailed one of the three-wheeled taxis that provided a marginally quicker transport than walking. Those irritating Earthers he'd shared his exile with would doubtless be amused. He supposed it was bound to happen eventually, but he'd expected that it be done by a member of one of the larger Imperial families back home. A mere human, though, he reflected . . . He must be missing out on his practice.

The Doctor was clearly right that they had to find out whether any of the missing people had been to the moon, Agni, but how was he expected to find out? He didn't know where any of them lived. And in any case, he doubted that anyone would want to answer his questions even if he did find their families. Certainly he knew he wouldn't, in their place. The thought occurred to him that, back home, space travel was closely monitored – as much in case of accidents as for defence. Surely an Earth colony shouldn't be all that different; they were all humanoids together, after all. If so, then perhaps whatever centre acted as ground control here might know if anything untoward had happened on Agni and maybe even who had been there.

'Take me to the spaceport,' he told the driver. It was mildly reassuring to be able to give orders to someone, and he relaxed slightly as the taxi hurtled bumpily along the road.

Nur's government ID allowed her and the Doctor to walk straight through the gatepost and into the spaceport.

A row of small golf-carts was available for the use of visitors, and Nur ducked into the nearest. The Doctor joined her, and they set off across the expanse of ground that separated the ultra-modern traffic control building from the more traditional marble passenger terminals. But instead of making for the charred main landing bays, Nur steered towards a fenced-off enclosure with a few walled-in bays.

'What exactly is this outpost on your moon used for?' the Doctor asked. 'Some sort of chemical or biological research base?'

'I'm afraid not. At least then we'd know the disease was from there. Actually, it's our key energy production facility. Agni orbits right at the heart of Indra's synchrotron radiation belt, and there are a series of collection antennae on the highest peaks which draw off the current from the magnetic flux tube that Agni's passage through the belt produces. The actual station is there to monitor the energy flow and its transmission back here.'

'Is that all the station does?'

'For most of the time. Every couple of years, though, it also hosts a harvest of airavata.'

'Airavata?'

'Creatures that live in the clouds of Indra. Their DNA contains a natural radiation decontaminant, which spacer corporations find rather useful.'

The Doctor looked appalled. 'So they kill the creatures? We'll see about that; wouldn't cloning the material from tissue samples be as effective, and cheaper in the long run?'

'Probably, but Raghi's a young colony; our economy couldn't survive without the income from the airavata harvest.' She didn't like it much herself, but she didn't make the laws. 'I've got Father trying to impose restrictions, but the other governors are against him, at least for the moment.'

The golf-cart passed into a concrete ravine between

71

the walls of two landing pads, and stopped outside a pair of doors. 'Well, here we are. My vimana's inside.' The vimana proved to be a small triangular ship about seventy feet long and ten feet thick at the edges, tapering to a sloped canopy at the nose. A hatch was set into both of the corners where the aft surface of the engine exhaust met the other two sides, but today a ramp was lowered from the belly of the ship, and Nur led the Doctor under the nose to ascend into the ship. 'Welcome aboard the *Garuda*.'

The Doctor's features settled into a nostalgic smile as he followed. 'She's an old Burro class planet-hopper, isn't she? I haven't seen one of these in years; in fact, I didn't know they still made them.'

'They don't. This one's older than me.'

'Ah, well, they certainly don't make them like they used to. What's wrong with older designs anyway, so long as they still work?'

'You tell me. You're the one who didn't trust his own ship to get to Agni.'

'Yes, well, the TARDIS is a rather special case. It would be rather analogous to you using the *Garuda* just to go from the palace to the city; obviously you'd take a boat or a skimmer instead.'

'Well, the *Garuda* may be just a skimmer in relative terms, but I'd trust her over any other ship any day of the week. Besides, nobody else flies me – ever.' She realized she had almost spat out the last few words, and smiled apologetically, forcing herself to relax. 'I'm sorry, Doctor, I don't mean to snap at you.' She rubbed at the bridge of her nose. 'My mother died in a shuttle crash a couple of years ago, and the inquest recorded pilot error as the cause. So now I don't trust anyone's skills but my own. I know I can rely on me.'

The journey was relatively short, but teeth-rattlingly bumpy, making Turlough wonder if the driver had some sort of lemming blood in him. The three-wheeler

72

eventually drew up in front of the sweeping arches of a long and grandly decorated building which had huge windows set into every arch. Inside he could see rows of seats, little shop stalls, and ticket desks. This part was obviously just the passenger terminal. Looming over it, however, was a truncated sandstone pyramid whose roof was forested with antennae. That looked a much more likely bet.

It took several minutes to circumnavigate the passenger terminals and find the indented entrance to the pyramidal structure.

Though fully air-conditioned, the sandstone walls and marble flooring made the reception hall feel as warm as it was outside. A man looked up as Turlough approached the curved desk before the alcoves that led to the doors and lifts into the building proper. 'Can I help you?'

Turlough wasn't sure, since in his experience people preferred to look after their own. Not to mention the fact that he undoubtedly wasn't cleared for the information he wanted. On the other hand, it wouldn't do to let the man know that. 'I expect so. Nur Pratapsinh sent me; you've heard of her, I take it?'

'Of course.'

'We're wondering about recent visitors to Agni. It seems there have been some irregularities there.' Turlough gave the man his best imperious look.

The man shook his head sadly. 'If you weren't a newly arrived offworlder, I'd almost believe you'd been listening to Karan. I imagine Nur has, in that case.'

'Karan? Does he know about this?'

'He's been making a nuisance of himself over some sort of meteoroid passing by near Agni.'

Turlough was intrigued. This wasn't quite what he was looking for, but he suspected that it might not be a coincidence. 'Where can I find this Karan?'

'Office 424.'

'Thank you.' Turlough walked towards the lifts.

'Wait, you can't go up there!'

73

Turlough had expected that. 'Of course I can, I'm Turlough.'

The image in the holographic monitor in Karan's office sparkled with jewelled pinpoints. While the stars all appeared basically white to the naked eye, even in space, the computer had automatically displayed them in their true natural spectra.

A silken ribbon of light was slowly creeping back from the position of the navigation buoy he'd just contacted, stretching in a long curve back towards the inner planets. The ribbon had only gone a short distance, but Karan could already see that it was not going to enter into any orbital path around any body in the system. Somehow he doubted that it would enter any slingshot path, either.

His ruminations were interrupted by a chime from his terminal. A uniformed Kshatriya stared out at him from the screen. 'Space traffic control, navigation and telemetry.'

'Sorry to disturb your work, but I have an instruction to pass on. You are to uplink a warning message to all nav buoys within a hundred million miles of Agni, repeating that Agni is under quarantine and all traffic is forbidden to approach.'

'Quarantine? In medical terms?'

'The order is signed by Preceptor Ambika and the Administrator of the Gul Mahal medical centre.'

'Consider it done.' Karan wasn't going to waste any time when it came to medical matters; you just couldn't take any chances with bugs and germs, he felt. He keyed in a quick and simple warning, and sent it up the relevant transmitter.

'Very efficient,' a new voice said approvingly. He decided to take it as a sign of approval, anyway. The speaker was a European-looking youth with a slightly haughty air.

'Offworlders aren't allowed in here,' Karan told him, wondering if he was some sort of spy. He decided that this couldn't be the case; that superior attitude would hardly help him blend in.

'I'm Turlough,' the stranger said, leaving Karan uncertain whether this was a name, nationality or job title. 'Nur Pratapsinh sent me. I'm told you're concerned about some sort of strangeness near Agni.'

That explained it. If the preceptor's family was involved, then perhaps they'd sent an offworlder so that they could deny any knowledge of him if anyone asked later. They must want something about Agni covered up. 'Of course, sit down, please.' He used one chubby hand to brush some papers off a spare seat, and shoved it towards Turlough. 'I've been working on backtracking this thing that seems to be heading for Agni.' He indicated the holographic monitor. 'A ship near Agni claims it's a meteorite, but it's too big and too regular for that.'

'Then perhaps I can help; I enjoy a good puzzle.'

'That'd be —'

'For a price.' Turlough gave a predatory smile. 'I came here looking for specific information on two people.'

Karan's smile faltered. This was irregular, to say the least. 'Most information here is classified . . .'

'All I want to know is whether a virologist called Phoolan Indrani or a biochemist called Pandit Lal have visited Agni within the last few months. A simple yes or no will do.'

Karne walked slightly ahead of Loxx and Sharma on their way to the hangar deck. 'Maintain continuous surveillance for any craft approaching from the colony. If anyone attempts to approach the station, jam their transmissions and destroy them immediately. Once that is done, use the colony's emergency frequency on the captain's ship to transmit a distress signal tagged with the intruder's transponder code. You, Captain, will then contact your superiors and inform them that all aboard were killed. They will then assume whatever is responsible for the quarantine to be the culprit for any losses of unauthorized visitors.'

'Understood sir,' Sharma replied, with a slight bow.

'Commander Loxx, keep our ship in Clear as far as possible.'

'Yes sir. Should I deploy the fighters to scan for incursions from outside the system?'

'Intelligence says the Rutan probes are still a couple of days away. Do you question their accuracy?'

'I simply thought –'

'A rim patrol might be detected by any incomers. If anyone comes here, you may still destroy them.'

'With pleasure, sir.'

Nur bounded up into the flight deck from her preflight inspection, and settled into her seat. The Doctor looked up from the read-out on Agni. 'Did your people build this energy station?'

'More or less. Our ancestors found the ruins of something similar to our own complex near some of the existing collection aerials, so they knew they had a good site on which to build our own. We never did find out who built them, but it was a long time ago, so I suppose it was a case of finders keepers.' She threw a row of switches on the panel before her, and the vimana began to vibrate faintly as a rising hum emanated from the engines. 'Strap yourself in; this is only a second-hand planet-hopper, not a yacht.' The Doctor snapped his harness tight. 'Raghi Control, this is Vimana tango four two one, requesting take-off permission on vector zero-zero-nine mark zero-six-zero.'

'Tango four two one, you are cleared for take-off on zero-zero-nine mark zero-six-zero.'

'Thank you, Control.'

The Doctor looked surprised. 'That didn't take long.'

'Privilege of having a government-registry ship.' With the engines at full power, Nur used both hands on the controls, and the *Garuda* rose upward. As the pressure of

76

acceleration pressed Nur and the Doctor back into their seats, the verdant hillsides tilted and dropped away below the edge of the forward viewport. The clear blue sky brightened ahead for a short time before darkening to purple, and finally faded as the stars winked at them from ahead.

Turlough was bored, trapped in a dull little office with a dull and slobbish man, waiting for the computer to spit out a one-word answer. He wondered if a few insults might brighten up the day, but his mind was deadened. Besides, he didn't want to do anything that might dissuade his host from helping out, as that would prolong the chore.

He glanced at the holographic monitor, where the scintillating ribbon had passed by the second planet in the system. There was something about the path that seemed odd, without symmetry. His mind clutched at this straw, seeking interest. 'What is this supposed to be?'

'I'm tracking back the course of this meteoroid,' Karan said.

'That's never come out of an orbit.' Turlough didn't recall much from the Academy before his exile, but basic astrography was drummed into every member of the Imperial families from the day they were old enough to open their eyes. 'I'd say it almost looks like it just appeared from nowhere and started moving.' He frowned. 'I'd say you're going to get it reaching a hyperspace egress point.'

'Meteoroids don't drop out of hyperspace.'

'Stranger things have happened.' Turlough wondered if this was something the Doctor ought to know about. It was a moot question anyway; he'd already gone out there. The computer beeped softly.

'Your answer. Neither of those people have been to Agni in the last five years.'

'Then that can't be the connection.' The Doctor would want to know this, but Turlough was drawn back to the image in the holographic monitor. The Doctor wasn't around to tell right now, and this might be even more important. 'Do you have an image of this so-called meteoroid?'

'Only very distant shots that don't show much. The nav buoys aren't really designed for that sort of telemetry.'

Turlough knew it was really only military technology that was designed to those sort of specifications. If there was some sort of link to those systems, then they might get somewhere. It seemed reasonable that there might be, since they might need traffic control's assistance in any major space-based operations. 'Can't you access data from military buoys?' He made sure to speak in a tone that implied he himself could, hoping it would inspire Karan to try and keep up.

'There's an emergency link to the defence grid, but that's only for use in the direst emergencies.'

'And of course a mile-long unknown intruder approaching your main source of power isn't an emergency?'

Karan hesitated, his chins wobbling slightly with their own momentum. 'It'll take time, but I could access the defence grid's sensor logs for that sector . . .'

'I won't tell if you won't.'

Sharma was slumped in his seat at the rear of the *Nandi*'s bridge, half-dozing with the relief of sitting after being on his feet for 36 hours solid. His seat was raised on a podium so he could see out of the armoured viewport that curved around the bridge, while the command crew's stations were splayed out before him on lower tiers.

He was in two minds about the quarantine order. On the one hand it meant that the aliens would remain undisturbed in their work, but it also meant that no more innocent bystanders should get hurt.

Why was he doing these things? he asked himself

constantly. He knew it was wrong, but it was as if he was a puppet. This must be what was meant by a fate worse than death. At least the aliens weren't telepathic, or they'd have killed him by now for these thoughts. He half-wished that they were, and that they would.

He didn't have to turn to register the presence of the one to his left. He could smell its greasy breath and inhuman pheromones from here. It was a lieutenant, as he recalled. They always sent officers with him, and he wondered why. Not as a sign of respect for his rank, as they had shown no honour at all towards the humans. Perhaps they didn't trust enlisted men. Or maybe they had their own castes. He supposed it didn't really matter.

'Outer boundary buoy of quarantine zone registers a spacecraft in close proximity,' Parvi reported. She didn't sound surprised, just bone-tired.

Damn, Sharma thought. 'Identify.'

Parvi checked the *Nandi*'s own long-range scanners, her greying hair hanging loose and unkempt towards the console. Sharma wondered if he'd even recognize his own face with a beard. There had been no opportunity to shave recently; the aliens' constant demands had seen to that. 'Sensors identify approaching craft as Raghi administration vimana *Garuda*. The vessel is on approach course to Agni.'

Sharma's stomach felt as if it was balling itself up. What was Nur Pratapsinh doing? The alien lieutenant hissed with displeasure. 'Your government has enforced a quarantine here; why send someone themselves?'

Sharma wished he knew, then decided he was glad he didn't, as he would have had to tell the alien. 'I'm not sure. Possibly they're medical experts sent to help, or perhaps they're coming to take up a blockading position themselves to keep others away.'

'Are they entering a holding pattern?'

'Negative,' Parvi reported. Sharma felt his stomach ball up again. The *Garuda* was Nur Pratapsinh's pride and joy. He looked across at the squat armoured alien which stood like an ancient bronze casting by the weapons console.

'We must warn them off,' he urged with feeling. At least he was able to say that, if nothing else.

The alien turned back to Parvi. 'Are they within sensor range of the third moon?'

'Our sensors would function at that distance, but a private light freighter –'

'We mustn't take any chances, Captain. Destroy them as soon as they are in weapons range.'

For a moment, Sharma thought he had screamed a vociferous 'No!' but he realized from the lack of reaction from the alien that he had only imagined doing so. 'Lock the *Garuda* into fire control and arm concussion warheads,' someone said. Sharma wished he hadn't recognized the voice as his own. 'Fire when ready.'

The curve of Indra's cloud cover rolled away to port as the *Garuda* settled on course for Agni, which was a tiny red disc ahead. A gleaming flash of white was visible among the stars ahead. Like a tanker on the distant horizon, it was little larger than a curved fragment of a chipped tooth. The Doctor looked on with interest. 'It would appear we're not alone out here.'

Nur squinted at the distant gleam, unsure whether it was natural or artificial. After a moment, she recognized the configuration of curved main hull and trailing wing. 'That's the *Nandi*, Captain Sharma's ship. He's been released from rim patrol duty to supervise repairs here. It's the same ship Jahangir was on before taking over Gul Mahal.'

'If we can talk to him, he might be able to tell us something about what's going on.'

'I've got a channel open, but he's not answering.'

'Not with words, perhaps.' The *Nandi*, by now coin-sized, was gently swinging around to face their approach, its arced nose tipping downwards.

Nur didn't like the look of it at all, and tried to deny what she was seeing, not wanting to believe it. 'He's moving into attack position.' She hoped he was just being cautious after the recent trouble, and wished she had a targeting sensor that would tell her if he was trying to lock weapons on to them. Just to be on the safe side, she rolled the ship off to one side, all her instincts telling her to run for home.

There was a distant flash from the *Nandi*'s trailing wing, and a glowing spark began growing in the viewscreen. Nur was dumbstruck; that could only be a missile, and it was heading for her ship.

'Get us out of here,' the Doctor urged.

'I think you're right.' Nur's hands leapt over the controls, and the *Nandi* began slipping away to the side. The missile was still homing, however, and grew in the viewscreen despite Nur's evasive manoeuvres. 'I think we're –'

There was a blinding flash.

Seven

The vimana bucked, snapping Nur and the Doctor forward in their seats. 'What the hell is Sharma doing?' Nur howled in outrage, blinking away the green and purple spots left by the glare. How dare anyone open fire on her beloved ship!

A second missile streaked from the launcher affixed to the *Nandi*'s wing. Wincing as her harness failed to follow the fast movement, Nur darted forward in her seat, punching controls frenziedly as the missile drew closer. A row of green lights flashed on the panel before her, and she immediately threw the vimana into a steep yaw.

The stars vibrated momentarily as the missile exploded just to port, and a howling alarm presaged the hissing discharge of the fire suppression system somewhere back in the main hold. 'They're closing,' the Doctor warned.

'Not for long!' Nur wasn't sure if it was possible to run away in a vindictive manner, but she was going to give it a damn good try. Leaving the inertial dampeners to try and catch up, she sent the vimana into a tight corkscrew spin, looping around the cruiser in a wide circle faster than the ship's masers could track them.

Powerful fists clenching with breathless anticipation, Commander Loxx jabbed at the small ship on the forward viewer. 'Amateurs,' he hissed smugly. 'They're out of their league. Raise forward shields. Transfer all power to meson cannons, and take the ship out of Clear.'

* * *

82

The exultant smile froze on Nur's face, as a second ship, all bulges and blisters, decelerated into visual range a few miles ahead. Acting almost independently of her brain, Nur's hands swept across the panels, inputting an evasive flight pattern in a flurry of movement. 'That ship looks familiar,' the Doctor muttered. 'I'm sure I've seen that design somewhere before.'

'Not in this system, then. That's not like any ship I've ever seen.' She saw that the Doctor was engrossed in examining the strange craft that loomed ahead, and assumed he thought they were finished – and why not, since they probably were. She gave him a reassuring nod, feeling a total hypocrite. 'This is a faster ship than it looks; they're not going to catch us.'

So saying, she slammed on the forward manoeuvring thrusters, sending the vimana into a wild spin for a moment, before shooting off at a right angle to the oncoming ship. Her outrage at the offence against her pride and joy was forgotten for the moment, as she let herself follow her instincts. This, she thought, was what flying was all about. She hoped she lived long enough to remember what it was like.

Loxx's bubbling breath escaped in an admiring sigh as the vimana peeled off at the last instant. There goes a brave one, he thought, with a tinge of surprise. Perhaps these human creatures did have some worthy qualities after all.

Nevertheless, his duty was clear, and a brave enemy was as dangerous as he was admirable. 'Track them. Open fire, all weapons.'

A shower of missiles and bolts of charged particles flashed across the intervening void from the less manoeuvrable ships, skimming the vimana's shields in sparkling discharges. 'If we can get into the rings, they'll never find us.'

The *Nandi* had swung around and was lumbering into motion after them, but Nur spun the ship into a series of sweeping zigzags just to be on the safe side. Ahead, the wide belt of Indra's rings pitched from side to side in the viewport. Tiny pieces of dust and rock glittered in the far-off sunlight.

Without warning, the Doctor slapped her hand from the panel and hurled the ship into a banking dive. Nur had barely drawn breath to curse him when the first volley of energetic particles seared through the spot where the vimana would have been, had the Doctor not acted. At least half a dozen of the glittering fragments that had been in the rings ahead became discernible as needle-like shapes converging on the area after the shots, and flitting past to swarm around the vimana as it tumbled away. 'Space superiority fighters,' he explained.

'Left there as picket ships.' She felt vaguely ashamed, though she knew there was no need for it. She was a commercial charter pilot, after all, not a combat flier. Regaining control of both the vimana and her breathing, Nur spun the ship around, and pushed the drive up to maximum output. The fighters overshot and peeled out of formation to get back into pursuit.

'Much as I hate to suggest this, shouldn't we try to hold them off with some shooting of our own?'

Nur wouldn't have hated to make any such suggestion; shooting back seemed like a fairly reasonable thing to do. 'An excellent idea, if we had any weapons turrets. Don't worry, though; I know a few manoeuvres. We'll lose them.'

The vimana swung back directly between the *Nandi* and the alien cruiser, and Nur banked to starboard, heading directly towards the turning *Nandi*. Bathed in Indra's glow, the *Nandi* grew out of the darkness like some metallic tumour, but there was no telltale sparkle of energy discharges from the weapon ports. This confirmed Nur's hope that they wouldn't want to risk hitting the other cruiser with a stray shot. The aliens had no such qualms, and one shot shook the vimana as a second sparked a small flash on the *Nandi*'s prow.

A quick look at the rear screen showed that the fighters were equally unconcerned, though they swooped and dived to avoid fire from the cruiser behind as they followed the vimana. They seemed to take quite a distance to turn, though, she noted with fear-heightened senses. 'They're built for speed along straight flight-paths. We can still outmanoeuvre them.'

Setting her teeth, she directed the vimana even closer to the *Nandi*, holding her breath as she made for the wing-mounted missile launcher. She let the breath go with a relieved gasp as the launcher passed overhead, the vimana having shot through the gap between the wing and the main hull.

Two leading pursuit fighters tried the same trick, but only succeeded in illuminating the vimana's rear viewscreen with a blinding flash when one hurtled through the missile launcher and the other buried itself in the port side of the main hull. A spray of molten droplets and buckled hull-plating hurtled out into orbits of their own. The remaining fighters hurtled past the spreading debris cloud that was already fading from around the shattered wing of the *Nandi*.

The swirling clouds of Indra's storm-tossed atmosphere rolled past above the viewport, and Nur rotated the ship until the arc of the planet was below them. The remaining fighters continued firing, but Nur was throwing the vimana around the sky so much that there was no possibility of them getting a clear shot.

Lightning storms flickering through the clouds vaguely imitated the blaze of weapons-fire from the fighters, while a quick glance into the rear viewer showed the alien cruiser getting under way as the *Nandi* slowly tumbled. The fighters were already spreading out to trap the vimana in a hemispherical formation, with the planet cutting them off. Nur looked back up at the looming cloudscape, trying to think of a cultured and educated way to ease her unwillingly diplomatic mind from worrying.

Her mouth quirked up slightly. 'Oh shit,' she grumbled at last.

Sharma had yelped in surprise when the vimana flashed past the bridge. But this was nothing to the screams that had followed when the fighter ploughed into the ship four decks below and to port, jackknifing the whole ship.

Now the bridge was lit with infernally red emergency lighting, and clouded with stinking smoke that didn't quite manage to choke off the moans of the injured. The dim redness was so thick that, just for a moment, Sharma was unsure whether he had actually opened his eyes. He pulled himself up from the floor, touching a hand to his forehead. His fingers were sticky with blood, but he couldn't feel any pain. Not yet, he reminded himself, but it would come.

Thank the gods, he thought, the vimana was unharmed. If only he could stop this madness. 'Come about,' he heard someone order. 'Major Karne's ship is out of our firing line, so resume firing at once!'

Major Karne? He remembered something, a pulsing and pounding in his head, urging him to obey. 'I can't.' Sharma rose unsteadily from his raised seat, and stumbled over to the gunnery pit. That had been a government vimana, he realized, let alone Nur Pratapsinh's; why had he fired on it?

'I order it. The major orders it!' Sharma looked over towards the source of the command. A squat figure was braced against a console, jabbing at the fleeing vimana on the main screen. The rest of the crew were already obediently checking over their consoles. Clearly he had to find out what had happened to him, and stop this insanity. Getting himself killed would just leave his crew under the control of that creature.

Evidently it didn't realize he was no longer under its influence, so perhaps he could twist the situation. 'I said *can't*, not *won't*. We can't fire, because the launcher system has been destroyed, and all main power is out. Can anyone give me a proper damage report?'

'All shields are down,' Parvi reported, ignoring the blood that streamed down her arm from a shrapnel wound in the shoulder. 'We have a hull breach on decks E to H, sections three to seven inclusive. At least 53 fatalities, and all port-side manoeuvring thrusters are out.'

'Transfer all weapons power to backup shields. Get repair crews to their stations. We can't give chase in this condition.' He looked back at the repulsive alien, trying not to let his distaste betray him. 'With your permission, it would be most efficient if I went down to supervise repairs personally.'

The alien waved disinterestedly. 'Permission granted.'

Nur gritted her teeth as the *Garuda* dropped with sound-less grace towards the murky field of Indra's ionosphere, with energetic particles sparkling brightly across the radiation shields. She knew she was coming in far too fast and too steep, but the pursuing fighters didn't leave her much choice other than to hope that the shields could take the extra strain.

'You know, it's not such a wise move to get too close to a gas giant,' the Doctor warned. 'Even at this distance, the radiation belt is putting out over a quarter of a million rads.'

'Well, I want to get closer yet.' On the forward viewscreen, the huge reddish patch of a phosphide storm was growing rapidly larger as Indra's horizon began to flatten out with nearness.

'Closer? Are you sure?'

'There,' Nur muttered distractedly, wishing a little selfishly that the Doctor would let her concentrate. She pointed at the growing storm, which, though a mere pinhead in comparison to the whole of Indra, was a good couple of thousand miles across. 'We should find some help there.'

'You don't have to do this to impress me,' the Doctor reminded her plaintively.

The ship rocked as a stream of projected energy from one of the pursuing fighters slammed into the shields. 'I'll settle for impressing them.' Nur smiled faintly, unexpectedly excited by the risk, as she tilted the vimana and plunged into the outermost wisps of sulphurous cloud.

A cone of glowing red began to form around the vimana's nose as the friction-generated heat began to build up with their steep entry. The thickening ochre outside merely made the flickering image burn brighter.

Behind them, one of the fighters dived after them at an even steeper angle, but quickly exploded into a shower of molten vapour as the friction from the thickening atmosphere got the better of its heat shields. Nur registered the flash with a controlled smile. 'Thought so. They're not built for atmosphere flight like this is.' She thought for a moment. 'We're not built for an atmosphere quite like this one, mind you.'

As if setting out to prove her words, the vimana was already beginning to shake and rattle, beaten by the growing turbulence of atmospheric currents around the huge storm. 'This is where the fun begins.' The ship shook again, and lurched downwards out of the haze, into a billowing patch of wind-tossed stormheads.

Nur kept a tight grip on the controls, reacting swiftly as the vimana lurched around the sky as if it was clawing its way through a mass of candy floss which was still in the whipping machine. The Doctor held on to the armrests of his seat with white knuckles, though his face was a picture of the innocent enthusiasm she herself had always striven to project. 'For a diplomat's daughter, you have a decidedly odd sense of fun.'

'How exciting can it be when everyone you pit your skills against, in any game or sport, lets you win so as not to risk being voted against at some trade talks? At least with the ship, I know it's really me that's doing it all.' A solid buffeting slapped her head back against the seat's headrest. 'Of course, it has its drawbacks . . .' She rubbed at the back of her head with a wince.

88

'Yes. Well, I for one would be delighted if those other pilots would let us win this little ga— Look out!' The Doctor's eyes widened in alarm as the clouds ahead solidified into a looming mass of protoplasm, which pulsed with soft pastel colours. The *Garuda* spun into a barrel-roll and hurtled underneath the huge expanse of delicate skin, threading its way between the mile-long tentacles which trailed out behind the enormous jellyfish-like creature. Nur couldn't help but duck involuntarily as the gelatinous mass flashed over the canopy.

Nur looked out at the billowing creature, soothed a little by the sight of the leviathan, as if its placid calm was contagious. Her smile softened. 'About time. I knew we'd find them here.'

'What on Earth is that?' the Doctor asked, sounding a little stunned. Sparing a glance over at him, Nur was faintly amused by the Doctor's somewhat awed look.

'Airavata. They feed on drifting protein strings in the atmosphere.'

The Doctor nodded, his expression clearing – somewhat understandingly. 'And the storms drag up more organic matter from the deeper layers?'

'Exactly. There are always herds at various points around the fringes of a storm, though they pass through into the calm eye for the birthing season.'

The clouds around the *Garuda* flickered and flashed as a brief series of energy blasts bracketed it, but Nur had already thrown the ship into a steep banking turn. Most of the fighters shot past the airavata and scattered for a moment before rejoining the chase. One, however, sliced through one of the creature's tentacles, which began to gently drift away and downward. The creature's reaction was instantaneous; it swelled, then shrank, and grabbed the fighter with spasming tentacles. They were too flimsy to hold on to the fighter for more than an instant, but that was all the time it needed to release a massive electrical discharge directly into the hull.

The fighter exploded, blasting a few chunks of

diaphanous flesh out of the airavata, which shuddered again, but then resumed its previous inscrutable course.

'It takes quite a lot to kill one,' Nur informed the Doctor rather unnecessarily.

Briefly trailing a phosphide umbilicus of cloud particles dragged along by the slipstream, the *Garuda* sped out of the clouds and into a clear patch of golden sky. Directly ahead, dozens of airavata billowed and pulsed delicate pastel communications at each other, drifting in huge and majestic dances around and around like some vaporous display of synchronized swimming. 'They're beautiful. Are those skin-colour changes some form of communication?'

'As far as we can tell, though we haven't deciphered it yet.' The vimana looped carefully around the huge creatures. Behind them, the fighters milled around for a moment, then followed, this time carefully avoiding the airavata. Nur nodded to herself. 'Here they come.'

'Space superiority fighters? Space . . .' The Doctor grabbed the copilot's controls and switched control of the ship over to them, tipping the nose downward. The vimana spiralled deeper into the atmosphere, shaking and juddering as they passed into a more turbulent pocket.

Nur looked daggers at him, feeling that he'd hijacked her ship. But she was unwilling to snatch control back right now lest the ship be torn apart while attempting conflicting manoeuvres simultaneously. 'And you're the one who said *I* was mad?'

'Yes, but there's method in mine. It's just a thought, I know, but if I'm right, then there's an advantage we have that they lack.' The Doctor canted the ship to curve back from the approaching far wall of the storm's eye. Going down wouldn't get them away from the fighters, but the Doctor had seemed to know what he was talking about so far. In the end, Nur thought, there wasn't really anything to lose. 'I hope you know what you're doing.' She pulled the vimana up briefly, flipping it over and diving deeper into the atmosphere.

'So do I. It's been a good few centuries since I flew anything like this planet-hopper.' Miles below was a flat brown carpet that was not ground, but the next layer of atmosphere. The image was strong enough, however, to unnerve Nur. It must be something in the genes, she thought, that gave a pilot pause when seeing anything remotely like ground rushing up at her, even when certain that it was just more cloud. Was the ship vibrating or was it her shaking, she wondered. She just couldn't tell any more.

An oval spot on the console began to flash amber. 'Heat shield's beginning to overload.' Nur looked over at another read-out, eyes wide in horror. 'Hull pressure reaching nearly twenty atmospheres. I wouldn't like to bet on which will blow first.'

There was a flash from the rear viewer, and Nur and the Doctor both leant in towards the screen. The last couple of space superiority fighters flickered and imploded behind them. Nur hoped that there were no others patrolling above, as the Doctor pulled out of the dive half a mile from the next layer of cloud and started climbing at a gentle angle. The ochre clouds above thinned out, turning gold before darkening as they neared the fringes of the atmosphere. Something popped back in the hold, and acrid smoke wafted up into the flight deck, but the vimana continued to climb.

The Doctor relaxed with a sigh. 'Unlike your vimana, which is designed for atmospheric flight, the fighters were built for zero-pressure environments. I suspected they wouldn't be able to go as deep into this atmosphere as this ship could.'

'We're not out of here yet. Hold her steady.' Nur left her seat and dashed into the hold. The hiss of a fire extinguisher was audible. Nur climbed back up into the flight deck with a scowl, and flopped petulantly into her seat. She had tried to resist that particular urge, but with little success. 'The heat shields have overloaded completely; there's no way we're making it into Raghi's atmosphere in one piece.'

'Sorry about that. Can't we repair it?'

She shook her head. 'The whole field generator has burnt out, and will have to be replaced.' She stared out at the stars, chewing on her lip. The vimana was old, but it was her pride and joy; it was, in fact, pretty much her freedom.

'I wonder . . .' The Doctor pointed out at the distant pinprick of Agni. 'Might there be spare parts there, for use by those airavata hunters?'

'Probably, but didn't we just try to land there?'

'As I remember saying to Robert the Bruce, if at first you don't succeed, try, try again. No, this time we'll have to try an approach without being seen.'

'Look, Doctor, this is just an intra-system planet-hopper. She doesn't have a cloaking shield.'

'No, but she does have radiation shields, doesn't she?' The Doctor smiled encouragingly.

'Only for certain wavelengths.' She wondered whether he was thinking what she suspected he was thinking. Light was a part of the electromagnetic spectrum, after all, and if the radiation shields could be tuned to its wavelength, they might just get away with it. 'The communications system, then. It's useless anyway with the antenna gone . . .'

'But it is equipment we can use for wavelength selection. I doubt that I can build a fully functional cloak, though; the wavelength will have to be specifically tuned. The question is, what do we most want to avoid? Sensors, or visual detection?'

'Sensors, definitely. Invisibility's no good to us if a general sensor sweep picks us up. Space is pretty big, though, and we're pretty small, so the odds should be against anybody seeing us by chance. Just in case, though, I'll cut the running lights and internal lighting when we make our approach. That way, if anyone *does* happen to see us drift by, we should be indistinct enough that they'd take us for a meteoroid, or maybe some kind of volcanic ejecta from the surface.'

'Lead the way, then. To the radiation shield power couplings, I mean.'

'Just a minute.' Nur made a few adjustments to the environmental controls. 'No time like the present to start repressurizing. It'll save time when we dock.'

'Repressurizing for what? Surely the station's atmosphere is the same as on Raghi.'

Nur shook her head. 'The station has a standard starship atmosphere; an 88:12 per cent nitrogen to oxygen mix, pressurized to one point six-six-bar. The extra pressure makes it breathable, but the lower oxygen content precludes the risk of fires breaking out and consuming the atmosphere or damaging the systems.'

'That's an interesting thought; I've been wondering why whoever they are hadn't landed on Raghi in force. Perhaps it's the atmosphere . . .'

Nur shrugged. She didn't care about what had happened to the station anything like as much as she cared about getting out of here in one piece.

Eight

Jahangir had never thought there was anything wrong with a long session of good solid work, but even he was beginning to feel his head swim with lack of rest. Fortunately, there had been no patients brought in in the past few hours, so his body decided to sit down when he ordered it to.

He leant back, gritting his teeth against the tears, and wondered what sort of monster he must have been in his last life to deserve this. To be made a healer with a passion for life, and then forced to kill the innocent. He certainly hoped this was punishment for a past life, anyway, since the prospect of being given a worse cycle next time was unthinkable.

A spark of life faded from the face of a young man, and he opened his eyes to dispel the vision; no rest for the wicked, he thought mirthlessly. There was still a sparkle on the terminal in front of him, however; a tiny icon flashed insistently. Jahangir's heart sank, knowing full well that this would be an inadvertent cry for death for some unfortunate innocent. Like a possessed limb in some Gothic fantasy, his hand reached out to open a file window on to whatever the icon was warning him about.

A single keystroke swept the main menu aside and left bare a display of the colony defence grid's file tree. The icon for the grid's sensor logs from probes directed in-system was flashing, indicating that someone was attempting to access the data there. The correct procedure would have been for Jahangir to notify the Kshatriya garrison of the hacking. Instead, as if in a daze, he executed a trace program to find out where the searcher was. He left the program to do its job, and took out a small communicator from his pocket.

'Report,' a gruff voice said.

'This is Jahangir; I have an urgent message for Major Karne, or Commander Loxx.'

'Wait.' There was a brief hiss of static, then a new voice came on-line. 'Loxx here; I trust this is important, human?'

'Someone is attempting to download the defence grid's in-system sensor logs. They may be able to backtrack your approach' – I wish, he thought – 'or that of the arrival you are awaiting.'

'That is of little immediate threat. Have you traced the source of the access?'

'The result should be through in moments.'

'I'll notify a squad to contact you. Give them the location of the target.'

The system defence grid's probes were more widely scattered than the navigational ones, which were mostly confined to well-travelled lanes. Once Karan had input his clearance, it wasn't too difficult for him to access the defence grid's sensor logs. Working out how fast the suppose meteoroid was moving, and thus calculating the point at which it would be most clearly logged, took only a little longer.

Within five minutes, Turlough was anxiously puzzling over the design of something that was definitely no meteoroid. The telemetry that accompanied the holographic image confirmed that it was precisely a mile long; hardly more than a grain of sand by the standards of nature, but quite remarkable for a constructed craft. It was like a squared-off submarine hull, with the scarred stub of some sort of connection on one of the narrow faces, implying that it had once been attached to something even larger. The wider faces, perhaps two hundred yards across, sparkled with a delicate filigree of blue fire.

'I've never seen anything like that,' Karan said in a hushed voice.

'That's not exactly surprising; humans are so parochial.'

'Have you, then?'

'As it happens, no.' It did seem familiar somehow, Turlough thought; more in style than anything else. He realized with a twinge of worry that the Doctor was heading in very much the same direction as this new arrival. 'We have to warn the Doctor and Nur.'

'How?'

'You do have communications equipment here? Or do you use smoke signals?' Turlough wasn't in the mood for reluctance, and at least taking charge would help hide his own anxiety.

Karan ignored the sarcasm, and hit the communications controls. 'Get me the *Garuda*.'

'Right – I'm sorry, there's some sort of interference . . .'

'They're being jammed,' Turlough said. 'Probably by your friend Sharma. Come on.' He leapt from his seat, and left.

Karan followed, with a more wobbly gait and confused expression. 'Where to?'

'To find a ship. We'll have to go after them.'

'You can't just take a ship.'

'We can if we let your esteemed leader know that his daughter's at risk.'

'Then we'd best take my car and visit the preceptor first. He'll probably send Kshatriyas along to help.'

'That'll be the first sensible thing he's done since we arrived.' *The first thing those troops will probably do,* Turlough reflected morosely, *is arrest me.* They entered the lift, Karan pressing the button for the garage below the building.

Karan's car was a typical electrolytic groundcar, and in moments they were humming quietly through the city of Kuru, paralleling the lakeshore. Turlough watched the pastel buildings pass by painfully slowly, while he wondered how Karan had managed to squeeze into his seat. 'I hope you know where we're going.'

'The bridge across to the island palace is further than any of the ghats, but we won't have to wait for a skimmer, so it should be quicker in the long run.'

Turlough grunted scoffingly. Running would probably be even faster at this rate.

The interior of the car suddenly flooded with heat, and Turlough ducked as he was showered with shattered glass. A whip-crack sound was his only warning before the car lurched, throwing him up to the ceiling. His muscles ached as the world came to rest upside down, and he flailed blindly. His hand caught the edge of the car window, and he dragged himself towards it, sliding through on to the roadside.

Karan was already staggering to his feet on the other side of the overturned car, and Turlough's lack of faith in humanity was reassured as no one emerged from any of the housing blocks on either side to see what the noise was. From what he'd seen here, there was a strong work ethic in the colony, but he'd have thought someone would be around.

Karan looked at him, and his mouth suddenly twisted from opening to speak to a silent yell, as a searingly harsh sound from behind Turlough drowned him out. Karan jackknifed and dropped below the car. A stunned Turlough turned towards the sound, but a broad dark shape lunged towards him, and a crushing impact spun him across a roadside wall and into a flowerbed.

On Earth, he'd heard of footpads using coins in a sock to assault people with. His shoulder, back and arm felt as if they had experienced something similar – a scaffolding pole wrapped in a towel, perhaps. Propping himself up against the low wall surrounding the garden, Turlough opened eyes that had instinctively closed in pain. Given the colony's location he half-expected to see an augmented Ph'Sor Tzun, or – marginally less worrying – a custodian come to punish him for breaching his exile.

Instead he saw two figures barely as tall as himself, but almost as wide as they were tall. Plain cloth robes hid their nature from the open street, but they lowered their hoods to reveal smooth domed helmets, featureless but for half-moon eyeholes. In a cold sweat, Turlough resisted the urge to make a run for it as one of them lifted the helmet from its head with three-digited hands.

The face underneath was as domed as the helmet, but formed of greasy olive skin. Tiny red eyes glared at him from either side of a lumpy nose, while its wide and lipless mouth parted to let out an oily hiss of satisfaction, which nearly choked Turlough. He had never seen these creatures before, but knew what they were all too well from lessons at the Imperial Academy before his learning was afflicted with the more parochial, yet perversely more complex, terrestrial Modern Studies at Brendon.

Every spacefaring race in the cosmos knew what a Sontaran looked like; they were a widespread menace to travellers and colonists. Since he couldn't run, Turlough's second most natural instinct was to bait – his teachers at Brendon would have testified to that. 'Can't you find a Rutan to push around?'

'How can he know –?' one of the Sontarans asked the other.

The second trooper pointed a scanning device of some kind at the boy, and peered balefully at the readings. 'His brain's electrical fields are not consistent with human life readings. Shall we eliminate him?'

'Check with Major Karne first. He'll probably want to know why an alien has come here at this time.'

Turlough looked from one to the other, thinking quickly. If the Sontarans were as confused as he was, then perhaps he could talk his way out of this. 'Wait a minute,' he interrupted hurriedly.

'Be silent.'

'I can show you where my ship is. I've just left it, so I could take you back there. Our flight recorder has details of passing some Rutan probes near here.' He wondered how good the aliens were at reading humanoid body language.

The Sontarans glanced at each other, fingering their weapons impatiently. 'Speak now.'

'I'm new here myself; I don't know the place names,' he told them, putting in just a hint of urgency. 'But I could lead you there.'

The troopers exchanged a glance, and drew their wand-like rheon carbines. 'Walk ahead of us.' Scrambling to his feet with a wince, Turlough started walking back the way he had come.

Once Sharma was sure that he hadn't been followed, he ignored the access corridor to the weapons bay, and slipped into a stairwell. He didn't want to risk any lift-monitoring showing that he was making for the accommodation decks.

He was almost at the door to his own cabin when the thought occurred that, if the aliens grew suspicious, it would be the first place they'd look for him. He continued past his own cabin and turned into one at random. He dimmed the lights that had come on as he entered, and made for the general-purpose terminal that was set into an alcove in the bulkhead. Every cabin had an identical terminal, though the tiny hologram of a family scene beside this terminal allowed him to identify the cabin as Parvi's.

He wondered wryly what her parents would make of his sneaking into her room, even when she wasn't in it. He activated the terminal and called up a communications menu. 'Enter password,' the computer demanded, loudly enough to make Sharma jump.

'Command override Sharma alpha one, password "shikara". Reduce speech volume by 75 per cent.'

'Password verified. Command override accepted,' the computer said quietly. Sharma was relieved.

'Align pulse-signal transmitter to tight-beam centred

on space traffic control on Raghi.'

'Beam-pulse transmitter is non-operational.'

'Why not?'

'Power conduit has been disconnected at source.'

That meant he was stuck with standard channels, he realized gloomily, and those could be monitored. Still, his duty had to come first. 'All right. Route the intercom for this terminal through to the main communications circuit and open a channel to space traffic control.'

There was a faint chirruping from somewhere inside the terminal. 'There is a malfunction on all external communications channels.' Sharma thumped the keyboard in frustration. Obviously the aliens were taking no chances. 'Can we still launch buoys?' It was worth a try, he thought — a buoy was so small that it would be difficult to shoot down, and no one had ever said its signal only had to beep.

'Negative. Launcher system inoperative due to collision damage from impact with space superiority fighter.'

Sharma almost laughed aloud at the irony: the one thing the aliens hadn't thought about, and it had been wrecked by someone evading their attack. 'Escape pods?'

'All escape pods are functional, except for units seven and eight, due to collision dam—'

'All right, I get the idea.' The escape pods weren't really a viable option anyway; the automatic transponder signal would be an irresistible target for the Sontarans to shoot at, and its launch would prove to them that someone uncontrolled was aboard.

What he needed was time to think. He shut down the terminal, and left Parvi's cabin. He headed back for the stairwell, reasoning that the Sontarans would become suspicious if he didn't show his face in the weapons section as promised. At the very least, the diversion should give him time to think.

Jahangir kept his eyes closed while the skin tab he'd attached to Chattar's neck drained away his strength, and his life. It didn't help, as he still saw the terrified eyes staring up at him from the midst of a twisted involuntary snarl.

He wondered if Chattar had known what he was going to do, or whether he believed Jahangir was going to cure him. He really hoped he never found out. He had been brought up to know that Shiva gave destruction an equal role in the scheme of things, but this didn't make him feel any easier. He knew that he was not Shiva, and nor were the Sontarans. If this had been the will of Shiva, he wouldn't find that his body refused to obey his mind.

He opened his eyes, when the sounds of the thrashing had stopped. Blood was oozing from the edges of the restraints, where they had cut into Chattar's flesh in the throes of the disease. Disease, he sneered mentally. He might fool Ambika with that, but he was cursed with knowing better.

Chattar's clouded eyes were still fixed lifelessly on Jahangir. Accusingly, even. Crying at his own weakness, Jahangir wondered whether life and death even mattered any more. His own certainly didn't. If he had learnt anything from this, it was that ending was quicker and easier than preserving. He just wasn't being allowed to bless the right people with this truth. Someday he would, he told himself hopefully. Someday the Sontarans would receive his tender mercies.

Despite the tears, he carried on with extracting tissue samples from Chattar's still lungs. After all, his masters needed them.

Dusk was slipping quickly by as Turlough emerged into a dusty square, noting the position of a flight of steps to his left and a shadowy alleyway to the right. Three lotus pools each had fountains springing from the trunks of life-sized marble elephants, the water from each cascading on to the back of the next and dripping down into that pool. The Sontarans had queried his certainty twice already on their half-hour walk, but Turlough had reassured them both times. Now, however, he reassured himself, since the aches from his fall had subsided over the journey.

Turlough stopped by the nearest low-walled fountain, and pointed up at the courthouse atop the stairs. He sagged into an exhausted posture. 'I registered my arrival in there only an hour ago.' The two Sontaran troopers turned to look up the steps, and Turlough's exhaustion immediately vanished, as did he, into the alleyway on the opposite side of the square.

Despite their ungainly build, the Sontarans were quick, and a burst of gunfire sprayed across the alley opening right on Turlough's heels. Turlough prided himself on being a survivor, and considered self-preservation to be one of his best features. The alley opened out into a maze of back streets, and he knew that he could lose the Sontarans there. Of course there was a risk that other people might be around there, and he didn't really like the thought of them getting in the Sontarans' way, but the choice between possible hurt to others and certain hurt to himself was an easy one to make.

Bolting into the maze, he dodged left and right more or less at random, taking care only to avoid going round in a circle. There were a few people around in a small communal square, chatting to neighbours or performing minor chores. Turlough slipped through them and out the far side of the square. A few seconds later there were a number of screams as the Sontarans rushed after him, but no sound of shooting.

Turlough's lungs felt raw by the time he stopped against the side of a building to catch his breath, but the solid pounding of the Sontaran troopers' footsteps showed no sign of slowing. There were still distant cries in the air, and sirens were screaming somewhere around. Turlough didn't trust himself to form an opinion on whether the Sontarans having ignored the bystanders in favour of pursuing him was a good thing or not. He suspected that he would probably come to a conclusion the Doctor would hardly approve of.

The heavy running steps were getting louder with proximity, presumably because the gravity that felt normal to Turlough was but a fraction of that which was normal to the Sontarans. He dragged himself along the cement wall, taking a few deep breaths to start his run off again, but then stopped as something metallic rattled against his shoulder.

It was some sort of drainpipe leading up to the typically flat roof. Grasping it firmly, Turlough rattled the pipe around a little to test its strength. The Sontarans were only under half their normal gravity, but they still each weighed about three times as much as he did, so perhaps this pipe might bear him, but not them. It certainly felt just about right. 'Halt!' The arrival of the Sontarans made up his mind for him.

Turlough scrambled up the drainpipe with relative ease despite his fatigue. Below, the nearest Sontaran trooper grabbed hold of the pipe with three thick digits and tried to pull himself up. The pipe buckled and came away from the wall. Grinning, Turlough turned to pick his way through the forest of clothes lines and air ducts that filled the night-cloaked rooftop.

Stranded at the base of the demolished pipe, the two troopers leant back to watch as the boy moved back from the edge. Drawing their rheon carbines once more, they both shouldered forward into the wall, punching through the thin cement sheet and kicking it aside.

A man pressed himself in front of a couple of screaming children, but the dust-coated troopers ignored them, concentrating on discharging short bursts up through the ceiling.

A series of potholes exploded into the roof around Turlough's feet as chunks of the roof were blown out from below. With no way of telling where the next shot would emerge, Turlough forced himself to hold back his fear until later, and made a dash for a slightly higher roof next door. He made the leap up on to the next level with an agility that surprised himself, and he began to wonder if the blasts from the room below had simply blown him clear.

Knowing that he would be better off considering his luck later, Turlough scrambled across the rooftops in the direction of some better-lit area he could see in the distance. Hopefully, he thought, there would be too many people around who could see the two Sontarans, and they couldn't risk being spotted. Self-reliance was one thing, but sometimes you really needed the presence of others.

With a muffled snap of cracking ribs, the sergeant batted the human father out of his way. The man crumpled into a groaning heap by the door as the Sontarans lumbered angrily back out through the hole they had made.

The failure was obviously his subordinate's fault, but punishment could wait for now. Finding a pitch-black alleyway, the pair retreated into the shadows. The sergeant unclipped his communicator. 'Team four to base.'

'This is Major Karne. Go ahead, team four.'

'Target has been eliminated, but there was another humanoid with him. The other escaped.'

'Imbecile!'

'Sir, he recognized us as Sontarans.'

'Are you sure?'

'He told us straight.'

'There has been no Sontaran presence this side of the Coal Sack for three hundred years. He must be an alien.'

'Shall we try to find him?'

'No. You've shown the limits of your usefulness. We'll divert the scanning bot from monitoring the water supply to scanning for alien energy sources. Return to observe the spaceport. If the alien returns, bring him to me alive. I want to know who else knows we're here.'

Nine

'I've set us in a low orbit, skimming just under the outer fringes of the atmosphere. That won't tax our heat shields, but those ships won't be able to track us through the radiation belts either.' Nur sat on a low case of first aid supplies, and leant back against the wall. She hadn't realized how much the recent crisis had affected her, but was now getting a faint urge to shiver that threatened to give her some idea. For the first time in as long as she could remember, she positively wished she was back in the palace suffering that wonderfully safe boredom.

'Hmm. This equipment all seems to be fairly standard material, so this shouldn't take long.' The Doctor had hung his coat over a fire extinguisher, and now stood on a crate, examining a tangle of fibre optics he had exposed by removing the casing of a junction box on the ceiling. 'If I can free this output line from the encoder chip . . .' He stretched up to undo a couple of small screws with a jeweller's screwdriver, and tugged a narrow cable free of the tangle that led up to the transmitter array. 'Do you have any pieces of extension cable?'

Nur handed him one wordlessly, thinking how useful it would be to have someone so intuitively inventive along on every trip. He attached one end to the severed encoder output, and jumped down from the crate, opening the inspection panel for the radiation shield. In a matter of moments, he had fixed the other end firmly in place. 'Ingenious.'

'Oh, hardly that. The tricky bit was paralleling the sensor cloak with the main radiation shield so that we wouldn't be fatally irradiated the instant we switched on.' He looked over the hasty lash-up with a faint frown. 'Well, it should hold, anyway.' Nur hoped she was only imagining the doubting tone she thought she heard.

'There's only one way to find out.' Nur climbed back up to the flight deck and settled into her seat. She felt a strong reluctance to try out the new modification, lest it fail and the other ships destroy them this time. On the other hand, they could hardly stay down here for ever. She began gloomily programming the communications system for its new role.

The *Nandi* settled into geostationary orbit over the Agni complex, tiny bluish pinpoints of exhaust from the manoeuvring thrusters sparkling here and there across the steely surface of her hull.

'All stations secure,' Nirad reported from the helm, his ·hands moving to shut down the controls on the horseshoe-shaped panel that enclosed him at the for-wardmost point of the crew pit. Sharma stepped back on to the bridge, startled out of his contemplation of the peculiar flashing lights which were the last thing he remembered before going into battle against the government vimana. He pulled himself together and nodded an acknowledgement.

He looked around the wrecked flight deck, resisting the urge to wince at the smouldering holes that used to be control panels, and the bloodied and sagging state of the crew. He would have given anything to be able to order them all to the infirmary to recuperate, but the dark and solid presence of the alien officer on the bridge suggested that this would not be the action of a safely controlled man. Hoping that ignoring their current pain would allow him to ensure their safety in the long run, he pressed the control for the ship's intercom. 'This is the captain; all repair crews report to weapons bays and fire control stations. All resources are to be assigned there first. Medical teams are to give aid as time and circumstance allow.'

His best hope was to get back to the Agni station; it would be occupied as well, but at least it was so large that he might be able to go to ground long enough to make contact with Raghi itself and issue a warning. He resisted the out-of-place urge to smile; he'd given up so many childhood pleasures to study to get this early promotion, and now he found it necessary to play hide and seek.

The Sontaran junior officer who had been assigned to keep the human crew in check strutted past the repair efforts at the weapons console, glaring at Sharma with the air of a dormant but not yet extinct volcano. 'Why are you not still assisting in the work?'

'I can't coordinate and take part at the same time.'

The Sontaran hissed disdainfully. 'The well-trained soldier can balance many tasks.'

'There is one other important repair task which I can fulfil, then.' Sharma fervently hoped that he was indeed keeping the same dulled tone of voice as the humans under control. He also tried not to hope too much, in case it showed. 'Replacement circuitry will be needed for some of the weapons power and targeting systems I examined. I must collect them from the complex below.'

The Sontaran lieutenant unclipped the communicator from his belt. 'Tell me what you need, and the parts will be brought here.'

Sharma dug his fingers into his palms behind his back, since he couldn't even curse this attempt to block him. A new thought occurred to him, however; why had the Sontarans kept a human crew at all? Perhaps they were unfamiliar with Earth technology. It wasn't such a silly idea, he realized; after all, he could put a complex communications system together circuit by circuit, but still needed to call out a mechanic to look at his much less complex groundcar when anything went wrong with it.

'Of course. We'll need a complete replacement for the targeting computer's mini bus from the firing pin to the ring modulator; the focusing system will need a new bifocal contact lens; and the cannonballs are all completely shot.'

The Sontaran flexed its fists for a moment, giving Sharma a chilly sense of failure, but then it released a greasy snarl. 'I am unfamiliar with these devices.' Sharma would have been surprised otherwise, of course. 'You will be able to identify and fetch these things for installation, human?'

'Yes, sir.'

The Sontaran shuffled almost indecisively, as if it were trying to reconcile the situation with whatever orders it had been given. 'Report to the main airlock. I will arrange for you to be sent to the complex, but –' he leant forward, hissing as if he could smell treachery in the air '– one of us will remain with you at all times.'

'I understand, sir.'

Nur's vimana tumbled slowly through the sky of Agni's dark side, no more than a dark blur, and even then only when it occluded a distant star.

The narrow stairwell that ran back down from the flight deck was a black pit now that the internal lighting was off. The only illumination in the flight deck itself came from the pastel twinklings of the controls.

Far below, scattered lights gleamed across the ruddily illuminated rooftops of the outpost, almost drowned out by the dully smouldering volcanic flames beyond the cliff. Squat towers flashed with constant discharges along the clifftops, the electrical sparks rippling across metal that was as smooth as liquid. 'There,' the Doctor whispered, though Nur couldn't see why. Habit, she supposed; the stealth of the approach did have a sort of covertly illicit air. 'Those would be the collection aerials?'

'Yes.'

'Surely your people didn't build them?'

Nur shrugged. What did that matter? 'We found abandoned foundations and repaired them, adding our own control complex. Does it bother you?'

'I'm not sure. The aerials look as if they're made of terullian, though it's hard to tell from here.'

'I'm a flier, not a navvy.'

'It means that, given the location of your colony, the original station might have been an old Tzun resupply station. Most of their technology was based on the use of terullian.'

'Well, I've never heard of them, or it.'

The Doctor pressed his lips together disapprovingly, and pointed at some charred sections on the roof of the control complex. 'Those damaged sections must have been defensive emplacements.'

'There were six twin-maser turrets,' Nur agreed quietly, not realizing that she was almost whispering herself. She was half-afraid that the slightest vibration would damage the cloak or radiation shields which had, unbelievably, actually worked.

'Didn't your father say that this Captain Sharma reported that there had been some sort of meteorite impact?'

'Yes. So?'

'So? All contact lost, then such very precise meteorites, to so neatly destroy all of the defences without damaging any other sections? What does that suggest to you? Hmm?'

She'd been trying not to listen to that sort of suggestion, which had been made by her subconscious several times over the past few hours. 'That those are the blast points of some sort of high-energy weapons? Not our masers, though . . . The ones on that cruiser?'

'Meson cannons, at a guess.'

'Who uses them?'

'They're fairly common around the galaxy; just the sort of blunt stick that no self-respecting galactic conqueror should leave home without.' He indicated a row of lights

109

on a protruding platform. 'That would be the hangar level, I take it?'

'It is. We can't land there, though. It'll be watched, even assuming it isn't already occupied by our friends from earlier.'

'Is there another landing area?'

'Not exactly, but that' – she pointed up at a corner where one step of the ziggurat-like habitat block met the cliff – 'looks a more likely prospect.' The pale blur to her right that was the Doctor leant towards the transparent alloy to peer out. Nur ignored him for the moment, gently rotating the ship for a clearer view. She'd hate to go in for a landing, just to discover a piece of the cliff jutting out from the shadows to trip them up all too fatally. The rock seemed smooth enough, blending neatly into the metal of the roof above them. She nodded absently to herself. 'Yes, that ought to do nicely.' She swept her hands across the glowing controls, and the ship vibrated slightly as its tumbling began to slow. 'If there's anyone in that section, they'll hear the vibrations when we set down, but it's the best I can offer.'

'How will we get in from that roof?'

'The habitat block was built in prefabricated sections, so there are airlocks here and there that will form interior bulkheads if ever another section has to be added to stretch it out further along the cliff-face. If I set us down on the end of level two's roof, we'll be able to walk directly into level one's current outer airlock.'

The Doctor threw her a barely visible look of healthy scepticism. 'How very convenient of the builders to leave the door openable from the outside.'

Nur shook her head. 'Safety. There are young children in the habitat block, so it wouldn't do to have them open up the doors from the inside and space the whole level. The outer locks can only be opened from outside, once an airseal is formed. It's intended for the construction crews to open them up once they've

110

pressurized the latest addition, but I know the codes, so it'll work for us once I've formed a seal with the ship's main lock.'

She hadn't stopped manipulating the controls during her speech, as the landing operation was so familiar as to be second nature to her by now. Barely glancing at the panels, she kept her eyes on the horizon as the rugged surface tilted up and away from the nose of the ship, and then gracefully spun around, circumnavigating the viewport until it was stretched out below.

She half-started to switch over to the reaction thrusters for the final approach, but then stayed her hand. The thrusters were small, but it was possible that the brief flickers of heated gases they put out might be seen. Besides, she thought, it would be more interesting to land on full but invisible ion drive; she knew what she was doing, so it was safe enough.

She could barely feel the glassy touch-screens under her fingertips, so engrossed was she in watching their rate of descent, yet they responded to her instinctive touch as if she was controlling them by mere thought. She swung the ship around to face outward from the cliff while the grey wall of the top level of the habitat block crept up past them to the left. There was a distant rumble as the ship settled on to the roof. Nur looked to her left, slightly guilty at feeling a surge of pride when she saw the habitat block's airlock lined up perfectly with the ship's port lock, a mere ten feet away.

The Doctor was already out of his seat and descending to the hold as Nur shut down all power except life-support. She suspected that he must be impatient to get on with doing something, since she'd been perfectly capable of flying the ship on her own. She couldn't really blame him. The hums and buzzes of the drive and its regulators faded, to leave the soft whispering of the atmospheric circulation pumps as the only sound, apart from a few faint creaks as the closed-down systems cooled. Pausing to conduct a quick search for any other

111

problems, and finding none, Nur leapt down to the hold in one motion.

The Doctor had retrieved a couple of torches that he'd come across during his modifications to the radiation shields, and was hunting around the inner airlock doors, presumably for the controls to extend the connection tube between the two doors. Nur took one of the torches from him, and shifted a small locker out of the way. The Doctor gave her a quizzical look. 'I've never needed to use the connection before,' she explained, triggering the mechanism. There was a dull groaning from somewhere inside the walls, and a bone-shaking clang that reverberated back along the connection when it locked on.

The Doctor winced. 'I can't say I blame you.' He opened the doors, and led her through and on into the connection tube and habitat block entrance. There was only a single set of doors there, rather than a full airlock, since this was intended to become an interior bulkhead. A keypad was set into the door, its protective panel frosted where the ship's air had touched the surface, still cold from the vacuum. Pulling on a flight glove for protection, Nur opened it and keyed in a code. With a grinding of frozen mechanisms, the doors slid apart.

The Doctor slipped through before Nur could move, and she followed with a sigh, closing the doors after her. It was a little warmer inside, but Nur couldn't tell what might be waiting for them, as they were standing in pitch blackness. They switched on their torches, casting the beams around. There was no one in the hallway with them, though a few low seats were clustered here and there which might have tripped them. The hallway's walls seemed to be in warm beige and pink tones, with doorways set into both sides at regular intervals. The whole place reminded Nur of a medical centre's waiting room.

The Doctor paused a few feet ahead of her. 'Is this level left unoccupied as a safety measure?'

She shook her head, then felt stupid as she remembered he couldn't see her. 'Not that I know of. Have you noticed how silent everything is? There isn't a single sign of life.'

'Yes, but there's no sign of death, either. I suppose the crew could all be hiding from whoever attacked them . . .' He sounded as if he was trying to cheer her up, and she wished it was working. 'Still, there's obviously no point in standing around here. What we really want to know should all be in the control section.'

'We also need a new heat shield, remember.'

'Yes, of course, but one thing at a time.' He strolled off along the wide corridor. 'Someone was very intent on not letting us in here, and they must have what they feel is a very good reason.'

'Evidence of three hundred murders?' What more reason did they need?

'They have a ship – two if we count the *Nandi* – so they could easily get away from any of your colony's forces, and an Alliance force from Earth Central would take several days to get here. There's a lot more to this, I'm sure.' He stopped at a pair of doors recessed into an alcove, a call button beside them. It didn't respond to being pressed. 'All power must be out. Is there a stairwell?'

'Round this corner.' Nur led the Doctor round a bas-relief pillar to a padlocked door. Like all the other pilots she'd met, Nur carried a small pouch of tools everywhere in case of need, and the pen-sized laser-cutter removed the lock while the Doctor was still searching his pockets.

'You'd best lead the way, then, since you know the layout.'

After a dizzying flare of nausea, Sharma had found himself standing beside a tripod-mounted device of alien design in one of the Agni complex's observation domes. A burly Sontaran trooper was waiting for him, his rheon carbine unholstered but not pointed directly at Sharma. The captain didn't really consider that much of an advantage in his favour, since the Sontaran certainly wasn't being courteous by not pointing the gun at him. More likely it was just being rather dismissive of such a low-key threat as a single human.

'Find your equipment,' the trooper growled, waving Sharma towards the door and following after him. Sharma went through obediently. He was reminded of the time when a shuttle he was piloting was hijacked by revenue dodgers. Everyone in the service knew that space pirates, as popularly conceived, didn't exist, since space travel was so lucrative that simply dodging import and export taxes on legal substances would turn in a tidy profit for even the greediest bandit.

On that occasion, he had simply feinted and over-powered his guard, before using the bandit's weapon to subdue the others. Then, of course, the dacoits in question had been as human as himself, but not as fit or well-trained. Sharma recalled enough of his arrival at the station to know that no human weapon would affect the trooper. Stun blasts had simply shown no visible effect, while bullets merely bounced from their armour. The Sontarans' weapons were very effective against the humans, however, and they obviously knew it. That sort of smugness made Sharma want to hit someone very hard.

What is the point? he asked himself, as they passed into the storage areas that formed a buffer between the operational complex and the habitat block. The trooper looked very solid to him. On the other hand, he realized slowly, its rolling gait implied that perhaps its balance left something to be desired. Those broad shoulders and thick metal collar and helmet might keep it top-heavy. Perhaps if he could wrestle it to the ground, the delay in its getting back up would allow him to make a run for it.

It would be taking a big chance, but as the captain of the *Nandi*, the crew was his responsibility, and he had to try whatever it would take to get them out of trouble. He was unfamiliar with the layout of the complex, but recognized that they were in a main connecting corridor between the sections. A group of lifts formed a dead-end to the left, while a cluster of seats and low tables were scattered around the relatively wide plaza created by the junction of three other corridors, all of which had turn-offs quite early.

Sharma smiled inwardly. All he had to do was get the trooper off-balance enough to shove him down into the lift reception area, and make a run for one of the corridors. The Sontaran would then have a choice of three routes to follow. Those odds were definitely in his favour.

'Over here,' Sharma said, stepping towards the lift reception area. 'We can head down to . . .' he broke off with an exertive grunt as he grabbed the Sontaran's gun hand, and leant back to swing the trooper around. The trooper gave an angry roar, and pulled back, sending a startled Sharma flying over one of the chairs.

Sharma landed heavily, his hip burning with pain, and wondered how the trooper could be so much stronger. The Sontaran levelled its gun, and Sharma hurled himself forward – gunmen always expected their victims to back away – and, as he had hoped, the trooper couldn't compensate in time.

His shoulder crashed painfully into the trooper's armoured chest, and they tumbled to the floor.

Nur switched off the torch as she saw the hair-thin outline of light shining around the rim of the door at the foot of the stairs. 'Main storage level, I think,' she told the Doctor. She opened the door and stepped through into a horseshoe-shaped area surrounded by lift doors. 'There's a direct corridor to the operational compl–' She pressed herself against the wall as she realized that they were not alone on this level. The Doctor followed her and did likewise, nodding grimly to himself.

A squat figure wrapped in some sort of quilted armour had lifted a uniformed Kshatriya clear off the floor by the

115

rest chairs, sweeping him aside as if he was a rag doll. Even accounting for the one-sixth gravity, this was impressive to Nur. The alien wasn't that much taller than herself, but was almost as broad as its height, with an impressively wide back and shoulders.

Looking back to the Doctor, she saw that his eyes were slightly widened, but he was nodding to himself absently. These aliens were interfering in her world, and if he didn't tell her what he so clearly knew about them, she thought she would probably go mad. 'What –'

'Keep your voice low,' he whispered. 'Their hearing is particularly acute; I suppose it would have to be, to make out anything through those helmets.'

'What is that thing?'

The Doctor sighed like a bearer of bad news who knew that, no matter what, the mail must get through. 'A Sontaran. Of course, the ship we saw was a Valt-class destroyer.'

Wonderful, Nur thought blackly. 'Maybe we ought to go back to Raghi and collect some reinforcements?'

'Brave hea–' The Doctor sighed. 'Chin up.' When he pursed his lips and dropped a hand into his coat pocket, the last thing Nur expected him to pull out was a cricket ball. 'I'd hoped for a disruptor at least,' she muttered reprovingly.

The Doctor slipped three fingers around the ball and hefted it experimentally. 'I thought we'd try something a little less excessive.' He breathed gently on to the maroon leather and polished it on his leg as the Sontaran finally tossed the Kshatriya aside and stopped to pick up its fallen weapon. He stepped around the corner, sighting along his free arm as the Sontaran straightened, its back fully turned.

The cricket ball flashed down the length of the corridor in the blink of an eye, punching into the back of the Sontaran's collar and ricocheting away. To Nur's astonishment, the alien spasmed and crashed to the floor like a falling tree. 'Out for a duck,' the Doctor commented, blowing across his fingertips.

'I've never seen anything killed by a cricket ball before.'

'You haven't yet. He'll wake up in a few minutes.' They hurried down towards the fallen combatants. As they passed the faintly twitching alien which lay face down in the middle of the floor, Nur noticed a small socket set into the back of its thick collar. The Doctor nodded towards it. 'Probic vent. It's the Sontarans' only physical weak point, but a surface hit to the rim only stuns them.'

Nur fingered the tools at her belt. Perhaps if she rammed a screwdriver into the vent, it would kill the creature. That would definitely make her feel safer, but the slight movements it was still making urged her to keep her distance. She let go of the screwdriver; having seen what it did to the Kshatriya, she definitely didn't want to get too close to the thing. Thinking of the alien's victim prodded her attention in his direction. He was groaning slightly as the Doctor looked him over.

With a growing sense of irritation, Nur realized that he was familiar; very familiar. For once she was glad she wasn't a diplomat, because if she was, she would have no excuse for what she felt like doing.

The insistent buzzing was back again. But this time it wasn't Parvi trying to page him, it was a dizzying rush of blood back to his brain. He seemed to be pressing himself up against a smooth wall, and was at a loss to explain why he couldn't step away from it no matter how hard he tried. His puzzlement was eased when a face lowered itself sideways in front of his watering eyes. He wasn't standing at all, and the wall was the floor.

He rolled on to his back with a painful indrawn breath. The Sontaran had been so strong it was unbelievable. 'It's all right,' the strange face – a Caucasian with fair hair and a reassuring smile – told him. 'No broken bones or concussion, just lots of bruises.'

117

Sharma sat up, grimacing at the protestations from his battered muscles, and allowed the stranger to help him up. 'I'm the Doctor, and this is —'

'Sharma, you bastard!' A burst of light behind his eyes blanked out the instant between the Doctor's speech and finding himself on the floor again. A sharp coppery taste insinuated itself between the teeth in the left side of his face.

He opened his eyes to see the enraged snarl of a dark-eyed girl with her hair tied back in the style of most female spacers. She was trying to refrain from wincing as she massaged her knuckles. 'Hello, Nur. Nice to see you again.'

'So you do still know me. You can hardly have mistaken my ship, then.' She tried to deliver a vicious kick, but the Doctor pulled her back out of range with a disapproving look. 'Why did you fire on us, Sharma?' He wished he knew what to tell her. Somehow he doubted that simply saying he was told to would placate her. He couldn't blame her, though, and thought that the Doctor ought to let her do her worst. He settled for picking himself up with a groan.

The Doctor took one arm around his shoulders and motioned to Nur to take the other. 'Save your argument until later; I don't think any of us want to be around when this Sontaran recovers.'

'Central control is this way,' Nur said with a nod along one of the branching corridors.

Sharma shook his head, but gently, so that it wouldn't fall off. 'They've set up their base of occupation there.'

'Hardly surprising,' the Doctor said. 'What about some sort of infirmary? The Sontarans aren't likely to use it, and you could certainly do with a few stitches.'

'This way,' Nur grumbled, grabbing Sharma's other arm with visible reluctance. 'You ought to lose some weight, Sharma.' Together, the three of them started off down the left-hand corridor.

* * *

Commander Loxx fumbled with the feeder hose at his station, plugging it into the probic vent for a refreshing energy burn as the scout cruiser descended towards the Agni complex. That burn was the perfect way to celebrate the victory. Admittedly, it was only an unarmed ship, but the pilot had been so fearless and inventive that Loxx felt the effort had been well spent.

It was unfortunate that he couldn't have ended the chase personally, with a clean kill from his own weapons console, but the exhilaration of combat was its own reward. He closed his eyes to the dim and cluttered flight deck, instead letting the energy burn fill his mind with the glowing fires of well-remembered enemy ships set aflame by his hand.

Every muscle pulsed with new strength as the vaporized hydrocarbons from the energy stream were reconverted and distributed by the mechanical glands implanted in his chest. His ears rang with the hoarse sounds of consuming flames and bellicose cries.

And then he staggered slightly with sudden disorientation as the feeder hose slithered back into the wall, and the harsh sounds of clicking buttons and boots on deck fell upon him. He opened his eyes, feeling renewed vigour surging through him. If only the feeder's safety cut-out was set to wait a little longer, he thought.

He had occasionally wondered what indiscretion he had committed to be assigned this skulking mission, which offered such little chance to taste the enemy's blood in the air. He would never voice the question, however, and knew that none of the others in the crew would either. They were soldiers, and wouldn't reason why. At least the major seemed to understand their problems. It hadn't really been pleasant or unpleasant to meet him again – they were soldiers posted on the same mission – but at least Loxx could take solace from the knowledge that Karne wouldn't have taken on an insignificant assignment.

There were other challenges, though, and his invigorated brain sifted through all of them. 'Put the complex on visual,' he ordered, settling into his unpadded seat. 'I will take us in manually.' The oval screen before him switched smoothly from a field of blackness – reflected light from the clouds of Indra and Raghi drowned out the starlight from this viewpoint – to one of the canted slab of the habitat block sliding past as the ship neared the more convoluted domes and cylinders of the operational centre.

Something caught his eye, and he gently tweaked the T-shaped control sticks to bring the ship in for a closer look as it passed. There was something different here, but he couldn't quite put his finger on what it was. Something on the habitat block, he thought, and then realized that it was the literal truth – there was something on the habitat block. 'Switch back to autopilot, and focus on that section there.' He pointed at the area of the screen in which he was interested.

The image cleared and grew larger, and Loxx's charged excitement faltered. The ship they had intercepted coming up from the human colony was instantly recognizable, perched though it was on a rooftop of the habitat block. His fiery enthusiasm turned to the flames of anger as he realized he had been humiliated. 'Contact the Major; tell him he has intruders.'

A couple of blank-faced technicians had ignored the prostrate Sontaran in the corridor junction. He resolved to teach the humans a thing or two when they were no longer needed. Admittedly, he couldn't be sure of getting the right ones – they all looked alike with their stick-like limbs and fur-topped heads – but the thought would do him good.

The numbing pain across his chest and back had subsided enough for him to lurch to his feet when his communicator buzzed. He tugged it from his belt. 'Alpha two here, sir. I must report that –'

'It can wait,' Major Karne's voice snapped. 'Join Commander Loxx at the main lock. Stay alert for intruders on your way there.'

'But sir, that's what I must report. Two intruders have abducted the human space captain. I was struck from behind –'

'Describe them.'

'One wore pale clothes. I think the other was a female.' How was he supposed to tell? He wasn't a biologist.

'Very well. Join Loxx.'

Karne shut off his communicator after contacting the last of the troopers needed for the search. The intruders put him in something of a dilemma; on the one hand they were a useful distraction for the bored Loxx, but they were also a dangerous diversion for himself. Or maybe he just thought that because it was what the others would feel. Perhaps they would make no difference. Sometimes these days, he wondered how many of his thoughts were still his own.

His mission on this benighted rock was a touch-and-go affair as it was, without the interference of woefully inferior pests. Still, if they gave the troopers some exercise, at least some good might come of it.

In the meantime, he had such a short time to work out the details for the use of the special equipment which General Skelp had informed him was en route. Logistics were all he heard these days, it seemed. He couldn't recall the last time he'd heard any real news from home on the progress of the war. If there had even been any real progress.

The matter was settled. Two humans were no threat to their plans, no matter how they managed to sneak in unnoticed. That was an intriguing thought to him; how did they go to ground on an occupied base when their very shapes were a giveaway, unless they could somehow alter themselves? Was that it? Two Rutan agents trained in polymorphism would be a catch that shouldn't be killed. They would have to be questioned. *There* was an amusing thought.

He thumbed the switch on his communicator. 'Major Karne to all units; I want the intruders taken alive. Repeat, I want them alive.' If Loxx would just give him some time alone with them, they might prove very useful.

Ten

There had been a few nasty moments for the Doctor, Nur and Sharma when other humans passed them. Sharma would have gone for his gun if his fuzzy mind had been up to it, and Nur braced herself to fight them off. The Doctor had simply ignored them, however, and they ignored the trio.

'They're all programmed, the same as you were,' the Doctor told Sharma as they entered the empty medical lab. 'I didn't think they'd bother letting anyone in here. The Sontarans won't consider humans worth treating if anything goes wrong with them.'

The lab was a wide chamber with bright lights on overhead rails, while rows of benches partitioned it off into smaller sections. A set of mortuary drawers were set into the outer wall, and a sealed cleanroom for work that required a particularly sterile environment was visible through a section of glass wall. A locker just about large enough to walk into held all the cleanroom suits next to a small interior airlock that linked the sterile chamber to the main part of the lab. A full airlock was set into the far wall, next to the drawers, for the arrival or departure of emergency cases which shouldn't travel through the complex to the main hangar for reasons of delicacy or possible infection. As with the lock through which the Doctor and Nur had entered the complex, there were no controls on the inside.

Sharma sat dejectedly on a workbench, focusing his mind away from the aches and pains from the injuries he'd sustained recently, while the Doctor stitched the long gash in the side of his head. Nur glared from across the room, eyes narrowed as if sighting a weapon. 'What you did wasn't your fault,' the Doctor told him, though he suspected it was more for Nur's benefit. 'It's standard Sontaran procedure to subject captives to a repeated ocular stimulus focusing neuronic activity in the brain centres that control autonomous function. It suppresses independent high-brain thought and leaves the victim extremely susceptible to suggestion.'

'You mean, he was hypnotized?' Nur scoffed.

'That's one way of looking at it. The Sontaran method is purely physiological, though; identifying the brain's electrochemical responses to external stimuli and then exploiting them.' He tied off the thread and handed Sharma an ice pack retrieved from a specimen freezer. 'If hypnotism is the equivalent of nicely inviting someone to invest in your business, the Sontaran version is more akin to sticking a gun to your head and demanding your money or your life.'

'I'd prefer both; he owes me now, for the damage to the *Garuda*.'

Sharma held the ice pack to his head, and tried to keep open the eye that wanted to close itself against the chill. 'Anyone would think you weren't happy to see me again.' He couldn't really blame her, under the circumstances.

'Look, it's been a hectic day. I suppose the Doctor might be right that you weren't in control of yourself, but I still can't help taking it personally when someone tries to blow a hole in my ship – especially while I'm on board.' She shook her head. 'Just give me some time to deal with this.'

At last he had a moment to marshal his forces. They didn't amount to much – two unarmed spacers, and his own machine pistol. He could hardly retake the *Nandi* with those, even if he felt he could live with killing his controlled crew. He doubted he could do that, especially since his own freedom meant that there was indeed some way to break the conditioning — preferably without subjecting everyone to concussion.

'All right,' Nur asked finally. 'Just what are these Sontarans?'

The Doctor looked up, roused from some private thought, and took a deep breath. 'They're an insanely aggressive military species from the southern spiral arm of the galaxy.'

'Then what are they doing all the way round here? They must be a long way from home.'

'Trying to gain some advantage in their war with the Rutan Host, I should imagine.'

'You sound very sure of that,' Sharma put in. 'They never mentioned that to us.'

'Really? Do you tell the toaster what sort of spread you're going to put on the toast? More or less everything the Sontarans do is with an eye to defeating the Rutan. They've been at war for longer than mankind has been walking upright, and they don't take prisoners.'

'Probably just as well.' Nur frowned. 'But Sharma, and the staff here; some of them are prisoners.'

'Are they, now? Not in the way you mean. They're just exploitable resources to the Sontarans — spoils of war — nothing more than that.' The Doctor strolled around the laboratory, peering into every corner. The benches and worktops were forested with stacked containers, microscopes and carousels draped with peculiar tools and instruments. 'Interesting.' He squatted down so that his eyes were level with the containers on the worktop. 'You know what these are?'

'Some sort of biochemical samples?'

'Yes. I wonder what —'

'There shouldn't be any here. All microgravity pharmaceutical research is done aboard specialized Corporation ships. What is it, DNA?'

'No. It looks more like some sort of polymerase chain.'

'Some sort of what?'

125

'An artificial molecular structure you can use for filling in the gaps in DNA sequences, as it mirrors the incomplete section to bond it to adjacent sections in sequence. Some food production facilities who've used gene therapy rather than husbandry to produce new strains mark the results with a sort of polymerase tag for legal purposes.'

'Copyrighting their breed of apple, you mean?'

'Basically.' The Doctor rose, wandering amongst the humming equipment. He stopped at a bulky computer terminal set into a less cluttered and more expensive-looking desk, which presumably belonged to whoever was in charge of this section. A slimmer terminal was next to it, with its keys inlaid into the desktop. The terminal the Doctor was peering at looked distinctly out of place compared to the rest of the colony's technology that was lying around. 'Ah, this looks more promising.' He settled into the chair behind the desk, and tapped experimentally at the keyboard.

The screen was displaying a menu inviting the user to examine a variety of subjects in some bizarre and blocky alien typeface which was stretched down the screen in thin columns. A flashing cursor in a box down the right-hand side was obviously a demand for some sort of password or clearance code. 'My Sontaran's a little rusty, I'm afraid, but it looks like some sort of selection of files on viral cultures.'

That was more than enough to draw Sharma across from the bench. His and Nur's expressions mirrored each other. You could always duck when someone pointed a gun in your direction, but viruses were another matter entirely. The chill that ran through Sharma had nothing to do with the melting ice that dripped down his neck. 'Germ warfare?'

'Well . . . That's not really Sontaran style. They have a theatrical streak that attracts them to weapons that make a lot of noise and colour, but if the war's been going badly recently I suppose they could be desperate enough to give it a try. I can't really tell from this menu though.' He tapped in a series of characters, and the box around the cursor flashed on and off while a faint static buzzing came from a speaker somewhere inside it.

'Well?'

'Oh dear . . .'

Major Karne peered at the flickering indicator that had suddenly started glowing on the panel of the station's mainframe computer. A note beside it identified it as being a connection to the main medical laboratory.

Karne was more than a little surprised; Lieutenant Vold of the medical and environmental division was currently conversing with him here on the upper level of central control. Of course, there were a few useful captives assigned to specific tasks, but surely not there? The risk of the samples being corrupted by skin cells of breath-borne particles was surely well known to Vold. 'Vold, have you left anyone in the laboratory?'

'No, the humans are fit only for labour. Is there a problem?'

'Possibly. Someone is trying to access the mainframe from a laboratory terminal.'

Karne swung around, stabbing at the security monitor controls with fingers far thicker than those the controls had been designed for. As a result, the screens remained filled with static as he couldn't depress fewer than two buttons at a time. 'We should have brought one of Intelligence's augmented technicians,' he grumbled, giving up. Nonetheless, he was actually glad that none of the genetically engineered, five-digited Intelligence operatives had accompanied their team; the enhancement of their skills and instincts was fine, but they had a dangerous tendency towards developing psychoses after a while. They were often as dangerous to their comrades as to the enemy. Besides, they were too suspicious of everybody, and would probably spend more time pursuing him than the intruders. 'Take two troopers and get

127

down there. It may be a crew member who escaped the initial sweep, but it might also be the intruders.'

Vold saluted and hurried out. Karne watched him go, and wondered how quickly they could get another biology expert. Preferably one with a more efficient sense of security. What was he thinking? There were far more important matters to attend to, such as ensuring that the supply of new technicians didn't dry up.

The walk-in locker full of cleanroom suits wasn't exactly comfortable, especially with two people squeezed into it behind the rack of suits. Although she couldn't see him on account of the dozen limp suits between them, she knew that the Doctor would be trying to be just as still on the other side of the locker as she was on her side. She certainly hoped so, anyway.

She also hoped Sharma was sensible enough to lie still. There hadn't been enough room for all three in the suit locker, so Sharma had dragged himself into one of the empty mortuary lockers directly opposite. In his current condition, she thought ironically, perhaps he felt more at home there.

The door to the medical lab finally slid open and three Sontarans moved heavily into the room, sweeping cabinets aside as if they were paper to look behind them. Two of them wore gun-metal armour and domed helmets that fitted flush with their heavy collars, the other wore green armour and some sort of rank band on its wrists. Its red eyes swept around the hangar from under thick brows that merged into a domed skull, which looked as if it was made of clay the colour of rotten whaleskin.

One of the troopers passed by the small honeycomb of mortuary lockers on the far side of the lab. Fortunately it didn't seem to notice that one of the drawer doors was open by a tiny fraction, where Sharma must surely be thinking that his demand for an ice pack was the worst request he'd ever made.

Drawing back its wide, lipless mouth over hooked grey teeth, the helmetless Sontaran turned slowly, wide nostrils flaring as if it could smell them out. Going by the degree to which Nur felt she was sweating, perhaps it could. It took a few steps towards the cleanroom suit locker, and Nur found herself frozen in indecision, afraid both that it would hear any movement and that it had already located her.

Her heart leapt with each of its heavy footsteps, and, just for an instant, its eyes met hers through the visor of a suit's hood. Gritting her teeth to hold in the incipient yell, she tried not to shake as it reached out a triple-digited hand to brush a couple of the cleanroom suits aside from the centre, and stared into the back of the locker.

Its gaze swept onward, and Nur sagged, as the alien continued circumnavigating the deserted lab. 'Has anything been disturbed, sir?' one of the helmeted aliens asked.

'Not that I can see. Nevertheless, wait out here and guard this area. If the humans attempt to interfere with the cell samples, I will want them alive for interrogation and proper execution.'

The others stepped back through the door and moved to either side. They saluted, right arms running along the trapezius so that their hands were level with the centre of their collars. Their leader lumbered out of the room and the door slid shut. The Doctor tapped Nur on the shoulder, and removed his disguising hood. Dragging her eyes away from the door for a moment, Nur looked to see what the Doctor made of this. He had drawn himself into a sitting position on a table. Sharma moved over to listen at the door, clapping his arms around himself in an attempt to warm up. After a moment, he shrugged and came back to the others. Apart from the guarded door, the only other exit was an airlock. 'Could we climb up to your ship outside?'

'Probably, but if that door is hotwired, the environmental systems board will hold its own Festival of Lights.

Couldn't we just knock out the guards or something? You said that vent was their weakness, so we can go for that again.'

'Possibly one, but I doubt we could deal with both. Sontarans are notoriously difficult to kill in hand-to-hand combat. How well was the good captain here doing against one when we found him? They evolved on a high-gravity world orbiting a G0 star, you see, so they're much stronger in this environment than we are. Do you really think that one of them would stand idly by while it takes all of us to overpower the other?' He returned to the samples by the microscope. 'This must be something to do with them, rather than the station crew.'

'A guess?'

'No, an observation. Green armour is the uniform of the Sontaran army's medical and environmental division. You don't see many of them in the field, because Sontarans prefer a clean death in battle to being patched up. Most of their medical officers are assigned to keep an eye on the progress of embryos in the cloning vats and hatcheries.'

'Could they be trying to set up one of those here?'

The Doctor shook his head, then froze and raised his eyebrows. 'I suppose it is possible. The Rutan evolved on a frigid world, so the high-energy radiation levels here might discourage them from coming to investigate. If they are planning to move in a hatchery, they'd certainly need to know what pathogens existed here, either native or brought from Earth by your people.'

'Like these samples here,' Sharma said from the door to the cleanroom. He held a sealed canister in each hand. 'The common cold?'

Nur drifted over to the microscopes. Curiosity had got her into trouble lots of times during her childhood, but she didn't think the Doctor or Sharma would chastise her for it now. And to think she'd been so bored by the very same things at the medical centre yesterday. She straightened, not knowing what any of the multicoloured

130

blobs in the lens were. They *were* the very same things, she thought suddenly, and bent down to the eyepiece again.

A faint thrill ran through her as she realized that she was literally correct. This substance was exactly the same as the sample in the microscope she'd peered through yesterday. 'Doctor! This stuff here; I've seen it before.'

'Really?' The Doctor came over and had another look through the eyepiece.

'I was on a civic visit to a medical centre yesterday. I mean, I didn't want to bother, but –'

A pained expression crossed the Doctor's face. 'Please, just tell me about this.'

'While I was being shown around, I took a look through a microscope and saw this exact substance. I remember the department head – ah, Jahangir, I think – got a bit jumpy at that point.'

'Jahangir?' Sharma exclaimed. 'Ageing, white hair . . .'

'That's the one. You know him?'

'He's the *Nandi*'s CMO. I haven't seen him since I first arrived on the complex.'

'Of course,' the Doctor breathed. 'Nur, has there by any chance been an epidemic of the common cold recently?'

'Actually, yes. At least in Kuru, I don't know about the other provinces; I mean, it's harmless and hardly newsworthy.'

'I have a nasty suspicion that it's anything but harmless. This is a cold virus with a polymerase chain attached, which will latch on to anyone who catches the virus. Your whole population could be tagged with it.'

'But it's not fatal or anything.'

The Doctor thrust his hands in his pockets and paced around for a moment. 'No, it isn't. And that's the strangest thing of all.'

Before Nur could think of an answer, something beeped in her pocket. Heart sinking, she drew out the electronic key to her ship. A red light was flashing on it,

131

and she switched it off. 'It's all academic anyway; someone's entered the *Garuda*, and I suppose we can all guess who.'

A couple of troopers bounded through the airlock with the surprising grace of those used to working in lower than natural gravity. Loxx followed with a purposeful stride as the troopers swept their rheon carbines around the cluttered cargo level.

One of the troopers consulted a small electronic device, and saluted Loxx. Loxx was in no mood for formalities; someone had humiliated him and he wanted to hit back as a warrior should. 'Well, soldier?'

'The tracker registers no lifeforms aboard, sir.'

'Scan the flight-deck control panels for bio-traces, then reset the tracker with the pilot's traces.'

'Yes sir.'

Major Karne was standing in front of a quartet of screens displaying the latest analyses of Indra's atmospheric conditions when Loxx bustled into the room. The trooper who had lost Sharma accompanied his squad, as they had run into him on their way back to central control.

'Sir,' Loxx began, eager to get into action, especially if doing so would help to gloss over the failure he had to report. 'The ship docked on the habitat block matches precisely the configuration of the colony vessel which was pursued into the atmosphere of the gas giant. We do have, however, a biological trace of skin cells from which to track at least one of the occupants.'

'The same craft,' Karne echoed. 'And how could it be that you failed to detect its approach from our cruiser?'

'The ship has been fitted with a sensor-cloak of some –'

'The modifications made to a ship by its pilot are of no concern to us, Commander. Our entire operation could be jeopardized if the occupants return to the colony with any information on our plans. According to this incompetent' – he gestured towards the trooper who had been felled by the intruders – 'there are at least two intruders, now in the company of a humanoid who has been involved with our work here.' Karne hefted his side-arm, and Loxx steeled himself for the blaze of pain that would presage a merciful if dishonourable death. 'I want those intruders, not apologies.' Casually, without even looking to aim, Karne swung the rheon carbine towards the recovered trooper, and fired. The trooper convulsed and thudded to the metal deck.

Loxx wasn't relieved as such, as he hadn't really been afraid in the first place, but he was grateful still to have the chance to fight the intruders. Karne stepped over the bulky corpse, jabbing at Loxx with the carbine as if it was an accusing finger. 'Don't fail me again, Commander.'

The Doctor threw open all the cupboards down at the end of the lab which contained a row of sinks for sterilizing and disinfecting. 'Find containers of some kind,' he instructed the others. 'Something solid but fragile.'

He dropped to his knees and rooted through the bottles and cartons that were neatly stored there, pulling out glass jars of ether and surgical spirits, placing them in the nearest sink along with a plastic carton of blue-tinted detergent and some petroleum jelly. Sharma handed him a pair of bulb-bottomed test tubes. 'Will these do?'

'Perfect, but find a few more just in case we miss the first time.'

'Isn't this a bit dangerous?'

'Less so than waiting here to be found by the Sontarans.' The Doctor started measuring the liquids into a kidney bowl. 'These should enable us to deal with the guards quickly enough, if the atmosphere doesn't prevent ignition altogether.'

'How so?'

'Well, the problem is to get both guards out of the way simultaneously, yes?'

'That'd be useful.'

'So if we blow those doors outwards?'

'The blast should take them out!' Sharma liked the sound of that.

'Not necessarily. I'm betting on it simply knocking them out of the way with the force of it. That should give us the chance to make a run for it before they recover enough to come after us.'

'Where do we go?' Nur asked. 'No way are you tossing homemade grenades around my ship.'

'We go back to Raghi, of course.'

'The intruders are sixty-eight yards away, bearing zero-two-zero mark two-two-seven.'

Loxx snatched the tracer from the trooper who carried it, and compared it to a layout of the complex on a small LCD pad he held. 'That puts them in the medical lab. I thought Vold checked there.' Vold could be disciplined later. 'Commander Loxx to Delta six and eight. Are you still guarding the medical laboratory?'

'Yes sir.'

'Get inside; there are two intruders for you there. Major Karne wants them alive.' Loxx beckoned his troops on, and set off towards the nearest stairwell.

The Doctor tore off the last piece of surgical tape with his teeth, and added it to the fourth of the bulb-bottomed test tubes, securing it firmly to the corner of the door. 'All right, Captain, are you sure you wouldn't rather I did this. I never miss, you know.'

'I'm sure.' I've got to do something, he added mentally, even if it's only detonating this explosive. A single shot into one of the four test tubes should do it.

'All right. Well, I suggest we all move back to the cleanroom. The armoured glass there should just about protect us.' Sharma looked back at the four tubes taped to the corners of the door, trying to judge which one he'd best be able to hit. The word 'should' wasn't very comforting here, and he wondered exactly what kind of mixture the Doctor had put in there.

As he looked backward, the doors started to slide open. It was just his luck, he thought; a few more seconds and the Sontarans would never have known what hit them. Why did they have to come into the room now? His body bypassing his numbed mind, Sharma fully turned, his back and shoulders barrelling into the Doctor and Nur and slamming them to the ground. They rolled to the side, behind rows of cupboards, and Sharma dropped to his knees beside Nur as the two helmeted Sontarans charged forward.

Sharma swept his gun up, the cylindrical magazine over his forearm balancing out the barrel's weight, and fired a single shot at the top right-hand test tube.

With a whip-crack, the air filled with a scarlet heat as the detonation of the first tube ignited the others. A blast of dry heat sent Sharma spinning backward as the benchtop clutter flew apart in smoking cinders.

Retching at the chemical taste in his raw throat, Sharma felt a tug on his arm. Nur pulled him up, while the Doctor shook his head and dusted himself down, before stepping gingerly through the ragged hole where the doors had once stood. Sharma tried not to look at the slightly steaming green and ochre mounds nearby, disgusted enough by the Sontarans' normal appearance.

Setting his gun to three-round bursts, he allowed Nur to lead him out of the lab, coughing as she did so. Bullets hadn't done any good against Sontaran armour when they first arrived, but the weight of the weapon was a comforting reminder that he could at least make his own choices again.

The Doctor paused in the pastel-hued plaza a short distance outside the medical lab, looking around with an indecisive expression. 'If the Sontarans are sending that concoction to Raghi, then they must have a direct link to the planet from here.'

'They have a ship,' Sharma pointed out.

The Doctor gave him a long look. 'Yes, but if one of them walked up to the front door of a chemist's, people would notice. Is there a transmat terminal here?'

Nur shook her head. 'Nobody in their right mind would travel through a matter beam with a terminus here. The energy discharges from the synchrotron radiation belt would scramble anyone who tried.'

'Then they must be using their own system, an osmic projector. That works by quantum tunnelling, so the energy coming down the magnetic flux tube shouldn't affect it.'

'They are.' Sharma didn't recognize the terminology, but he had certainly used some sort of matter beam to get here. He shuddered at the thought. 'I came down it from the *Nandi*.'

'Where did you materialize?'

'In a dome with an open view of the sky.'

'Observation dome,' Nur said. 'It's at the top of the central hub of the operational block. Didn't you see it when we landed?'

'A clear dome with a garden inside?' the Doctor ventured.

'Right.'

'Good. Then all we have to do is reach the central hub and climb up.'

'There isn't a stairwell the whole way, just lifts, and they're all shut down.'

'Think positively, please.'

Loxx kicked a piece of parboiled trooper aside, and took in the devastated state of the lab in a single glance. 'Where now?'

'Head for the central hub. They'll reach the maintenance bay in moments.'

'Come on. Shoot to wound.'

Nur looked to both sides as she passed under the wide entrance arch to the storage cells' maintenance bay. There was no sign of Sontaran activity, though a couple of grimy humans were pushing a dumpster-sized cart along. The vaulted bay was mostly in shadow, but there was still a distinct flicker of electrical life in the bluish crystalline columns that passed through the wide pit. On the far side, around the catwalk, the doors to the cargo lifts were clearly visible. Sharma seemed to have recovered, and followed a little more vigorously. Nur supposed it was probably for the best, and he did seem genuinely upset. She would let it go for the moment, and see about his transgression later.

The Doctor bounded ahead with unlimited energy, tapping at the cargo lifts' call buttons to no avail. She wondered if he had any idea how high the complex really was, because such a long climb wasn't something *she'd* think about lightly.

He turned to call back to them, and she felt her blood chill as his eyes widened. 'Take cover!' he yelled.

She hurled herself behind the cargo cart, as Sharma spun to fire ineffectually at the Sontarans who were clattering into the bay. A blast of energy blew one of the grimy workers off the cart and the body slid into the wall a few yards away. Sharma grabbed the other one, and pulled him into shelter.

The Doctor took a flying leap, chunks of pitted metal being blasted from the supports of the column beside him, to join them sheltering behind the cart. He looked curiously at one of the chunks of metal, and picked it up.

Nur stifled a warning, as the expected cry of pain failed to come from the Doctor. 'Not even warm,' he told her. 'What do you make of it?'

She looked at the piece of metal. It was the colour of quicksilver, but there was a smooth patina to it that was more reminiscent of ceramic. 'Some new alloy? I told you; this section was found the way it is, and we added the complex around it.'

'This is terullian. The whole support structure for these storage crystals is built from – How deep do the columns go?'

'Several miles.'

'And all gift-wrapped in terullian. What does that suggest to you?'

How could it mean anything to her? she thought. She'd never heard of it. 'That there's a lot of it about?'

'Yes. I wonder why that makes me so nervous.' He tapped at the dumpster.

'Ordinary steel.'

'Start pulling it this way. Sharma, you cover us.'

The Sontarans had raced into the maintenance bay just behind the intruders. Loxx had immediately raised his gun and opened fire; his troopers followed suit. Particle bursts blew showers of sparks from all around the chamber, fitfully illuminating the dusty recesses of the cargo loading bay as the humanoids had flung themselves behind a cargo cart.

Now the escaped captive returned fire with his machine pistol, but Loxx grinned contentedly to himself under his helmet as he stepped unhesitatingly across the open space between them, ignoring the heavy punches of bullet impacts against the outer skin of his armour. This was the sort of thing that war was all about, he thought, as he circled around for a clear shot at the intruders. His squad kept up a barrage of covering fire from flanking positions, encouraging the humanoids to keep still.

He unleashed a roaring stream of fire into the side of the cart. The cart exploded in a spray of flame and sparks, forcing Loxx to roll further aside, while the flash threw off his squad's aim. By the time Loxx sat up, pieces of wreckage were smouldering all over the floor, and the humanoids had vanished. 'Tracker!' he bellowed.

The trooper with the lifeform tracer pointed off to the right. 'They are moving parallel to that wall.'

Loxx felt a moment's puzzlement, then noticed a grating near the place where the cart had first stood. They must have gone into some sort of vent or service shaft. Attaching his rheon carbine back on to his equipment belt,

Loxx removed his helmet and walked over to the wall. The rest of the squad followed as he walked steadily along, listening for the slightest sound. After a moment, he identified a very faint muffled thudding from an area about three feet off the floor. The humanoids were obviously trying to be quiet, but he was glad that they had underestimated the efficacy of superior Sontaran senses and training. He waved the squad forward a few yards, and beckoned two of them forward. 'You two get into that vent and follow them, just in case there are any turnings.'

The troopers saluted and jogged back the way they had come, bending to squeeze themselves through the grate. Loxx paused to check on the progress of the fugitives' sounds. They seemed to be a few feet short of the squad. He could taste the sweetness of victory already, even as he reloaded his carbine.

He fired at the wall, the shots shearing clean through the thin surface. His squad followed his lead, pouring a steady stream of energy blasts into the wall.

Nur flattened herself against the floor of the narrow shaft as sparks and bursts of charged particles exploded in through the side of the vent, flashing within inches of her face as they passed through and on out the other side. She hoped they wouldn't be passing any depressurized areas if this was going to happen.

The Doctor and Sharma fell flat as well. The shots remained a few feet ahead, and it gradually dawned on her that this was no accident; they knew exactly where the humans were. It naturally followed that an attempt simply to stop them must mean that someone had come in after them.

Nur could just make out – courtesy of the limited light entering via the holes blasted by the Sontarans – a shaft ascending to a higher level. It was wide enough to squeeze into, but meant venturing into the fringes of the area which had been riddled with shots.

If I'd wanted to be captured, I'd have stayed in the

medical lab, she told herself. She twisted her head round, painfully constricting her neck. 'This is a bit risky, but follow my lead, OK?'

Rolling on to her back, she sat up once directly under the opening, and reached up. Slithering her way into a standing position, she felt a lid of some kind shift under her palms. Pressing upward, she moved it aside. A faint light spilled down through a hexagonal gap, and she grabbed hold of the rim to pull herself up.

Puffing a little at the exertion, she found herself standing at the base of a hexagonal shaft some twenty feet across. Sealed hatches were set into one wall at regular intervals, and a ladder stretched up into what looked distressingly like infinity to the left of the hatches on the same wall.

This was obviously some kind of service shaft for the five main lift shafts round the hub, with the laddered sixth wall providing an entrance on every level for maintenance teams. 'Come on, hurry,' she called back through the hatch.

Loxx had ordered a cease-fire. The major wanted them alive, so the major would get them alive. The troopers should have caught up with them by now. 'Squad two, report.'

'The intruders have ascended into some sort of service shaft. Shall we follow?'

'Of course, you fool! Use your initiative!'

When the communications circuit beeped, Major Karne leant on the railing that separated the supervisor's raised gallery from the control deck.

'The humanoids have entered a service shaft rising through the hub of the operational block,' Loxx's voice reported. 'They must be heading for the osmic projector in the observation dome at the top of the hub. Two of my men are in pursuit, and the rest of us are preparing to go in after them.'

140

'Where does the access door at the bottom of the shaft emerge?'

'According to our scans, an emergency lifeboat launch bay on the hangar level.'

Karne smiled, as any good Sontaran officer should when about to dispatch an opponent. 'They want to get out? I have no objections to that. Don't pursue them. Just use the emergency override to open the inner and outer hatches of the lifeboat bay.'

'They are no longer wanted alive?'

'Their inventiveness shows how dangerous they are. Depressurize the shaft.'

Red lights dotted along the length of the hexagonal shaft began pulsing ominously, and a wailing howl started to sound. This was quickly drowned out by the hollow whoosh of air rushing past. All five climbers halted briefly, looking around at the lights.

An unfixed chair from the dome above suddenly tumbled past, bouncing from the metal walls. A cloud of papers, pads, pens and other bric-a-brac swept by the climbers like a surreal snowstorm, and the three fugitives huddled against the wall as a variety of sharp objects assailed them.

The Sontarans continued to ascend, their armour protecting them from the flying debris. 'What the hell?' the still-sluggish Sharma shouted.

Nur looked down at the others, a wild-eyed look of fear on her face. 'That's a depressurization alert. The bastards are spacing the shaft!'

The Doctor's stick of celery parted company with his lapel, and was stolen away by the buffeting rush of air. He ignored it, grimacing as he pulled himself up on to the next rung. Above him, Nur was scaling the ladder with a surprising turn of speed born of desperate terror, while Sharma, weakened by lack of food and rest while under Sontaran control, was gasping for what breath he could snatch from the airstream, his legs trailing away from the rungs.

A burst of fire from the Sontaran's rheon carbine flickered up through the red-lit shaft. Sparks exploded from the rungs by Sharma's head, and the exhausted captain jerked backward, losing his grip with a yell.

Eyes slitted against the buffeting, the Doctor snaked out an arm around Sharma's chest as he dropped past. The airstream whipped the Doctor's strained cry away with the constant howling of the siren as he fought to hold on to the ladder with one arm and Sharma with the other. Rocking his body from side to side, he slammed Sharma into the ladder, and the captain had enough presence of mind to grab hold of it with both hands.

Heaving himself up another couple of rungs, the Doctor stabilized his hold on the ladder, and offered a hand to help Sharma up. Sharma shook his head, looking back down the shaft with a scowl. He started climbing more aggressively, as if the fall was a personal insult. The Doctor leant aside to let him pass, then followed. Up ahead, Nur had disappeared through the round patch of light that marked the end of the shaft.

Sharma reached the top of the ladder and started to crawl out, moving slowly in the suction of air that led down into the shaft. The Doctor was just a few feet from the top, when a crushing grip folded itself round his right ankle. The first Sontaran had closed enough to grab him, and was trying to pull him free from the ladder.

The Doctor tried to kick the alien away with his left foot while hanging on with both hands, but the trooper ignored the impacts on its heavy helmet. White-knuckled, the Doctor strained to pull himself up, but could already feel his sticky palms slip around the rung while his throat was raw from a hoarse cry that was inaudible in the howling wind.

A bloom of sparks suddenly splashed across the Sontaran's helmet, to the accompaniment of the harsh rattle of Sharma's machine pistol. The shots ricocheting around had no chance of penetrating the Sontaran's armour, and one burrowed bloodily through the Doctor's calf, but the force

142

of the impacts was enough to startle the trooper into loosening its grip. With a last desperate tug, the Doctor pulled his foot free as the surprised Sontaran fell back into the darkness.

Right leg trailing behind him, the Doctor pulled himself over the lip of the hatch just as a volley from the second trooper tore across the roof of the shaft. Nur and Sharma were both spread-eagled on the floor on either side of the hatch, hanging on to nearby cabinets so as not to be blown back into the shaft. As soon as the Doctor's feet were free of the hatch, Nur pulled the emergency closing lever that was set under an open floor panel. The hatch slammed shut, and the three of them gasped for breath in the calming air.

Hardly had his comrade flailed past the Sontaran trooper in a hail of bullets than the hatch slammed shut above him, trapping the screeching alarm sound and causing it to echo around the shaft agonizingly. The trooper's hands involuntarily clapped themselves around his helmet in a vain attempt to block out the pain, and he toppled back off the ladder.

Worse was to come. The air whooshing downward suddenly vanished, setting the trooper tumbling in his fall. His throat contracted, unable to draw breath, but this was nothing compared to the acrid burning across his gullet that spread out through his chest and shoulders. Too late, he tried to reach around and clamp a hand over his probic vent, but a stream of bile, blood and elementary lung tissue were already spraying out, forced by the positive pressure applied to his body by the armoured pressure suit.

Leaving a trail of cooling organic graffiti stretched out along the sides of the shaft, the thrashing trooper hurtled into the darkness after his comrade.

Nur tentatively let go of the table-leg she was clutching, and sat up, her breathing ragged. Sharma blinked several times, as if he couldn't keep his eyes open, and propped

143

himself against the wall. The Doctor, she was glad to see, had already pulled himself into a chair, and was taking a few deep breaths. He rolled up his trouser leg and examined the torn flesh critically.

Sharma looked surprised, then groaned. 'I'm sorry, I –' He shrugged, lost for words. 'I'll see to it; make it up to you somehow . . .'

'No, I'm perfectly capable of tending to it myself,' the Doctor told him, tying a handkerchief above the wound as a tourniquet. 'And, considering the alternative, this is certainly the lesser of two evils.'

'But get some practice with that thing, and soon,' Nur recommended. Sharma only winced. She turned to the Doctor. 'What now?'

Sharma gestured towards the door of the room. 'I think it's through there.'

The Doctor tested his weight on his injured leg and grimaced, but remained standing. 'No time like the present, then.' He limped over and through the door. Beyond, there was an incongruous plain of grass, with a small brook and a few shrubs under the harsh light reflected by Indra.

A device not unlike an antique movie camera was mounted on a pedestal on a flat piece of concrete at the junction of some meandering paths. 'Perfect,' the Doctor sighed, with a weary smile. 'Quantum tunnelling bends the laws of causality a little, but this is hardly a time to split hairs about it.'

Nur eyed the device doubtfully. It didn't look like any matter transmitter *she'd* ever seen. 'Causality? This is a time machine?'

'No, but you can use it as one in a limited way, if you're really desperate. It works by isolating the person or object to be transmitted as a quantum wavepeak and then' – he waved his free hand as if trying to reel in the right word – 'tunnelling through to the destination before the wavefront, which picks up all the relativistic effects quite harmlessly. It's not unlike the Lorentz Transformers used by hyperspace engines to iron out potential paradoxes in faster-than-light travel.'

'Lorentz Transformers?'

'You'd know if you had an interstellar ship. Remember, it's FTL journeys that were once thought impossible, not FTL velocities. They reconcile separation by relative time with that by relative space, to ensure a mean causal sequence regardless of relative position. It used to be thought impossible because a wavepeak effect could occur before its wavefront cause. Nowadays, of course, any schoolboy knows that such paradoxes can be lived with, since you just have to listen to, for example, a gunshot on a neighbouring hill. If you listen over the phone or radio, you'll hear the shot before the sound reaches you. To all intents and purposes you've heard it before it's happened.' He closed the panel, and switched on the power to the controls. The sudden silence surprised Nur; she had just about got used to the Doctor's subconscious need to talk while busy, no matter what he was doing. 'We'll only be able to go through one at a time.'

Sharma nodded. 'I'll stay here and watch our backs.'

'Actually, I was rather thinking that you would go first. For one thing, you're best equipped if there's anything nasty waiting for us at the other end. And secondly, you don't know how to operate the machine.'

Sharma shrugged. 'You've been right so far . . .'

Eleven

The baleful red glimmer that was Antares smouldered coldly in the distance, its colour scarcely tainting the sour milk shade of frozen methane that enveloped the outermost planet in its system.

The planet was not alone in its orbit; a necklace of sparkling jewellery encircled it and its tiny moon. Huge sheets of icy crystal like diamond butterflies swooped around the even larger clusters of gemstone minarets and buttresses that were laced together with glassy lace as fine and fragile-looking as a glass spider-web.

Far below, methane monsoons lashed across the ice fields from nitrogen and methane clouds. A field of craters marred the smooth surface of the southern pole. Vapour rose from the carefully maintained shafts of rippling water that tunnelled deep into the ice sheet.

In the depths below the miles-thick ice sheet, the blackness of the sunless waters was dispelled by fuzzy organic luminescences flickering and pulsing all around the underside of the ice. Here the ice itself was illuminated from within the fantastically buttressed spires that reached downward like the roots of a plant.

Throbbing masses, whose veins flickered with a glowing nimbus, could be seen shifting around inside the inverted crystal citadel as the Rutan busied themselves with the complex task of choreographing the flight plans of their orbiting fleet.

The Rutan also perused the data being transmitted back from their scattered probe, their thoughts echoing through the statically charged organic molecules in their atmosphere so that the entire Rutan in the base could work on their duty.

So far, the probe had sensed no Sontaran, though several systems had been memorized as being of interest for other reasons. Another thought was received by the communications array on the surface, and translated into electrostatic pulses in the atmosphere that became a thought.

Another part of the probe was about to be deposited.

Turlough was disappointed to discover that the well-lit area he had seen so distantly turned out to be a floodlit water filtration plant. Warehouses stood amidst a scattering of small silvery lagoons, all surrounded by chainlink fences and low walls.

A low bridge led across from the rooftop where he was to the roof of one of the warehouses, and Turlough edged his way across as fast as he dared. Pipes stretched out across the gravel unnervingly far below, while a stretched black ambulance was parked next to one of the small lagoons. A number of white-coated figures milled around with the faint crunching of gravel underfoot.

Turlough wondered if there had been some sort of accident, and was beginning to wonder if he shouldn't go down to investigate. A faint series of whistling chirps helped him postpone the decision, and he settled for ducking below the low parapet that edged the warehouse roof. He was glad he had, when a floating trapezoidal machine with trailing insectoid legs and a matt finish of mouldy bone drifted across the gravel.

It slid up to the medical orderlies – which is what he presumed the white-coated figures were – without disturbing the gravel. Several of the orderlies had lifted a small powered pump of some kind from the ambulance, and one of the others opened a panel on the robot's trapezoidal body. He removed some sort of glistening container from inside, and this was quickly attached to a socket on the pump.

The orderlies then fitted a pipe from the pump into a socket in the wall of the lagoon. The pump whirred for a few minutes, then the orderlies disconnected it, and put it back in the ambulance. Without speaking to each other, they then all got in and drove away.

The robot remained behind for a few moments, turning slowly and chittering softly to itself, then it gathered up its thin legs and floated off towards the main gate in the fence. Turlough was torn between three choices. Should he follow the ambulance, the robot, or should he just thank the gods it hadn't seen him, and get out of here?

Obviously there was only one common-sense answer: he should give thanks and get out.

But who ever said he had common sense? he asked himself. The robot didn't look like the same style of technology as that of the colony, so perhaps it was a visitor, too; and that meant it probably belonged to the Sontarans. If that was the case, the Doctor would want to know.

He slipped round to a skeletal fire escape down the side of the warehouse, and descended rapidly. The robot might have the answers just by virtue of its presence.

The Sontaran probe that orbited the fourth-magnitude star of Lambda Serpens Caput was too small to be picked up by sensors, unless one knew exactly where to look for it. No larger than a bar stool, it was a stark metallic lump of glowing silver on the sunward side and heatless shadow on the outward side.

It was really little more than an energy detector tuned to very specific frequencies, and a tight-beam hyperwave transmitter with just enough computing power to send the beam accurately.

It had been trailing its six-mile monofilament antennae – each a single conductive long-chain molecule too small to be detected – in a polar orbit around the star for several weeks without disturbance. As a mere machine, though, it didn't become bored or discouraged, but simply continued in its endless path.

Until now.

The heat from the star was a threatening tingle leaching through the translucent walls into the Rutan scout, even though they had come into realspace a million miles above the system's plane of the ecliptic.

The scout was safe at this distance, however. A little discomfort was bearable for them, not to mention far preferable to discovery by the grotesquely solid enemy.

The scout dissociated, parts of themselves powering off into the darkness outward of the sun to seek out any worlds that were there for the taking.

The Sontaran probe's onboard computer compared the energies radiating from the scout's drive units to the energy signature it was to scan for. Computing a perfect match, it aligned itself carefully, and routed a stream of data into the tight-beam transmitter.

Turlough peered round a plaster-walled corner and squinted through the masking darkness at the matt trapezoid of the robot, which now hovered under a streetlamp. It didn't seem to have detected him, not least – he hoped – because of his careful choice of distance at which to follow it.

It had been easy to track, once he had picked out the light and airy tinkling hum that emanated from it. The streets, so colourful in the daytime, were like pale and faded photographs in the spare light. The colourful murals which had disguised whether a building was a home or office were now just shifting patterns of lifeless grey shades. The nocturnal ghost town had been eerily silent in the cool and calming air, but Turlough didn't feel particularly relaxed by the ambience of the streets. There had still been no sign of nightlife, and Turlough had begun to suspect that people simply didn't have nights on the town here. Or at least not in this quarter.

Not for the first time, he wondered what he was doing following this spindly mechanical prowler through the dusty maze of mural-clad walls. Maybe selflessness was a disease and he'd just caught a dose of it.

The robot chirped softly to itself, and flexed its legs in a disconcertingly arachnid manner. Turlough was just about to move across to a small archway across the street for a better look when an answering chirp came from the cloaking darkness beyond the robot. Shrinking back slightly, he watched as two Sontarans – there was no telling if it was the same pair – emerged into the cold grey light in the centre of the crossroads. One of them opened a panel on the side of the robot, and made some adjustments.

The robot remained silent and still until the Sontaran closed the panel again. Then it unfolded its whip-like legs, and accompanied them back into the darkness. Turlough was half-tempted to follow again, still wishing to know what they were up to.

The other half, which felt that enough was enough and there *was* such a thing as tempting fate, was the part of his brain in charge of his legs.

The misty ribbon of the Milky Way ran far under the southern hemisphere of the blue star Spica, which burnt in the darkness like a fiery sapphire. Many of the starlike pinpoints which ringed the sky slid across the sky far more quickly than any stellar or planetary body, too distant from each other to be any more distinct than a distant star.

Above a dead world whose noxious atmosphere had already been transferred to energy by a plague of Von Neumann machines, a huge triple sphere was impaled by a vaulted spire, the severed end of which burnt with the intensity of solar fusion. A sextet of War Wheels, their double-disced forms not unlike a tank's rollers, flew as close escort around this most valuable of Sontaran warships.

Like so many of the drifting points of light, the Linx-class cruiser was composed not of natural rock, but of unnaturally smooth metal surfaces and scattered fields of illuminated viewports and running lights. A faint cloud of gunboats and tiny fighters buzzed around the huge ship like insects around their queen.

The bridge was busy, the officers going about their duties with an icy single-mindedness that left no room for conversation. It was anything but quiet, though, with equipment humming and beeping, boots clattering on the deck, doors clashing, and the constant throbbing of the engines rising up from the depths of the ship. The operations ring set between the main viewscreens was almost empty, as most of those on duty were working in the adjoining port and starboard command and control blisters, which were graced with an open view of space through the transparent domes that formed one whole side of each chamber.

A blue-armoured trooper hurried on to the bridge, making straight for General Skelp. He saluted, and proffered a data chip. 'Sir, urgent from the monitoring section. Transmission downloaded from a probe in the Lambda Serpens Caput system.'

Skelp took the chip disinterestedly; Intelligence had predicted this timetable of events remarkably well for a change. 'Carry on.' The trooper saluted again, and left as Skelp inserted the chip into a viewer, and peered at the screen. He had barely started to skim through it when Commander Vulg stepped up from the port-side blister into the fenced-off operations ring with a salute.

Skelp shut off the scrolling decryption of incoming data from the probe. 'I ordered no interruptions.' There was so much to do before the fleet was fully ready, that he hated the idea of wasting even one second on unnecessary affairs.

'A frigate is approaching, sir, Strag class. Its transponder codes identify it as a courier direct from Sontar.'

'Carrying what?'

'They did not say; the information is classified for you only.'

Perhaps, Skelp thought, the Council were finally going to give him another combat mission. It had been so long since he had tasted the tang of a good fight that he had occasionally considered mustering excess hatchlings so that he could conduct combat drills under live fire. In any case, the message must be important. 'All right. Issue instructions to listen for Rutan communications to and from the coordinates in this chip.' Leaving the operations ring, he stepped into an arched alcove that was just large enough to completely enclose him.

A recharge nozzle was recessed into the rear wall, but he ignored it, since it would be the height of insubordination to plug in for a burn while in communication with a superior officer. Instead, he tapped his private identification code into the communications terminal that was flush with one wall.

The reptilian-patterned wrinkled face of a member of the Gunar Clan brightened on the screen. Skelp saw that it was another general, though where his own rank was marked by shoulder boards on his gun-metal army uniform armour, the new arrival's rank was represented by the silver collar attached to his brassy uniform of the elite Koda military security branch. 'General Skelp, this is General Kragg of the Koda, speaking for Fleet Marshal Stentor of the Grand Strategic Council. We require permission to board.'

Skelp's temper simmered slightly, but he kept it tightly controlled. The Koda seemed to think they could bully anyone, even those of equal rank, he thought. What was more galling was the fact that they were right in thinking that. Skelp prided himself on fearing no enemy, but had no immediate urge to join a penal battalion after the next loyalty purge. 'Permission granted,' he said bluntly, and cut the transmission. He had no fear that the other general would be offended, since that bluntness was precisely the behaviour they encouraged.

152

He almost opened the door, but changed his mind. A burn would do him some good now.

A moment of blackness presaged a nauseating shortness of breath, but Nur immediately felt two pairs of hands grab her shoulders before she hit the floor. 'Don't worry,' the Doctor's voice reassured her. 'It'll pass in a moment, once you get used to a normal gravity and oxygen content again. Just be grateful the integration field compensates for the different atmospheric density.'

I will when I'm certain it has, she thought. Getting her breath back in the cloying air, she saw that they had arrived in a circular room that was empty other than a couple of unused trolleys. Going by the way she felt about 30 years older, Nur was confident that at least they were on Raghi again.

Sharma had opened the door by a crack, and was looking out, while the Doctor tightened the tourniquet round his leg. 'Where are we?'

Sharma shrugged. 'I've no idea.'

'You wouldn't,' she scoffed, shoving him aside. Through the slight gap between door and wall, she could make out a familiar procession of bas-relief elephants on the far wall, while a set of smoked glass doors to the left opened on to a courtyard of sandstone cobbles. 'This is the Gul Mahal medical centre. We're only about two miles from home.' With a creeping sensation of *déjà vu*, she wondered how close she had been to undergoing a journey in the opposite direction yesterday.

Sharma checked the rounds remaining in his gun. 'If the Sontarans have a bridgehead here, we might as well be three light years from home.'

The Doctor looked out as well. 'Yes, but if it's just this Jahangir, with the rest of the people here unaware of what's going on, then we could just walk right out of here.'

'Either way, I suggest we get out of this room before they follow us down.'

'Well, they might find that a little difficult.' The Doctor looked a little sheepish. 'I've set the projector we used to operate on a jamming frequency. It'll take them several hours to fix it, I'm afraid.'

'I'd have thought if they were smart enough to build it, they'd be smart enough to fix it.'

'All things being equal, you're probably right. Fortunately there's not much equal about Sontaran ranks.'

'They all looked the same.'

'That's just because they're clones. Now, if you were a military hierocracy with virtually limitless foot soldiers who did all the dirty work, what would be your biggest fear?'

'Revolution.' Sharma shrugged; everyone always wanted to be the boss instead of settling where they were.

'But if you could control the nature of soldiers right down to the genetic level, say during a cloning process?'

'Then you could leave out the desire for greater power? I don't think so.'

'Not literally, but you could simply leave the brain simplified and open to suggestion, rather than able to think for itself. It's an obscenity, but it provided the Sontaran clans with an easy answer. When they first started cloning millennia ago, every clan introduced an enzyme into their main racepool that inhibits the development of higher brain functions. Naturally, the officers are cloned from an uncontaminated racepool. It gives them an instant difference between the officer caste and soldier caste.' Nur and Sharma exchanged looks of shocked dismay. 'Fixing the osmic projector isn't very likely in the near future. Even if they contact ground allies, they'll assume we've tried to make a break for it, so right now we're safest in here. Nur, tell me exactly what happened on your visit here.'

A dimpled globular scout cruiser had slipped from the frigate before it had even fully stopped relative to the flagship, and swept under the larger ship's hull as the frigate accelerated on its way again and leapt back into hyperspace.

The scout cruiser was settling into the docking ring prepared for it even as the hangar doors ground shut and the bay started to repressurize. General Skelp stepped forward to the foot of the scout cruiser's ramp, with Vulg and the other senior officers flanking him. The main hatch slid up on its runners as soon as the ramp touched the deck. Half a dozen brassy-armoured Koda junior officers emerged, taking up positions matching those of the flagship's command crew. Skelp recognized the covertly hostile moves immediately, though none of the new arrivals actually made any direct threat.

Metallic footsteps announced the emergence of another passenger, and Skelp was surprised – and more than a little honoured to meet this great war hero in the flesh – to see that it was Fleet Marshal Stentor himself, his status asserted by the gold-trimmed blue sash he wore. The Fleet Marshal ignored him for a moment, not even deigning to acknowledge his presence, the Koda armour looking almost golden under the harsh lights. 'Permission to come aboard, General?' His voice was rasping and hoarse despite the presence of all of Sontar's natural atmospheric compounds. His blubbery skin had long since turned to the texture of worn leather, while the reptilian pigmentation that marked him as belonging to the Gunar Clan of Sontar's southern deserts had faded to a blurry vellum shade.

'Granted, sir.' Skelp couldn't recall ever meeting another Sontaran who was anything like as old as the Fleet Marshal. The fact he had never led a sheltered life made his advanced years all the more incredible to Skelp, and he felt almost as thrilled by the meeting as by the victory of a battle.

'Good. Why have you dragged your command crew away from their stations?'

'The honour of your visit –'

'Honours come after the battle, General. Being torn

from their posts just to greet some visiting brass is a cruel insult to members of my army.' Skelp waved his staff away with a sinking feeling. 'That's better, General. I know you meant to show respect, but bootlickers are no match for combat-ready fighters.'

'In that case, Fleet Marshal, if you'd like to review the disposition of the fleet . . .'

'I'm not here for any mere inspection. By order of the Grand Strategic Council, I am hereby relieving you of command for this mission.' The Fleet Marshal signalled to one of his aides, who handed Skelp a data chip. 'That is my authorization. You will remain aboard as captain of this cruiser, but I shall take charge of all strategic planning decisions regarding the assault on Antares.'

'Yes, sir. I understood there was to be a ground assault by my troops to take their data stores intact.'

'We've decided to hit faster and harder than that. G3 Intelligence have finally done something useful for a change; they've taken time off from playing around with captives to break down and analyse the Rutan access codes. We're going to simply siphon off the contents of their data core, then crush them from orbit.' He smiled thinly. 'Don't worry, Skelp. I know your blood cries for combat. We'll find some Rutan for you to kill among their fleet support vessels.' He paused, looking at Skelp. 'I almost pity them, General.'

Skelp couldn't have felt worse if the Fleet Marshal had polymorphed into a Rutan there and then. Pity was for fools and humans. 'Is this a test, sir?'

'Not at all. I'm serious. I pity them because you and I are not just going to kill them. We're going to tear them from the fabric of space and wipe the humiliation of their very existence from the galaxy.'

Skelp sighed in relief. 'Of course, what a shame it will be.'

'From what you said, it seems that Jahangir and a couple of orderlies are the only problem, and if I can find the

156

right – Ah, here we are . . .' The Doctor pulled out a couple of small pen-torches from a storage drawer, and handed one each to Nur and Sharma.

They had left the empty room a few minutes earlier, as soon as Nur had finished telling her story. The few nurses they passed in the hallways acknowledged them with polite smiles, but otherwise ignored them.

'What good are these?' Sharma demanded.

'The conditioning process you and your crew were subjected to depends on a repeated pattern of stimuli, and can be circumvented by a different pattern. When we run into Jahangir, all we have to do is hold him long enough to decondition him.' The Doctor pointed his own torch at them, flashing it on and off in a rapid but steady sequence of four long and three short, over and over. 'Just shine your torch into the eyes of anyone under control, and flash your torch in this polka beat until they come round.'

Nur experimented briefly until she found the right beat. Sharma, meanwhile, jerked a thumb back towards the main lobby. 'Shouldn't we just get out of here and report in?'

The Doctor fixed him with a weary look. 'We could, but then we'd just have to break in here later to find out what the connection is. Now, wouldn't it be better to just investigate first, then escape with that information?'

'I suppose so . . .'

'Then come on. Nur?'

'Yes?'

'Did they show you the administration centre for this place?'

'No, but I think it's round the back; there are some signs outside.'

'Lead us there as best you can.' He ushered her on with an enthusiastic smile. Unable to resist returning it – he did have rank, after all – she led them out of the storeroom.

Fleet Marshal Stentor finished reviewing the disposition

of the remotes which were busily stripping the nearest planet down to its most basic hydrocarbons. The fleet that had been assembled here would require as many raw materials for fuel and sustenance as the entire molecular and chemical composition of the system could provide.

Skelp stepped up to the operations ring with a salute. 'Sir, the cyphers section reports that the Rutan comnet has confirmed the arrival of their probes in the Lambda Serpens Caput system.'

The Fleet Marshal turned slowly, easing his weight by leaning on the battle standard he carried everywhere. Better to look foolish at times than to allow the legacy of his years to get the better of him by forcing him into a command couch, he thought. If anyone disagreed, well, as the Gunar's representative on the Grand Strategic Council, he had the authority to re-open the duelling pit on deck 37. 'What progress has Major Karne made?'

'His last report stated that the tagging programme was on schedule.'

'And the generator?'

'Has arrived in the Unukalhai system and is being ferried to Karne's position from the inner part of the system. That should lessen the likelihood of its detection by the humans' border sensor probes.'

'Good. Show me the overall view – latest update.'

Skelp manipulated some controls, and brought up a representation of the entire quadrant in the holotank. A cone of green pixels marked the fleet's position near the blue pinpoint of Spica at the top right corner of the cube on the side they were standing on. A series of concentric red circles surrounded Antares, nestled some way in from the centre of the cube's side. A yellow circle ringed Unukalhai off in the bottom left corner of the far side. A scattering of red pinpoints arced through the left-hand side of the cube. 'This is the progress the Rutan scouts have made into the former Tzun domain, according to the communications traffic we've intercepted from their comnet.'

'That one?' The Fleet Marshal pointed to a red tag that was pulsing rapidly.

'Type 62 scout cruiser, according to the messages we've decoded; currently surveying Lambda Serpens Caput. If they follow standard Rutan procedure, they'll make the jump to Unukalhai in two days, local time.'

'Then tell Karne to redouble his efforts. I want Unukalhai IV prepared for nucleosynthesis within 36 hours.'

'Major Karne is the only officer with sufficient experience in planning this project to determine its timescale.'

The Fleet Marshal gave him a withering look. He had been instructed to lead, and lead he would. 'No individual makes decisions here. This army is a team, General; a machine made of closely interlinked precision-made elements which must operate in synch. Now stop talking like a human, and transmit the order.'

Twelve

The Doctor, Nur and Sharma started winding their way back towards the exit of the medical centre, albeit by a circuitous route. The only area of the administration building they hadn't already checked turned out to be a locked door at the end of a short cul-de-sac. The door bore a sign in flowing script. 'MORTUARY,' Nur said with a faint grimace. She tried the door handle. 'Locked.'

'I wonder why,' the Doctor said quietly.

'Perhaps the dead have something to hide?'

'We really must do something about this morbid streak of yours.' The Doctor held out a hand. 'Government ID?'

She handed over her smart card. 'It won't work without the right code.'

'That depends on what you intend to do with it.' He slid the rigid plastic into the gap between door and wall, and shuffled it around for a moment to slide the bolt back before slowly drawing the door open. He handed the card back. 'Don't leave home without it.' He held the door open for her, and she slipped reluctantly into the chilly room. Sharma followed, and the Doctor brought up the rear.

The morgue was a very plain, tiled room, with three rows of hexagonal drawers on one wall. The opposite wall was bare but for a long and empty noticeboard, while a computer terminal squatted at the far end of the room. The Doctor bent down to examine the label on one of the drawers. 'Look at this.' He grabbed the handle and pulled.

Nur shook her head and switched on the terminal in the corner, while Sharma went over to see what the Doctor had found. Let the boys have their fun proving to each other what strong stomachs they had! All the important information would be here in the database. 'Anybody we know?'

'It's Chattar – the man whose house Turlough and I came from when we first met you and your father. A blacked-out ambulance collected him.'

Nur turned round as they closed the drawer. 'So, he was brought here. I saw that ambulance when I was here before. I knew it!' Being proved right didn't seem particularly cheering this time. 'He should be in here somewhere . . .' She entered the name into the database as a search parameter.

A form appeared on-screen, with an image of Chattar's face, and various bits and pieces of personal history. 'CAUSE OF DEATH; TISSUE REJECTION.'

'Are you certain?' the Doctor asked.

'It's what it says here.'

'Put that in as a search parameter.'

She did so, and a list of names and numbers flashed up on-screen. The Doctor peered at the list of names through half-moon spectacles, then went back and scanned the line of drawers. 'Every name on these drawers is on that list.' He leant over Nur's shoulder and typed quickly. A new form came up, listing names, admission details and causes of death. 'Interesting. All these people were admitted for a simple viral infection, yet died of tissue rejection.'

'So?'

'So,' Sharma said pointedly, 'what virus adds anything new to body tissue?'

'Of course,' Nur exclaimed. 'The stuff from Agni.'

The Doctor nodded in a pleased manner. 'Exactly. Some humans must have an adverse reaction to the polymerase chain, and they're all being brought here out of the way, where their own doctors can't get so much as a blood sample from them that would expose the chain.'

'But how would anyone know what was responsible for their illness?' She fell silent, the truth dawning. They'd know if they had a hand in it themselves. That could only mean Jahangir, and perhaps her father. 'No, it must be coincidence.' She would not allow herself to believe that her father could be involved, no matter what happened. After all, he hadn't been to Agni in years.

There was a sudden clicking at the door as someone unlocked it from the corridor. The Doctor and Nur stayed where they were, but Sharma dashed across and pressed himself against the wall behind the door. The door opened, and Nur was not entirely surprised to see that it was Jahangir himself. He was carrying a clipboard, and froze in comical surprise when he saw the two intruders.

His expression was bland, even when Sharma put his gun to the back of his head, but his eyes held a haunted and pleading look. Nur realized that the spark in there wasn't a spark of life, but of incipient madness. Sharma smiled grimly. 'You're under arrest, collaborator.'

'Oh, he's no more a collaborator than you were,' the Doctor told him. 'There's no need to hurt him.' He took out his pen-torch, and shone it into Jahangir's eyes, flashing it on and off to the beat he had showed them earlier.

The effect on Jahangir was startling. He began to breathe in ever-shorter gasps, and a drawn-out howl burst forth from him as he hurled himself into a corner, racked with sobbing. The Doctor bent to help him into the chair by the terminal. 'Why don't you kill me?'

'Because I'd rather help you. I'm the Doctor, and I believe you know Nur and Sharma.'

Jahangir shuddered. 'All doctors would rather help, but some of us kill instead.'

'Is that what the Sontarans made you do?'

Jahangir's sobbing ceased immediately, and he looked up with a feverish expression. 'You know them?'

162

'Oh yes; far too well.'

'They're demons, you know. Rakshasi. I know. They've been making me one of them,' he spat, 'making me kill and spread disease like an emissary of Rudra, and pass on new workers for them, because they can't be bothered to look after the ones they captured with the station.'

'Yes, we know about the cold virus and the polymerase chain.'

'You understand such things?'

'I've been known to dabble.'

Shaking, Jahangir nodded rapidly. 'Ambika allowed the virus to be introduced into the water supply of the lower caste areas, as I had told him that the tag would simply provide a caste marker.'

'A what?' the Doctor asked, disbelievingly.

Jahangir scowled in a pained way. 'I was ordered to suggest to him that giving each caste a distinct genetic marker would be a more efficient system. The marker was engineered to be carried by a simple cold, but some people rejected the tag, and I had to kill them. I couldn't help myself. I tried not to do it, but I wasn't strong enough . . .' His words dissolved into a fit of sobbing. Nur could almost feel sorry for him, but her father's complicity – and he had no mind control as an excuse – had shocked any other feelings out of her.

The Doctor sighed and handed Jahangir a handkerchief. 'Did they tell you what the polymerase chain is really for?'

Jahangir tried to speak, but couldn't form the words. He shook his head mutely.

'What now?' Sharma asked. This was all getting too discomfiting for him.

'Now we go and have some words with Preceptor Ambika.'

Karne watched with mixed feelings as the mile-long mass of metal drew alongside his comparatively small Valt-class destroyer. Being so close to such a dangerous structure

163

was, he had to admit, less preferable than a straight fight.

The destroyer lurched slightly, and there was a series of distant hollow sounds from somewhere in the distance. 'Grapples locked,' Loxx reported. 'Docking clamps attached.'

So, it was finally here. Karne wondered what part he would have to play in its role. Only the technical crew was scheduled to work on the final preparations, and no doubt Loxx would keep reminding him of things he had to do elsewhere. If he could just get five minutes aboard on his own, he was sure he could do more for the war effort than any number of his comrades at the front. 'Notify the tech crews that they can get to work immediately.'

Turlough woke from a troubled but exhausted sleep as he heard footsteps approaching. The small upturned boat under which he had sheltered wouldn't provide much protection from Sontaran gunfire, but it had hidden him successfully enough from prying eyes.

He didn't dare risk returning to the villa in case the Sontarans found him again and thus followed him to the TARDIS, but it seemed logical that whenever the Doctor and Nur returned, they would want to visit the palace again to see her father.

Playing the odds, therefore, he had made his way to the ghat nearest the bridge across to the island palace. There he could keep out of sight in one of the boats, while watching for the Doctor or Nur.

There was, of course, no point in showing himself until he was sure of who was out there. The footsteps were quite slow. Not the lumbering tread of the Sontarans; more like tired humans. He lifted the edge of the small boat slightly to look out at who was approaching the bridge. To his delight, it was the Doctor and Nur, with a Kshatriya and a white-haired man whom he didn't recognize.

He rolled the boat over to get out from under it, and

forced himself to take the steps up to the bridge at a normal pace. He was delighted to see the Doctor, but he wouldn't want the Doctor to think he was incapable of getting on on his own. 'Oh, it's you,' he said.

The Kshatriya looked surprised, but the Doctor merely raised an eyebrow. 'Turlough, I don't believe you've met Captain Sharma –'

'I've heard of him.' Turlough immediately moved himself protectively in front of Nur and the Doctor, hoping it wasn't really necessary. 'Back away, he's working for the Sontarans.'

'Not any mo–' The Doctor looked at him in surprise. 'You've seen some here?'

That's one way of putting it, Turlough thought. 'They've been chasing me over half the city, not that I've done anything to offend them.'

'Sontarans don't need a reason. How did you run into them?'

'I went to space traffic control to check the passenger lists to and from Agni. None of the people Nur mentioned had been there. The man who was helping out had detected a large new arrival in the system, and we accessed the defence grid's sensor logs to try to identify it.'

'And did you?'

'It looked familiar, but I couldn't place it. Didn't you see anything?'

'No, we were under some pressure ourselves.'

'So it was you,' the white-haired old man said wonderingly. 'Your data search was registered on my machine, and I notified the Sontarans. I'm glad to see you're unharmed.'

'Well, that warms my heart.' Turlough wasn't violent by nature, but if he could just get a weapon of some kind . . . 'It won't do much for the traffic controller they killed.'

'The Sontarans seem to have been busy,' the Doctor commented. 'Mental conditioning is a standard technique of theirs. Now, I'd love to stand around here in the dark and exchange gossip, but there are more pressing matters.'

They hurried across the bridge, and Nur escorted the foursome into the main hall. The gilt-trimmed room was normally used for receptions and dinners. Immaculately set tables lined the walls, while a white grand piano, as solid a part of the building as the walls, was positioned off to one side of a raised area for guests and dignitaries. 'There's to be a civic reception tomorrow – today,' she explained. 'I'll go and fetch father.'

Ambika was already entering, flanked by Arjun. Turlough steeled himself for the usual barrage of threats that always seemed to come at around this point. 'What is all this?' Ambika demanded. He noticed Jahangir and Sharma. 'Is there a problem?'

Jahangir nodded with a sob. 'I have betrayed you, Excellence, and led you false.'

'What do you mean?'

'He means the illnesses, father,' Nur said icily. Turlough admired the way she did that. It was very polished, and worthy of any family ruler back home. 'You lied to me. You said there were no other cases, when all the time you knew that a percentage of the Sudras were coming down with it.'

'I –'

'How long have you been contaminating the Sudra water supply with a bacterium carrying the common cold?'

Ambika paled. 'Who told you this?'

'I did,' Jahangir answered. 'It was not my doing; I was told to suggest it to you.'

'By whom?'

'By the Sontarans,' Turlough sneered. He'd had enough of Ambika's innocent posturings.

The Doctor nodded. 'I'm afraid all the crew of the *Nandi* were compromised months ago. Since then they've had you dancing to their tune to infect your own people. To be honest, though, I doubt they found it very difficult, if you *really* thought that separating your people's social groups into genetic types was a good idea.'

'The question now,' Turlough added, 'is what you've really added to those people.'

'Jahangir said it was a simple marker. He suggested that each caste should carry a genetic marker that was easily detectable, so that the census and administrative tasks were simplified.'

'Yes,' the Doctor said, as if to a child. 'But Jahangir was told to say that by someone who doesn't know the difference between a human life and a watch looted from a corpse.'

Nur stared at her father, shaking her head slowly. 'How could you? You're making our people just like them, with their clan tags. What next? Control the physical and mental attributes of each caste group?'

'But Nur, I just wanted to simplify things for everyone . . .' Ambika looked as if he felt the entire mass of Indra was pressing down upon him. Turlough hoped it really was as painful as that for him. 'It seems I have little choice. This infestation must not be allowed to spread to Raghi.'

The Doctor leant over the table towards him. 'Haven't you been listening? There are already several Sontarans operating on the surface.'

'I heard. But so few can't do much on their own. The others on Agni are of more important concern. If they interfere with the energy transference from the collection aerials to here, they could burn off huge patches of the colony. I can't take that risk.'

'If that was all they wanted, they'd have done it by now. Besides, how are you going to get them off the station? There are two cruisers out there waiting to destroy anyone you send.'

'I'll order an agneya to be prepared. That will be small and fast enough to avoid being shot down.'

'A what?'

'A missile with a fusion warhead,' Nur explained. She turned back to her father. 'That's the stupidest damn thing

167

I ever heard. We can't destroy our primary energy facility. That'd be suicide; johar for half the population.'

'We can replace the output with the fusion satellites our great-grandparents brought from Earth.'

'If they still work?'

'All right, maybe it's not a perfect solution, but what else can I do? Let these aliens burn us to death or shut down our energy supply?'

The Doctor coughed discreetly. 'Might I make a small suggestion?'

Thirteen

Loxx flanked Karne impassively as they both stepped through their ship's main lock and into the narrow access conduit in the new arrival. A short walk brought them to a cramped engineering station, in which several bits and pieces of Sontaran technology were crammed as best they could be amongst a network of more finely tooled electronics.

A lieutenant in an engineer's blue uniform saluted as they came in. 'Lieutenant Bolg reporting, sir.'

Loxx barely noticed, so engrossed was he in admiring the almost magical alien technologies to which their own had been piggy-backed. Karne looked more closely at the Sontaran additions, then saluted back. 'Has there been any damage to the systems en route?'

'No, sir. The drive units we fitted have functioned perfectly.'

'I never doubted that. How long will the arming process take?'

'Assuming you have acquired the technicians that were requested, about two shifts.'

Loxx was surprised as he, for one, had expected that the structure they were standing in would be ready for its job simply as it was. 'What's to prepare?'

'Mostly it will be necessary to improve stability. When we activate, the entire system must function equally smoothly in every section of the hull.'

'I'll see what can be done.'

Night on Raghi lasted while Indra was below the

horizon, leaving the pale buildings shrouded in gossamer starlight, the sandstone and marble now tinted a pastel blue. There were distant sounds of voices and vehicles from the residential areas around the spaceport, where hotels and clubs catered for offworld visitors. The remainder of the city was dark in the few short hours before the requisite early start to the working day.

Although most of the streets were silent, a faint humming and beeping did blend in with the gentle chirping of nocturnal insects as a dark mass hummed slowly along the deserted byways. Essentially a squared-off trapezoidal lozenge, it had four hydraulic arms folded under a platform set into the base of its lozenge-shaped body. Several whip-like metal tentacles were carefully folded away as it drifted along, antennae twitching.

The Sontaran sergeant monitored its progress on a small hand-held scanner, though he privately thought that all the dwellings looked very much the same. The searcher robot had certainly picked up something, however, as the telemetry from its energy sensors was spiking repeatedly as it quartered the area in an ever-shrinking spiral search pattern.

The energy signature was unfamiliar, but had been compared to the craft at the spaceport with negative results. If they were lucky, the sergeant thought, perhaps it would turn out to be a Rutan scout. The energy readings spiked again, and the robot swung round, accelerating towards its source, which registered as very close now. On-screen, the robot's sensors focused past a low wall, and locked on to a tall rectangular box sitting in the garden of a lakeside villa.

The sensors must be mistaken, the sergeant thought. The box couldn't have that mass and energy . . . Still, orders were orders. He reached for his communicator.

Another technician collapsed from his post in Agni's central control as Loxx and Karne returned, and Loxx prodded the filthy unshaven body with one foot. The human didn't stir, so Loxx shoved him aside and waved over a replacement. These humans had hopelessly inefficient biological systems; he wondered that they had ever mastered space travel at all.

Besides, they had surrendered, and so were worthless. Anyone stupid enough to surrender instead of fighting to an honourable death deserved to be treated like the refuse they were. Personally, he couldn't understand how any species could stand for that.

The communications station chimed, and Karne went over to reply. 'Major Karne here.'

'Team four, sir. The bot has found something, but I don't understand how it could be what we're looking for.'

'Of course not, you're not bred to understand.' Karne remained silent for a moment, and Loxx wondered what he was thinking. He did seem to consider things more than most officers, Loxx had noticed. Perhaps his near-death back in the nebula all that time ago – just before Loxx had rescued him – had given him some deeper perspective. Or maybe it was delayed concussion.

If a Rutan probe had already reached the system, then all their plans would be jeopardized. On the tiny screen, a shaky picture of the patio of a villa flickered into being. At first, Loxx thought the troopers were imagining things – if it weren't for the fact that they had no imagination – but the picture swung round suddenly, and he saw what had so concerned the troopers. Karne obviously saw it too, as he started slightly. 'Patch through the bot's telemetry to my station,' Karne snapped. 'Show me every detail of this energy source.'

Karne hurried back to the office he had appropriated from Chandra, and punched up the robot's telemetry data. It took a few moments for realization to dawn, but Karne had always paid particularly close attention at intelligence briefings, so the tall blue box in the hedge-bounded garden was not entirely unfamiliar to him. He recalled that it had been witnessed several times during the course of the war, each time near an operation that was subsequently disrupted by a third party. A very specific third party, in fact − a Time Lord called the Doctor.

Karne was well aware of the power that had been ascribed to the Time Lord, and felt a faint thrill of dangerous excitement. The Doctor's whole file showed that he would be a threat, of course, but if he could be taken in one piece . . . A Time Lord and his TARDIS would be an unparalleled boon to the war effort. 'Are there any occupants inside?'

'It is sealed, but there is no one in the native residence.'

The Doctor could be inside, but Karne doubted it. He would simply have moved the TARDIS when the troopers approached. 'Fetch a transport beacon and affix it to the TARDIS so that it can be brought here by the osmic projector, then leave the robot to watch the residence. Apprehend anyone who tries to enter.'

'Yes, sir.'

Karne cut the connection, ignoring the activity around him as he considered this development. Perhaps it was just the turn of luck he needed to make his mark, or perhaps it would destroy all that he had worked for. 'Sir?' Commander Loxx interrupted him.

'Yes, Commander?' There was a fine line between a first officer's duty-bound opinions and the job demarcation with his superior. As far as Karne was concerned, Loxx was treading on a razor right now.

'There is a standing order that information regarding the Time Lords must be reported along the chain of command as soon as possible. It is to take precedence over everything else, by order of the Grand Strategic Council.'

Why did Loxx have to remind him of these things in the open? Karne glowered at him. 'Take the ship out of the synchrotron belt so that we may send a clear transmission without electromagnetic interference, then open a secure tight-beam subspace link to the flagship.'

'Yes, sir.' The image of Indra on the main viewer slid away. Loxx worked at the communication console. 'Fleet Marshal Stentor is in a planning briefing. His aide says the Fleet Marshal will contact us as soon as he is available.'

'Very well. The human medical officer; is he still on the planet?'

'Yes, sir.'

'Have him brought to me on the ship.'

Jahangir awoke as the insistent beeping of the communicator battered its way through the soporific influence of the sedative which the Doctor had given him in the hope that sleep would do him some good. He tugged it from his pocket, staring at it as if it were a live cobra. No, he wouldn't obey any more. Not again. He put the communicator down.

He sat up in surprise. He had been able to put it down; nothing had stopped his resistance. He was free at last, he realized with elation.

He came back down with a bump. If he failed to answer, Karne might realize that something was wrong. Perhaps he would attack and kill others, and that would also be Jahangir's fault. He might be free of control, but he felt he would never be free of the pain.

Unless, like any good surgeon, he removed the cause rather than the symptom. Yes, if Karne believed him to be under control, he would be able to get close to him, and then . . . He supposed he was fated to be cast down in the next life anyway, so one more killing wouldn't make much of a difference.

He picked up the communicator. 'Jahangir.'

'Why did you not answer?'

'I was . . . unconscious.' It was more or less true, and Karne must have noticed the draining effect of constant work without rest.

'Weakness. Report to me at once; there is some information I require.'

'Yes, sir.' Jahangir put the communicator back down.

Now it was time to work from the inside again, but this time against the invaders. Making sure that no one was watching, he slipped out of his room.

There were guards on duty, of course, but as one of Ambika's advisers, he had been here regularly and knew their patrol patterns. Crossing the causeway back to the city was simple enough, and there were still a few taxis around. Flagging down the nearest, he slumped into its passenger seat. 'Take me to the Gul Mahal medical centre,' he commanded the driver.

Ambika couldn't bring himself to look Nur in the eye when he rejoined the others in the main hall. He couldn't really blame her for feeling betrayed; his judgement had been somewhat soured recently. He wished he could think of a way to set things right again. 'I've reported the situation to the Colonial Office and asked for assistance. They're sending an Alliance cruiser and escort ships, but it will take at least a week for them to get here from Earth Central.'

The Doctor looked up from examining the sheet music that was lying atop the piano that stood to one side. 'That will probably be too long, but I doubt it'll make much difference. The world is ruled by letting things take their course. It cannot be ruled by interfering. Well, not much, anyway.'

Jahangir had never been aboard the Sontarans' own ship, and took the opportunity to examine every cluttered corner of the cylindrical corridors and domed chambers through which he passed. He and the escort who had been waiting for him at the osmic projector terminal eventually reached a bulging doorway embossed with the increasingly familiar symbol of four diamonds in a diamond pattern which graced every door he had seen on board. The door rolled open, allowing them into the tightly packed bridge.

Karne was watching an image of a wild-eyed, curly

haired man in a long brown frock coat and trailing multicoloured scarf. He seemed to be standing slightly below the level of the source of the image, at the foot of a short flight of steps in a huge jade chamber, surrounded by a number of people in an odd mixture of animal skins and stately robes. Jahangir wondered who this was. Had Karne and his people attacked other colonies? Karne turned as a trooper escorted the Brahmin in, and gestured to the man on screen. 'Do you recognize this man from the planet below?'

Someone else resisting these aliens, then. He had no idea who the man was, but was determined not to give the aliens any information that might help them. A negative answer hardly counted, though. 'No,' he said calmly, his mind still raging silently in shame at having been betrayed by his weak will earlier.

'This man?' The image had changed, and now showed a white-haired man wearing a ruffled shirt. He leapt from side to side across a mouldy stone wall, while some sort of projectile weapon blasted chips out of the ancient blocks.

'No.'

'Perhaps this?' The scene changed to what Jahangir recognized as an old spaceliner's main recreation hall, where a mop-haired man in a baggy tailcoat raised his hands in a gesture of surrender.

'No.'

Karne hissed in displeasure, and Jahangir ordered his limbs to launch him at this unclean invader. He stayed where he was. 'Are you certain you are telling me true, human?'

'Yes, I have never seen any of those men before.'

Karne glared for a moment, then called up an image of the two intruders. 'What of these two?'

'I've never seen either of them before, but the man is clearly not Raghi.'

'Good. He must be the Doctor. We will use this information to our advantage. Return the human to his work.' Jahangir resisted the urge to nod to himself at the confirmation that these creatures and the Doctor knew each other. He would save his emotions until the joyful moment of vengeance. Killing Karne wouldn't fully atone for his treason, nor would it cleanse his corruption. Somehow he had to kill all of them. Every single one.

To do so, however, he would need a plan. He allowed a trooper to escort him out.

The doors slammed shut behind Jahangir. 'Major,' Loxx said, 'Fleet Marshal Stentor is on visual.'

Karne turned to face the main viewer, and saluted. 'Why have you broken the communications blackout?' Stentor rumbled threateningly.

Karne stared back unblinkingly. 'We have detected the presence of the Doctor on the colony world. Standard orders are –'

'I am conversant with the orders, Major. I posted them myself. What proof have you of the Time Lord's presence?'

'We have located his TARDIS.'

Stentor's eyes brightened from embers into tiny flames. 'You have this TARDIS?'

'A detachment is bringing it to our ship now.'

'Excellent work, Major. However, as we have known since Marshal Stike's abortive stratagem four centuries ago, the TARDIS will be of little use without the Doctor as well. You must divert as much of your resources as possible to his capture without engendering any further delay in the operation.'

'Capture may be impossible. The Time Lords are excessively jealous of their secrets.'

'As is everyone. If his death occurs, I will expect a report on why it was so necessary, and I will want proof of your actions. I don't want the victory of our analysts having cracked the Rutan communications code to be balanced out by the loss of a chance at time travel.'

'The communications code has been cracked?' Karne was quite shocked at that; he had always thought the code to be impenetrable, and for him to be proved wrong at a time like this was distressing. He recovered quickly. 'Yes, sir.' Karne fixed Loxx with a burning glare as the screen went blank. 'Send a detachment down in the craft left behind by the Doctor and his companion. If the Doctor is collaborating with the ruling clan, he may be at their headquarters.' He stepped forward warningly. 'See to it personally, Commander, and deliver the Doctor directly to me – alive.'

'It would be safer to kill him. Never leave a live enemy behind you.'

Another disagreement, Karne thought irritably. He would have to do something about this upstart. He was beginning to become too independent, and that might be dangerous. But, first things first. 'Perhaps you would like to share that opinion with the Fleet Marshal?'

Loxx hesitated. 'No, sir. I simply hunger for combat.'

'Ah. That could be arranged . . . There will be a battle soon enough, but we must take the Doctor first.' He looked away, lowering his voice as if he was talking to himself. 'Together with his TARDIS he would make us invincible.'

Fourteen

A black speck high against the night-veiled face of Indra slowly resolved itself into the triangular form of the *Garuda* spiralling gently downwards.

Inside, the pilot's seat was almost flattened by the wide bulk of a blue-armoured Sontaran, who thudded at the controls with graceless efficiency. The sergeant in the copilot's seat peered down at the shimmering reflective patch of water far below. 'You're sure you're guiding this thing to the right place?'

'A simple matter of accessing the flight computer's memory core. The vessel's home base is there.'

The sergeant grunted wordlessly. Let the engineering and ship's services division have their fun, but it was he and his squad which would snatch the fugitives. It was also they who would die if anything went wrong. This prospect didn't bother him unduly, but there was a big difference between coming off second in a fight and being blasted by aerospace defences before even getting to shoot somebody. 'Just get us down in one piece and don't bother me with the technical details.' He swivelled the seat around to look down to where his troops were clustered in the hold, hanging on to any reasonably solid furnishings as the ship bounced occasionally. 'You've all seen the pictures of the three we want to take alive. Kill anybody else who gets in the way, but don't bother chasing any runaways.'

'But sir —' someone protested in a vaguely affronted tone.

'Shut up! The orders were to grab those three and get

out. Now I don't like it any more than you do, but orders
is orders, and any of you who tries anything funny will
answer for it in the duelling pit.' He glared at them
threateningly, but couldn't tell whether it was having the
desired effect, as the expressions of their blank helmets
never changed. What did I expect, he asked himself. A
bunch of fresh hatchlings still damp from the nutrient
tanks. If only he had a troop the quality of the one he led
at the Madillon Cluster. Unfortunately they had been
wiped out, but at least they knew how to die fighting. 'All
right. Who's got the lifeform tracker?'

There was an uneasy silence, whose gradually increasing length started the sergeant visualizing his opponent in
the duelling pit. 'Do you mean this?' someone asked
finally, holding up the tracker.

The sergeant balled his fists to resist the urge to go for
his gun. 'Yes, that. Now –'

'I've got it.'

The lieutenant who was piloting the ship rolled his
eyes slightly. The sergeant just felt more murderous.
Perhaps the trooper was doing him a favour, he decided,
as the humans were going to be so much worse off when
he took out his ire on them. 'I can see that, you cretin.'
He wondered what the odds were on trapping the moron
in a crossfire. 'Now, we're going to land in an open space
by the main building. You two' – he pointed to the
troopers nearest the landing ramp – 'will toss out a couple
of grenades to deal with any resistance at the LZ, then
secure the area. The rest of us will take out the front doors
and enter the building. The tracker should lead us right to
the three we want, and anybody who gets in the way is a
legitimate target. Once we've grabbed the humans, we'll
call for projection back to the cruiser, and get out. Any
questions?' He regretted the words the instant they passed
his lips. Troopers weren't supposed to ask questions, and
inviting them to do so was just going to confuse them.

'Wha–'

The anonymous pundit was interrupted by a chirp

from the flight console. 'What was that?' the sergeant asked suspiciously, if admittedly with a twinge of relief.

'Ground control interrogating the flight computer about who we are and where we're going,' the pilot told him.

'What are we supposed to say?'

'Nothing. The transponder code and flight plan will be transmitted back by the flight computer and we'll be allowed through their aerospace defence grid. This is one of their own government's ships after all. The human here has ensured that its captured status has not been logged.'

'No? Good.' He turned back to the troop. 'Fence in. Check your weapons and prepare for landing.'

Ambika's usually neatly side-parted hair was slightly ruffled as he paced around his formal reception hall. The Doctor sat on the piano stool, frowning at the keyboard. A pair of guards stood by each door, and a few trolleys of buffet foods were dotted around like cars abandoned in the aftermath of an earthquake.

Nur felt that her father's predicament was sauce for the goose; the reception he'd been planning was very important to him, as he was meeting the full city council, and even a delay might embarrass him, let alone a cancellation. Not that it would make much difference once his role in the Sontarans' schemes got out. A hesitant version of 'Chopsticks' darted across the room.

Ambika sat, finally, and steepled his fingers. 'Doctor,' he began, 'approximately how many of these invaders are on the station?'

'Hmm.' The Doctor rattled a key experimentally. 'We only saw about a dozen, all told, but I'd assume there's a full company. Perhaps a hundred of them.'

Nur tried hard not to imagine that. Ambika pursed his lips. 'Did they tell you this? Or did you have a lifeform scanner to determine their numbers?'

The Doctor lowered the lid over the piano keys with an innocent expression. 'That's the standard support

180

complement for a Sontaran Valt-class destroyer. Thirty crewmen, six fighters and a hundred ground troops.'

'That could pose us some problems, Excellence,' Sharma said with a glower. That wasn't quite the way Nur would have put it. Hours of training in civility restrained her from putting it more simply. A distant whine that had niggled at her ears for a few seconds was growing louder by the moment, and was now a howl overhead, muffled by the marble roof. It was still a sound she'd recognize anywhere – those were engines she'd tuned and maintained herself, after all. She held up a hand to silence the others. 'Listen.'

Everyone cocked their heads to concentrate on the sound from outside. 'A vimana heading for the spaceport,' Ambika said with a shrug. 'You of all people should be used to that sound by now.'

'Exactly. Very used to it. That's not just any vimana; it's the *Garuda*. I'd recognize its pitch anywhere. Sounds like it's coming into the courtyard itself.'

'But you left it on Agni . . . ' The Doctor and Turlough exchanged a look, and Ambika called out to the nearest guards. 'You two, get a squad together and detain the ship now landing in the courtyard.' The guards bustled off, whispering hurriedly into communicators.

The Doctor looked out into the foyer after them with a concerned expression. 'Your guards may not be able to hold them. How quickly can you get reinforcements?'

'Quickly enough, I hope.' Ambika hurried over to his personal table, which had a small terminal set into it. He tapped at a few keys. 'This is the Preceptor. We have a possible intrusion here at the palace, and my daughter's ship has been stolen. Have three gunships sent over, along with two platoons of Kshatriyas. Have them all placed under the command of my chief of security.'

'Tell them to bring grenades filled with coronic acid; that's about the only thing that gets through Sontaran space armour.'

'What acid?'

'Of course, you've never heard of it.' The Doctor sat at the terminal. 'I'd better pass the formula along.'

A number of scarlet-garbed guards were taking up positions suitable for giving covering fire, sheltering behind the elaborately carved pillars that supported small pavilion roofs at each corner of the wide courtyard.

The courtyard was mostly greenery, but the far end was a Tarmac helipad. It hadn't been designed for spacecraft landings, but everyone was familiar enough with Nur's ship to know that it was just about small enough to fit in the courtyard. A pair of guards started setting up a tripod-mounted cannon of some kind in front of the main doors, while others laid down their rifles for a moment to build up a defensive wall of benches and large plant pots around the cannon.

They snatched their weapons back instinctively as the dark pointed slab of the *Garuda* dropped low over the roof. The guards ducked behind their cover, shading their eyes from the whirlwind of dust and leaves that slammed into all four sides of the courtyard as the *Garuda* settled, her wide stern on the helipad, her nose crushing a statue in a small fountain near the doors.

The guards held their weapons ready, and peered out at the vimana as the landing ramp lowered from below the starboard airlock. A pair of stubby cylinders sailed from the shadowed hatchway into the nearest clutch of guards. They didn't even have time to duck as the air turned white with a blazing flash, sending streamers of organic vapour into the air where the men had been standing.

A squad of lumpy figures tumbled from the *Garuda* as the smoke settled, their rolling gait carrying them with remarkable speed and agility for such an ungainly bulk. The surviving ground crew scattered, leaping for the dubious shelter of the drainage trench around the border gardens as bursts of light from the attackers' weapons played across the pad.

A furious exchange of fire erupted, with the invaders'

gun-metal armour briefly reflecting the fiery colours of their opponents' energy blasts. The air itself smelt burnt by the searing bolts. Another alien grenade made short work of the cannon before it could even be fired, and the cover built up around it was blasted across the corpse-strewn courtyard. When the smoke cleared, the doors were seen to have also succumbed to the blast, with one having fallen away entirely and the other hanging by only one hinge.

A last couple of guards scrambled back to the doors, ducking inside for further cover as they shot back ineffectually at the invaders. The aliens ignored all available cover, but simply jogged forward, firing whenever they had a clear shot. Just as the first few aliens reached the wreckage of the cannon, the first gunship loomed over the south wall on humming repulsor-lift fields, quad rotary chain-guns panning to either side. Two alien troopers armed with larger and bulkier weapons opened fire, and the port side of the gunship shuddered and blew out with a spray of molten shrapnel. With one repulsor field generator torn apart, it listed to the side, the rotary quads churning several furrows of turf, marble and polymerase-chain flesh out of the southeast corner of the courtyard. The firestream lasted only a few instants before the gunship collapsed into the lake, sending out a billowing cloud of steam that obscured the source of the sharp bangs and pops which emanated from it.

The other two gunships had cleared the outer wall, but the guards at the main door had already been cut down, and the Sontaran troopers were pouring in.

Alarm bells rang furiously as the sound of gunfire echoed through the palace. Several Kshatriyas ascended from their basement barracks, weapons in hand, but they were no more effective against Sontaran armour than the warriors on Agni had been.

Another ship howled over the roof, and the sergeant was just about intelligent enough to recognize the sound as a heavier ship, which therefore probably meant a transport with reinforcements. He blasted a couple of guards from the curved marble staircase to the left and snatched the lifeform tracker out of the hand of its operator. The target humans were only a few yards away. He looked in the direction the scanner indicated, and saw a barred door with a couple of dead guards before it. He smiled under his helmet, and hefted a grenade.

A surprisingly muted rumble accompanied the charred fragments of the barred doors across the elegant room, a cluster of squat figures following the sound into the room, their armour making them seem like darker patches of the smoke that dissipated rapidly.

A cacophonous roar of explosive impacts tore apart one side of the white grand piano as Nur hurled herself under it. Smoking chunks of upholstery burst volcanically from the hand-carved chairs to her right as full automatic fire from a pair of rheon carbines pursued the Doctor and Turlough up the length of her father's pink-hued reception chamber.

Turlough ducked at the last minute, leaping into a relatively sheltered alcove. That kept enough pillars between him and the guns to stop the magnetic bullets of irradiated particles before they reached him. The Doctor took a flying leap across Ambika's podium, knocking him and his chair over and down the few steps on the other side. Nur wished she could reach them, hoping that the Doctor would know how to deal with the Sontarans.

The firing continued down the line, and one of the Kshatriyas spasmed in a cloudy spray of blood from grotesquely distorted bruises before bouncing off the wall under the impacts.

A fallen weapon was lying just a few feet away, and Nur hooked it with a broken piece of piano stool, dragging it back towards her. It seemed simple enough, with a three-setting fire selector and safety. Uncertain of what effect each setting would have, she set it to the highest setting, wanting to be sure. Then again, it seemed reasonable that the Kshatriyas had also set to kill, and it hadn't done them any good. Maybe the sheer surprise of returned fire would scare them off, she thought doubtfully. At least she wouldn't have to aim at anything that way. Cocking the gun, she poked the barrel up above the shattered piano, holding it steeply towards the ceiling as she opened fire.

The gun roared and bucked surprisingly violently in her hand as a wide furrow of plaster rained down from the ceiling, and the air clouded with dust and splinters of glass from the exploding chandeliers. The other shooting had stopped, and she risked a quick look that showed her the two Sontarans turning this way and that, seeking the source of the new firing.

The gun's power pack died, even though it had been but a few seconds, and the Sontarans lumbered across the room, past a couple of serving trolleys laden with buffet foods. 'Sharma!' Nur shouted. She wasn't sure how he would handle a combat on the ground, but he couldn't possibly be any worse than her.

The patrol ship captain had been waiting for just such an opportunity anyway, she knew, and was already scuttling up the length of the hall. The two Sontarans reloaded hurriedly as Sharma snatched a brandy bottle from the trolley, hurling it at the nearest one's head. The Sontaran ignored it, the bottle smashing against his forehead in a wet shower without provoking so much as a blink from the alien. The Sontaran brought up his rheon carbine. Sharma swept a wok-like pan from the upper bed of the next trolley and released it in one smooth motion even as he rolled aside to avoid the gunfire. The pan jerked and spun in midair as the bullets hit it, sending a spray of burning oil across the room.

With a soft whoosh, the brandy that had soaked into the Sontaran's fibrous armour caught fire. His rheon carbine started blazing after Sharma as he swung around, unhurt, but blinded by the bright flames obscuring the eyeholes of his helmet.

The Doctor had risked poking his head over the dais, with Ambika right beside him. Nur hoped that neither of them would get their head shot off. A cricket ball flashed through her mind on the way to an earlier Sontaran. 'Remember the probic vent,' she called to Sharma in an urgent tone. 'The small opening at the back of the collar.' Sharma rolled straight back up and pumped half a dozen shots into the Sontaran's helmet. Sparks exploded harmlessly from it, but then the alien screeched, and clapped its hands to its helmet as a splash of pale fluid spattered out from one of the eyeholes. It spun around blindly, and Sharma fired again the instant its back was fully turned.

The Sontaran hit the floor and burnt more quietly as Sharma emptied the rest of his magazine at the other alien, then ducked back to reload his pistol. He looked out to make sure that the first one was well and truly out of commission. Nur wished, not for the first time, that her father had allowed her to take that training as a child. In fact, if she'd been his son instead of his daughter, he would have insisted on it.

A sudden cry of alarm from her father drew Nur's head round immediately, and she saw the Doctor slip from Ambika's attempt to hold him back, and lock his arms around the other Sontaran's collar.

The Sontaran lurched drunkenly, trying to unbalance the Doctor and throw him off, but without success. The Doctor's habitual relaxed smile had been replaced by a look of intense effort, and he gritted his teeth in an effort to hang on and prevent the alien from getting a clear shot at Nur or Sharma. 'Turlough!'

'Oh no,' Turlough muttered from his alcove, darting out with a look of nervous reluctance. Ducking under a flailing blow, the youth grabbed hold of the Sontaran's forearm, trying to peel the two thick fingers away from the wand-like rheon carbine that it was discharging across the room.

Determined not to be left out, Nur scrambled out from

186

under the shattered piano, reaching the Sontaran's free arm at the same time as Sharma. The creature's arm was absolutely solid, and she doubted she could hold it alone. Sharma had wrapped his arms around the Sontaran's elbow, however, and together they held it back from knocking away Turlough's hands.

'Get away from there, Nur!' Ambika shouted, moving shakily towards them. He stared at her as if she were holding a cobra. She rather wished she was.

'It's all right, Ambika,' the Doctor gasped, shifting his weight slightly. 'Give me a bottle from one of the trolleys.'

'What?'

'Do it, man!'

Ambika looked around blankly, then proffered a bottle of cooking brandy to the Doctor. The Doctor took it carefully in one hand, and smashed the neck against the Sontaran's helmet. Hanging on for dear life, he poured the brandy down the Sontaran's probic vent, and the creature redoubled its struggles.

Half the liquid splashed to the floor, and the Doctor's feet slipped across it, sending him tumbling from the Sontaran's back. Nur felt her heart leap into her throat as the alien swung its arms' human baggage around jerkily. Ambika's face cleared of its panic, though she was pleased by the concern still etched around his eyes, and he lifted a broken splinter of the piano from the floor.

Nur was appalled, wondering if his mind had snapped, but he thrust the wood into the flames licking around the fallen alien, and it caught fire. The preceptor looked around at the three young faces. They all nodded, Nur convinced that all knew exactly what he was silently asking. The Doctor, however, rose unsteadily, shaking his head. 'No! The alcohol will destabilize its enzyme productions and force it to leave for recharging.'

'Not good enough.' Ambika thrust the burning wood into the Sontaran's probic vent, and the three others instantly threw themselves to the ground. The Doctor looked unharmed, Nur noted, and was watching with obvious disgust as a blue flash burst from the probic vent.

The Sontaran stiffened, a low howl drawn from somewhere deep within the creature, and it suddenly twisted and jerked spasmodically as acrid smoke curled out from both the vent and the eyeholes in its helmet. With the noise of a collapsing elephant, it toppled to the floor, twitching and howling a little less with each passing second.

The Doctor glared at Ambika. 'A few more seconds and it would have been incapacitated and harmless.'

'A few more seconds and it could have shot everyone in the room.'

Behind the tinted canopy, the blue-armoured Sontaran pilot was slashing furiously at the *Garuda*'s controls. The supporting oleos of the landing gear were starting to stretch out as the vimana's engines started to lift her clear. Before the feet of the landing gear parted company with the ground, however, one of the gunships completed its swing around the island, and was arrowing straight for the courtyard.

An almost solid stream of rocket-assisted explosive projectiles from the gunship's rotary cannon gouged a channel across the *Garuda*'s nose. The canopy flew apart in a cloud of glittering dust and Sontaran organic vapour. With its controls destroyed, the vimana's engines cut out, and it slammed heavily back to the ground, the nose leg oleo snapping at the joint under the sudden compression. The *Garuda*'s nose crumpled into the flowerbed as the gunship continued overhead.

The remaining Sontarans now milled around the dust-scattered vestibule, firing upward at the roof as a flurry of booming thuds under an all-encompassing roar marked the arrival of reinforcements.

A rain of glass jars filled with a viscous yellow liquid pelted down on to the troopers, smashing on helmets or marble floor and sending gouts of the stuff lashing through the air. Several Sontarans started withdrawing back through the doors into the courtyard, clouds of acrid smoke wrapping around their heads as their armour started to dissolve into their flesh.

As soon as they stumbled out of the doors into the clearer air, the two gunships opened fire on them, the rapid fire ripping the already weakened troopers into gobbets of ragged ochre.

A few managed to pull up before reaching the outside, but more Kshatriyas had already gained entry to the palace through the roof, and were firing from the cover of the balustrade at the top of the staircase. This time, with the Sontarans' armour full of smouldering gaps, their fire was sufficient to bring them down.

As the shooting died down in the foyer outside, Nur's face was screwed up in revulsion, and Turlough felt his bile bubble and rise. Somebody should have wiped them out long ago, he thought irritably. The Doctor got to his feet, breathing a little shakily as he surveyed everyone. 'Are you all all right?'

'We're not injured, if that's what you mean,' Turlough replied, fighting down his own revulsion. Since when was getting shot at all right?

Sharma bent to recover the fallen Sontarans' weapons. The movement saved his life, as a sweeping burst of fire raked along the wall. Another Sontaran had kicked his way in through the French windows. Sharma quickly hurled himself full-length on to the nearest serving trolley, rolling on to his side as it moved and firing back with both of the confiscated rheon carbines. A field of swollen bulges burst across the new Sontaran's torso as he pitched backward through the window, his weapon clattering into the pink carpet. There was a distant splash from somewhere outside.

Nur hugged herself as Sharma swung himself back on to his feet and made both guns safe. Ambika took a ceremonial lance from the wall, and prodded the Sontaran he'd assaulted. It didn't stir, though a few wisps of rancid steam drifted from its helmet, which then rolled off.

The creature's lumpy head was even more grotesque than any of the recorded images Turlough recalled from the Imperial Academy, with acrid slime spreading from every orifice. Ambika gagged slightly. 'I've never seen anything like this . . . thing before.'

'You've been lucky then,' the Doctor told him. 'There are rather a lot of them about.'

'If they're warriors, then they should suffer losses.'

'You saw how difficult these were to kill. Besides, they're a cloned species; every one of their incubation complexes can produce up to a million hatchlings in four minutes. Fortunately for most of us, they're so wrapped up in a blood feud with the Rutan Host that they don't really have the opportunity to turn their attention to anyone else, though quite a few races have been caught in the crossfire from time to time.'

'The Rutan must breed just as fast, then, if they haven't been wiped out yet.'

'Worse, if anything. They're a race of amphibious amoeboids, which reproduce by division, so their numbers increase exponentially. As a matter of fact, the Arcalian exobiologist Crahin on Gallifrey has speculated that, since the Sontarans are a genetically engineered species, they may have been created with the express purpose of keeping down the Rutan population. Otherwise they'd have overrun the galaxy millennia ago. Personally, I don't believe a word of it.'

'Then what did start their war?' Nur asked.

'Nobody knows,' Turlough put in sagely. He didn't want these humans to think he was as ignorant as they were.

The Doctor nodded in agreement. 'Probably not even themselves. I think these days it's become more a cultural habit for them than anything else.'

He started towards the doors, and the others followed, choking on the stinking smoke and dust. Turlough lifted a fallen weapon just in case. The shooting had stopped, but it paid to be careful. Several uniformed men were carrying or supporting dead or injured colleagues from the scene. A Kshatriya officer with sweat-damped hair moved towards them, carefully stepping around the splashes of acid which were already blackening the marble flooring. 'We count half a dozen aliens in here, Excellence,' he reported. 'We're not too sure about those outside, as the gunship cannons haven't left much to work with. We've lost about 40 men, all told, including one gunship, with at least a dozen wounded.'

'There are another three Sontarans in there, and one at the bottom of the lake,' Sharma said. 'Are there any survivors?'

'Not that we can tell, sir; they're hardly inconspicuous.' Turlough drew on all his strength of will not to scoff at that. No one had caught the two who had chased him through the streets. 'We're conducting a thorough search all the same.'

'Good,' Ambika said with a nod. 'Go over this area with a fine-tooth comb; find out everything we possibly can about these aliens.'

'Yes, Excellence.' He frowned, then held out a small box. 'There is one other thing . . . One of them had this.'

'If you'll allow me?' the Doctor said, taking the box. He activated it, and a tiny screen lit up with three glowing spots – one in the exact centre. He turned around slowly, and the other two spots moved around the central one, which remained still. 'Interesting,' he said, looking between Nur and Sharma. 'It seems this tracker was set specifically to home in on the three of us.'

'How is that possible?' Nur asked. Turlough had to wonder at her naiveté.

'I imagine they got traces of our particulate cell structures from skin cells in the *Garuda*, and tuned the tracker to look for the same signature.' His eyes widened, and looked at the tracker as if it had suddenly transformed into the holy grail. 'Of course!' The others looked at him,

191

the same wordless question in their eyes. 'Do you have medical equipment here – a microscope, that sort of thing?'

Ambika made a so-so motion with his hand. 'There's a small first-aid room, and the gardener has some microscopes for his husbandry experiments.'

'Good, that'll do. Get a tissue sample from one of the Sontarans and bring it to me, then fetch a microscope. I think I have an idea.'

Fifteen

Turlough and the first shaft of dawn light found the Doctor at the same time. He had set up a small microscope in the first-aid room, and was comparing two specimen slides. 'Any luck?'

'Success, yes, but I wouldn't call it luck. Not for the people here anyway.'

'Then you know what's been done?'

'I suspected all along, but a tissue sample from one of those dead Sontarans has confirmed it.' He held up the scanner that the Sontarans had used to track them down. 'Look at this.' He switched the scanner on, and left the room.

Turlough followed, curious in spite of himself. He had nothing against helping these people – no one deserved to be caught in the Sontaran–Rutan crossfire – but he couldn't see how this would help. The scanner started beeping softly. 'Well?'

'Watch.' The Doctor pointed out a large mass of blips on the tiny screen. 'Two-four-zero degrees, nine yards.'

Turlough looked behind and to the left. A number of Sontaran corpses had been piled there. For some reason, Turlough found it disturbingly creepy that the flies were leaving the bodies alone. 'It detects Sontarans. So what?'

The Doctor pointed to a pair of smaller blips. 'Zero-three-five degrees, fifteen yards.'

Turlough dutifully looked to the right. Ahead, two gardeners were clearing up some of the shattered stonework from the wrecked fountain. He had a nasty suspicion that he knew what this meant. He hoped he was wrong. 'Gardeners are Sudras?'

'Yes.'

'You've set the scanner to look for the polymerase tag?'

'Exactly. For some reason, the Sontarans have been infecting the people here with the artificial marker that identifies the hatchery from which any given clone was bred. According to Ambika, they were going to spread it to each caste in turn.'

'Presumably with a different Sontaran clan's tag each time.'

'Not necessarily, but I shouldn't be surprised. Makes you think, doesn't it?'

'It makes me think I'm glad we have our own water supply.' Turlough knew this was rather selfish, but wasn't everybody? 'The question is why?'

'I'm not sure yet. What I do know is that we have to stop this before it goes any further.'

'Then we have to destroy the lab on Agni.' At least it would be a useful act, though Turlough could think of better ways to spend his time than getting shot at again.

'Right.' The Doctor unrolled his hat, and put it on. 'Time to see Ambika and Sharma. We'll need transport and probably some backup.' The Doctor didn't sound happy about the idea of needing any military support.

'You know there's a saying about the only good reason for going into the jaws of death.'

'Well, we'll ask Jahangir if he knows a good supplier of dental pliers as well.'

The Sontaran Valt-class destroyer orbited alongside the larger new arrival like a remora cruising alongside a shark. A slim transfer tube was suspended between the destroyer and a roughly welded makeshift cabin atop the longer ship.

Karne was just about to step into the transfer tube from the destroyer's main airlock when Loxx paged him. Karne

194

was tempted to not answer, but such a breach of regulations might have unfortunate consequences. He would just have to hope that he got an opportunity to go across alone later.

The bridge was a hive of activity when Karne returned to it, and busy voices were constantly calling out checks to each other. Loxx was waiting by the communications console. 'Well?'

'Fleet Marshal Stentor is on hold.'

Karne thought a moment. Didn't they trust him to do his job on his own? 'Put him on.' Stentor's ancient features came into vision on the main screen, and everyone fell silent. 'Fleet Marshal.'

'I see you're hard at work. Good. Is the generator ready?'

'The tech crews finished preparations an hour ago. I would prefer to personally examine –'

'There will be no time. Our sensor net has detected the approach of a Rutan scout heading for your current location. You must withdraw your force and execute the plan within twelve hours.'

'But only one human clan grouping has been –'

'It will have to suffice. The Rutan scanners will be sensitive enough to detect them. There is one other thing. We can't risk an equipment malfunction in the generator's automatics; someone will have to remain behind and activate manually if need be.'

'With your permission sir, I volunteer,' Loxx said proudly. Karne seethed inwardly; this would have been a perfect chance for himself.

'Ah, your sacrifice is noble, Major Loxx.'

'Thank you sir.' Loxx sounded half-unable to believe his luck in being granted the promotion. 'I shall die gladly, to take the Rutan with me.' Obviously no one had told him that you didn't win wars by dying, but by making the enemy die. Karne, however, had no particular desire to correct him.

* * *

195

The Doctor stood aside resignedly as Sharma led his squad into the villa's grounds, each member of the team keeping at least one of the others covered. 'This isn't really necessary, you know.'

Turlough, for one, was glad of the added measure of protection. Armed guards had never been a favourite choice of company for him, but given the choice between them and another bout with the Sontarans, he was willing to let them follow. 'We don't know whether there are any more Sontarans down here.'

'Even if there are, I'm sure they've got better things to do than hang around waiting for us.' Ignoring Sharma's frantic hand signalling, the Doctor strolled across the cropped lawn, curving around the villa. Giving the others an embarrassingly apologetic look, Turlough followed. At least if there was any trouble they just had to pop into the TARDIS and go. A soft rustling of cloth accompanied movement behind Turlough as Sharma led the Kshatriyas after them.

That was almost a pity, Turlough thought, since it would be far more difficult for him to try to convince the Doctor to leave for somewhere safer if the warriors were around. He rounded the sandstone pillar that held up the shady porch overlooking the courtyard, and realized with a plunging feeling of disappointment that the question was purely academic now.

The Kshatriyas shuffled off to either side, looking suspiciously around as the Doctor prodded a hand into thin air ahead of him on the lawn. Behind him, the sculpted topiary peacocks were clearly visible in all their splendour, without the TARDIS obscuring them from view. Turlough looked aside at Sharma. 'Can you get your men to search the house for a large blue box a little larger than one of your public information cubicles?'

Sharma nodded. 'Not going well?'

'You could say that.' Turlough walked over towards the Doctor. Sharma's men wouldn't find anything, of course, but it would keep them too busy to ask questions whose answers they probably wouldn't understand anyway. 'So, the TARDIS has gone?'

The Doctor grimaced. 'You really must tell me where you came by your deductive skills.' He straightened, and pointed up to where the bright pinpoint of distant Agni was crossing the twilit sky. 'They must have picked it up as an anomalous energy reading and decided to take a look.'

'Will they know what they've got?' Perhaps if they thought it was merely a human construction they might forget about it.'

'We have crossed paths on occasion. I imagine the TARDIS's form will be registered in their enemy recognition manuals somewhere.'

And I said the chameleon circuit wasn't important, Turlough thought. 'Could we get a message to Kamelion? He might be able to fly the TARDIS back here.'

'Kamelion only responds to mental commands, and it would take weeks to build a psionic relay which could let us do that.'

'Then we're stuck here?'

'Not necessarily. We know the location of their osmic projector terminal. A few of us could teleport up and secure the TARDIS, then let a ship land to pick up the surviving humans.'

'Always assuming we know where they're keeping the TARDIS.' Turlough didn't like sounding pessimistic, but he knew how uncertain plans could be.

'They must have transported it up via osmic projector, since a ship would have been seen. That means that if we're quick enough we should still find it at the projection terminal in the station's observation dome.' He turned, and froze. Turlough wondered how he was supposed to talk himself out of the way of the machine that had emerged from the hedge.

He didn't have to. A barrage of explosive rounds from the Kshatriyas' weapons sparked off the trapezoidal body as he and the Doctor sprinted for the shelter of the patio.

197

The Doctor patted his pockets anxiously, then grimaced. 'I'll never forgive those Terileptils for that. Sontaran robots are vulnerable to high-frequency sound.'

The robot's soft beeping rose to a frantic screech, and it exploded in a shower of razor-sharp fragments. Turlough peered out from one of the patio's pillars. 'Loud bangs seem to disagree with it as well.'

Nur returned from the requisite morning dip off the palace's private ghat, and felt sick to her stomach as she approached the *Garuda*. Her vimana was tilted nose-down like a cartoon boxer who has just been knocked cold; the landing gear under the wide rear hull was still firmly supporting the ship on the helipad, but the churned and twisted prow was tangled on the ground along with the wreckage of the forward landing leg and the rubble of the fountain.

Chunks of damp Sontaran flesh were putrefying in spots both inside and outside the shattered wound of what used to be the flight deck's canopy. The collapse of the forward landing gear had buckled the ramp, so she scrambled up the cracked chunks of stone from the fountain on to the battered nose of the ship, and carefully lowered herself into the cratered flight deck.

Careful not to lose her footing on the debris-strewn floor – or slip on any Sontaran fillets – she surveyed the damage with an aching heart as well as a burning anger. The consoles and avionics had all been smashed clean out of existence, and the seats were just twisted fingers of charred metal. The steps were now the only level part of the floor, and she moved slowly through into the canted hold. The small lounge was riddled with holes and scorch marks, but was at least recognizable, while the main area of the hold was battered and every surface was dented. At least the bulkhead to the engineering compartment had held.

Deflated, she sat on a hardened mound of sealant foam whose tank had been ruptured. It might be theoretically possible for the ship to be repaired – new furnishings and panels installed, the avionics system replaced with an upgrade, new consoles and hull plates for the nose – but it wouldn't really be the same ship.

After so long, the pilot's seat had been almost moulded to fit her; the controls and flight computer were riddled with short-cuts and hotkeys that enabled her to fly with the maximum of ease. It had its own moods and temperament – such as the air conditioning's tendency to go for scorching midday temperatures – that were inconvenient but unique and bearable.

She supposed it had really been her friend, in a way. In a life where people fêted her because they wished to curry favour with her father, or because they thought it was their place or rank to do so, the *Garuda* had always partnered her well on its own terms and without any ulterior motive or ritual deference.

She wondered what sort of sad and lonely person she must be to care so much about what was, after all, really only a lump of metal. She supposed she should be glad that Shiva had chosen to remind her of the *Garuda*'s nature, especially since a new creation would be required to follow it. That was its karma, she told herself.

There was a rattle of activity from the buckled landing ramp, and the Doctor climbed aboard. She brushed her still-damp hair away from her face and gestured around. 'It seems my freedom is at an end.'

'Perish the thought,' the Doctor said with a smile. 'I'm rather afraid I'm going to need your help again.'

'What? On the ground?'

'No, I need you to fly a transport.'

'Do I look like a bus driver?'

'I don't know. It takes all sorts, I suppose.' He sat down. 'The Sontarans have taken my ship. Not only do I want it back, but we'll also need a ship to ferry all the prisoners on Agni back home.'

She'd almost forgotten about them, she realized guiltily. 'Why not come down the osmic projector?'

'You might recall we had to come one at a time; bringing three hundred people back could take longer than they or we have got.'

Perhaps it wasn't such a bad idea; keeping herself busy might take her mind off her loss. 'If it's got a cockpit, I can fly it.' Besides, a pilot is *what* I am, not who I am, she thought; it's my dharma.

'Good. Your father has promised us the use of a military ship. I'll rig another sensor cloak and then go with Sharma and some of his men to secure the station. You and Turlough will come up to collect the captives, and we'll shut down any defences the Sontarans have left to let you in.'

'How are you going to deal with them all?'

He smiled boyishly, like a grade A student having opened his exam results. 'Well, like anyone else, they have their weaknesses.'

The Gul Mahal medical centre looked like some sort of exclusive country club in the morning light, but Sharma wasn't going to take any chances. Not after discovering how strongly the Sontarans' conditioning held its victims. 'Remember,' the Doctor told him, 'no shooting unless the Sontarans attack personally. We can easily decondition anyone who's under their control.'

'Right.' Sharma waved his men forward, and they dashed up the drive and into the reception area. A couple of startled nurses suppressed yelps of surprise as they were hustled out. 'All right. First platoon with me; the rest of you carry out the operation as planned. Decondition everyone – if they weren't controlled it won't do any harm. Then evacuate the centre, just in case.' He turned back to the Doctor. 'I hope you know how to work that transmat the opposite way.'

'Yes.' The Doctor strolled unconcernedly in the direction of the storeroom with the osmic projector terminal.

Nur guided the assault transport off the ground, and

headed out of orbit. She grimaced as she shoved the power up further and further just to reach escape velocity. 'I don't believe that somebody bought this thing for the military,' she grumbled. 'It's a piece of junk: overweight, underpowered, and the fuel system leaks like a sieve.'

Turlough had no real experience on which to base any comparison. It had been so long since he had flown in an ordinary ship that he would have found fault with the most luxurious of yachts if it had a G-force like this on take-off. The TARDIS might not be fully reliable where navigation was concerned, but at least it didn't purée you when leaving a planet.

At least the company was pleasant. 'I didn't think there could be another planet like that.' Not that he'd had much chance to enjoy it. Still, once this was over, perhaps he could explore without being chased.

'Like what?'

'Like Trion. Kuru seems very like the Meridian city, but with fewer castes.'

'Never heard of Trion. Is it an Earth colony?'

'No.' Thank the Gods, Turlough added mentally.

'One of the Alliance worlds then?'

Turlough was about to respond negatively, but then recalled that this was three hundred years in his future. Added to the fact that he didn't know what the Alliance actually was . . . 'Alliance?'

'It was formed after the Dalek invasion; Earth, Centauri, the Cyrennhics . . .'

'Oh, probably. You seem to know a lot about the Agni station.'

'Going on a tour there is part of the training to qualify for a spacer licence on Raghi.'

'And Sharma? You've known him long?'

'I should do, I've been engaged to him since I was eight. Arranged by our parents, of course.' Turlough didn't know what to say. Or rather, he could think of many things to say, but none of them would have improved the situation at all.

Something glittered outside the narrow viewport. 'There are some other ships there.'

'It's all right, we're invisible to their sensors. I'll have to be careful on approach, though, in case they see us directly.'

'Yes . . .' The largest of the three ships was familiar, and Turlough realized it was the thing that Karan had been tracking. It was even more worrying when seen dwarfing the other ships. There was definitely something familiar about it, he repeated to himself. He didn't like it at all.

Each Kshatriya dropped into a combat-ready crouch as soon as the hospital room faded away to reveal the starlit grass of the Agni station's observation dome. A man in a lab coat was lying prone on one of the gravel paths, his face drawn and unshaven, but no one else, human or Sontaran, was around.

Once all twenty had arrived, the Doctor crouched to examine him as the Kshatriyas spread out to check the dome's bulkhead doors. He looked up with a faint nod to a curious Sharma. 'Oh, he's alive, but only barely. The Sontarans won't have bothered to allow anyone rest or food. That's why they've had to keep abducting scientists from Raghi – refills. You and your crew were lucky that there are at least twice as many of you as there are jobs to do, so you can still rest when each shift changes.'

They left the dome, and descended cautiously to the main corridor at the base of the hub. There were no Sontarans around, though there were plenty of exhausted and dead or dying prisoners. Sharma was disgusted; this could so easily have been him and his crew, and as it was, many of these people were his friends. One thing nagged at him, however. 'What about the families that were stationed here? We've seen no sign of any spouses or children of the workers.'

The Doctor avoided his gaze sadly. 'I'm not sure. Neither Nur nor I saw any sign of them when we were here. We can scan for them from central control, but the chances are that the Sontarans simply killed them, being of no use to them.'

Sharma hurried on ahead when they reached the main corridor linking the habitat block to the operations section, not wanting anyone to see tears welling up. He was going to hurt the Sontarans very badly, he promised himself. He stopped as something caught his eye from outside the armoured viewports that lined the main passageway.

Three shapes hung silently above the magma fields outside. The scarred white form of the *Nandi* sent a twinge of heartache through him, while the swollen Sontaran destroyer inspired quite different feelings. He wished he could hit it from here. The third shape was more of a mystery. It was a long slab, like some sort of silver girder, inlaid with traceries of bluish highlights which glowed faintly. A delicate wing sprouted from one side of this object, about halfway along. The wing didn't stretch very far, however, as it soon dissolved into a mass of jagged and twisted fragments.

'I don't really like to worry you,' Sharma said in an almost, but not quite, matter-of-fact tone. 'But compared to the *Nandi* I'd say that thing's about a mile long.' The Doctor said nothing, and simply gazed out of the viewport with a wide-eyed expression of fascinated shock. 'I've never seen a ship like that.'

'It's not a ship, just a part of one,' the Doctor said quietly, blinking as if to clear away the cobwebs. 'That is the main graviton drive nacelle of a Tzun Stormblade. I wonder . . .' He turned away quickly. 'Come on, we have to get to central control.'

Loxx methodically extracted data chips from the computers in central control, depositing them in a small container ready to be taken back to the destroyer. Around him, a couple of troopers rather clumsily removed the bits and pieces of equipment that they had added to the humans' facilities. The damage caused to the humans' equipment didn't matter, so long as their own technology was all recovered intact.

Everyone else had already withdrawn to the destroyer, but Loxx had stayed to ensure that the clean-up was done was proper efficiency. In any case, some of those data chips would be used on the Tzun nacelle once he transferred over, so he thought he might as well collect them personally.

He was slightly surprised, therefore, when he heard the doors slide open. He turned, as one of the troopers fired with admirable reflexes. A glass canister crashed into the troopers armour as the invading humans dived for cover behind the consoles. The first trooper was already collapsing into a thrashing mound of decomposing matter as the second was knocked off his feet by the combined blasts of a dozen guns. Even Sontaran armour couldn't withstand such concentrated fire, and the trooper spun across the room, dead before he slammed into a terminal and hit the ground.

After surreptitiously pressing a button on the box on his belt, Loxx raised his hands as half a dozen guns were trained on him. The position felt remarkably strange, and he seethed with anger, proud of the fact that Sontarans never surrendered. Anyone who did – such as the human crew of the station – deserved all they got. Unfortunately, however, some duties were even more important, and there was nothing too dishonourable about playing for time.

The angular and bearded human who had been in charge of the ship they had captured was in charge here as well, and Loxx turned to him. 'Jingo Loxx, Commander, four-four-three-two-seven squared.'

A paler humanoid, who could only be the Doctor, smiled charmingly, not that it had much effect on the Sontaran. 'Stay right where you are, resistance is useless.' The Doctor shrugged and leant conspiratorially closer. 'I've always wanted to say that.'

* * *

The Sontaran lieutenant had vanished by the time Jahangir boarded the *Nandi*. Jahangir was disappointed; it would have been so much more satisfying to have killed the lieutenant himself. He could almost sense the pressure of the Sontaran's flesh resisting some sharpened piece of a support strut as he spitted its brain by way of that little vent at the back of its collar.

Instead, he settled for healing. He was relieved – and surprised – to discover that he could still do it. He could easily recall the pattern of lights that had freed his own soul from slavery, and had found a torch with which to release the others. It would have been an impossibly long job, but each crew member so released went on to release others. Within an hour, everyone on board was free of Sontaran control.

Jahangir huddled himself into Sharma's command chair. Now he had a ship and crew. The Sontarans couldn't get away from him now. He sagged slightly. He couldn't really ask the crew to die for him; they deserved their chance to recover, or else the Sontarans would have won in some way. Still, with any luck it wouldn't come to that, since they had surprise on their side. No doubt the Sontarans would be expecting the *Nandi* to remain where she was, tended blindly by a crew who would simply keep watch until they died of exhaustion.

'Parvi, lock the Sontaran ship into fire control, and make sure that all repair priorities are given over to the weapons systems.'

'Yes, sir.' Though all of the crew were bone-tired, it was as if their new-found freedom had invigorated them.

Sharma watched impatiently as the Doctor plugged the Sontaran scanner into the station's own monitoring system. Its only register was in the control room with them. 'We might be too late,' the Doctor said warningly. 'They seem to have left, apart from these three.'

'Any sign of the families?'

'There's a large concentration of human life-signs in

the habitat block's hangar level . . .' The Doctor skipped through several internal monitor channels, showing pictures of dead or unconscious scientists, until an image of a large room packed with people came on-screen. The inhabitants, including many children, looked half-starved. 'There they are. Luckily there seems to be some sort of food dispenser there. I imagine the Sontarans simply locked them in there to ensure the cooperation of the more useful humans, then forgot about them once everyone they needed was put under control.'

Sharma took a few moments to find the meteor shield controls, but deactivating them took only a few keystrokes. 'All right, Nur,' he announced over the communication channel. 'You're clear to come in. According to our scans, there are no Sontarans left here, except for one prisoner we've got. I'm clearing you for the habitat block's hangar, because our monitors show several families held there.'

'I copy, we'll get them aboard first.'

Nur settled the wide-bodied transport on to the deck, having retracted its stubby wings. On the far side of the transparent blast shield, dozens of weary and filthy people were staring out at them in amazement.

That was much more refreshing than a handshake from some civic official, but Nur would have preferred the civic handshake, if it meant that there wasn't suffering like this. She probably wouldn't sleep for a week, she thought. She got out of her seat, and descended to the cavernous passenger hold, which was filled with rows of folding seats. A couple of Kshatriyas were there, and preceded her out of the wide cargo doors.

This was the sort of thing that really needed a good organizer, and she wished one was here. Unfortunately there wasn't really time; the Sontaran warship was still out there, and could pick them off at any time. 'All right, Turlough, take charge here. Get these people on board as quickly as you can. I'll go and see what the others are up to; and bring back the station staff they've found.'

'I think it would be better if I went. This ship is your responsibility, after all.'

'Fine. Do you know where you're going?' Turlough groaned. 'Exactly. I won't be long, and you've got the Kshatriyas to help.' Without giving him a chance to answer back – and she was certain he would think of an answer – she disappeared through the hangar's inner airlock doors.

The trip to central control didn't take long, despite stopping to decondition the occasional prisoner and telling them where to find the ship. A group of Kshatriyas helping more freed prisoners passed her in the main connecting corridor.

She entered the amphitheatre that was central control to find the Doctor poring over a computer. Sharma looked at her with an expression of relief, and she decided that he'd earned a smile from her. Duty was duty, though, and she joined the Doctor in Chandra's office. 'Found anything useful?'

The Doctor continued tapping absently at the keyboard. 'Hmm.' He looked up, as if hearing the question several seconds late. 'There's a link to their ship's mainframe which our friend there hadn't quite disconnected yet. Captain, would you be so good as to find some storage medium on which to download this? There might be something in these files that could help.'

'I don't know if you've noticed, but there's another new arrival out there. A big slab-like ship.' She didn't like to remind him of it, but its presence had been unnerving her.

'Yes, I saw it. Graviton drive nacelle from a Tzun Stormblade.'

'Tzun? You used that name before.'

'Yes.' The Doctor nodded. 'This whole sector used to be Tzun space, so I imagine that nacelle is part of the wreckage left over from their destruction at the hands of the Veltrochni.'

'You've met them before?'

'Leela and I had some trouble with them on Mimosa II.'

Sharma repressed a shudder. 'Then what do the Sontarans want with an old Stormblade drive nacelle?'

'I have a rather nasty suspicion. Look.' He brought up a holographic analysis of Indra's composition on the main screen. A graph spiked up across it. 'This was in those files. It seems to be a progress chart of some kind, or a projection of expected events.' He looked into the distance, as if searching for a form of explanation that the others would understand. 'Tzun ships travelled along the wavefronts of gravity waves. They'd use the wavefronts of two adjacent waves rather like tramlines. For longer journeys, they'd use the main nacelle to direct a graviton stream at their destination, taking into account all the interference from other bodies, of course . . . You're both familiar with the rubber sheet model of the universe, where a heavy object makes a deeper gravitational dent?'

Sharma and Nur both nodded. Nur hated being treated like a dirtsider that way.

'Good; it's not actually very accurate, but it'll do for now. Unlike a normal warp or hyperdrive, where the engines simply quantum-tunnel through space and form a briefly localized Einstein–Rosen bridge from A to B, the Tzun gravity drive grabs the destination point of this hypothetical sheet and drags a flexible extrusion of it back towards the current position. When the sheet snaps back into place, it takes the ship with it. Technically, you could say that the ship doesn't actually move; it's the universe that shifts around it.'

'Well, whatever they're up to, it obviously involves Indra, and that thing.'

The Doctor suddenly leant in towards the image of the graph. 'How massive is Indra?'

'A little more than Jupiter. Maybe 1/400th of Solar mass.'

'Look at this,' the Doctor suggested quietly, indicating the starting point on the graph. 'This looks about right for

Indra's mass, but the curve increases exponentially.'

'You can't mean that Indra's mass could increase exponentially? It's not possible. Anyway, what would be the point?'

'Well, it could be done if something like a naked singularity were to be introduced to the core. As for the point . . .' He tapped a red mark further along the curve. 'It must have something to do with this stage – everything is directed towards it.' He gazed unblinkingly at the monitor, and his eyes widened slightly as he mulled over the possibilities. 'Nucleosynthesis,' he breathed. 'Of course. A Stormblade was over five miles long, because they needed at least that length to focus the graviton beam precisely enough. Without the conductive sections of terullian built into every Stormblade hull, all that gravitational force will stay exactly where it is, building up continuously. All the Sontarans have to do is get that nacelle within about a thousand miles of Indra's core, and set it running towards overload – the massive artificial gravity field produced will compress Indra enough for nucleosynthesis to start, and the eventual explosion of the nacelle will just give it that extra kick-start to do more damage to the system.'

'Nuclear physics was never my strong point. I land on planets or take off from them. I don't usually need to know how they work.'

'It's a process by which you build up heavy particles from fusing base hydrogen atoms together, and the largest supply of hydrogen in this region of space is Indra itself.'

'I don't see what good altering Indra's mass or makeup would do them.'

The Doctor straightened. 'No, but it's what harm it could do *you* that bothers me. According to this chart, Indra could reach fifty times its present mass in a matter of moments once the reaction is triggered. Fifty times Indra's mass would be about point zero five of Solar mass, which seems like overkill.'

'Overkill? Of us?'

'Basic physics. The lowest mass limit for a true star to ignite is point zero six of Solar mass, if it's going to be a main sequence body, but a lower amount would ignite briefly.' Pausing for breath after the rapid flurry of words, he fixed her with an urgent look as her blood began to chill at the dawning realization of where he was leading. 'If the Sontarans can trigger this reaction, then when it reaches point zero one of Solar mass, nucleosynthesis will begin.' He took a deep breath. 'Indra will explode and, in effect, become a star.'

'You're not serious!'

'Oh, it won't be main sequence' – he put some lightness into his tone, as if he was trying to cheer her up with that restriction – 'and it will only burn for a couple of million years, but the swelling of the outer atmosphere as it becomes a solar corona would be more than enough to engulf Agni and Raghi. And, of course, in the long term it could do some quite terrible things to the orbital stability of everything else in this system.'

'But why? I mean, why create a new star just to blow up a colony?'

'I doubt that your colony is really the ultimate target of all this. It just doesn't have enough relevance to the Sontarans. They wouldn't waste their time here while the Rutan are still in existence.' He stopped. 'Of course. If the Rutan were here . . .'

'What would they want with us?'

'The missing element. That polymerase DNA tag that's been spread by the virus, it was identical to that in the Sontaran cell structure.'

'So?'

'Well, the Sontarans tracked us by a lifeform scanner cued to our cell structures. If a scan was done for Sontaran polymerase – the building blocks of cloned flesh . . .'

'It would pick up everybody who's had the virus. They'd think they had found a Sontaran base?'

The Doctor nodded. 'And send a battle fleet to destroy it, which would then be wiped out in Indra's explosion.'

Nur held up her hands in a 'wait a minute' gesture. 'Wouldn't it have been easier for them to turn Unukalhai nova?'

'Possibly, but it's almost a light-hour away, so the Rutan would have time to jump back into hyperspace.'

'An accurate assessment, Doctor,' a new voice added from behind them. A sharp rattle of gunfire flashed across the room, and the remaining Kshatriyas spun to the ground, as several Sontaran troopers fanned out through the control centre, shooting anything that moved.

'Loxx,' Sharma growled.

'Sontarans do not surrender. I merely awaited the answer to my signal.' He pointedly reset the button on his communications box. 'Major Loxx here. The control centre is secured.'

'What happened?' another voice asked over the air-waves.

'Captain Sharma and the two intruders have returned with troops to evacuate the station crew. One of the intruders is the Doctor.'

'Excellent. Bring the Doctor and the other intruder to our ship.'

'And the captain and the others?'

'Seal him in a room with a view of Indra. He should enjoy the spectacle if he went to such trouble to get a closer view. Ignore the others; they are harmless and will be destroyed when nucleosynthesis begins.'

211

Sixteen

Turlough looked at his watch. The last prisoners had been brought in nearly half an hour ago, but there had been no sign of the Doctor or the others returning. They could hardly have returned to Raghi via the osmic projector, since Nur was needed to fly the ship.

Then again, perhaps she'd run out on them. It wouldn't be the first time a human had betrayed his or her comrades. He was half-tempted to try taking the ship out himself, as it was much more primitive than any Trion ship. Unfortunately, the hostile vessels out there were a constant reminder of how bad an idea that would be.

He could hardly sit around here and wait to be captured, though. He wasn't in the heroic mould – too intelligent for that, he told himself – but going out to see what had gone wrong was beginning to feel like an increasingly attractive option. At least that way, if the ship and prisoners were captured, he could always try to make for the osmic projector.

That was his reason and he would stick to it, he reassured himself. But if central control was near the way, he might as well check up on it. He turned to the Kshatriya sergeant who had brought in the last group of prisoners. 'Can you find your way back to central control?'

'Of course. Do you want me to go and check for the others?'

Respectful obedience, Turlough noted. It had been a while since he'd experienced that. It was quite flattering, he supposed, for what it was worth in the current situation. 'No, I want you to lead me there.' He couldn't believe he was saying that. Maybe when brave actions were described as rash, it was meant literally, and infectiously. 'Bring a couple of your men, just in case. Armed.' That was more sensible, he thought.

'What about the ship?'

'I'm not a pilot anyway, so I don't think our absence matters.'

The sergeant shrugged and beckoned to the nearest two soldiers. They left quickly.

Jahangir could feel the power that hummed through the fabric of the ship, and already envisioned it tearing through the Sontarans' hull. The destroyer had now docked directly with the emergency airlock at the station's medical lab, and Jahangir hadn't dared to fire even though the weapons were now on-line.

He was puzzled as to why they had returned to the station, but reasoned that something unforeseen had cropped up. That most likely meant an attempt by his own people to retake the station.

He couldn't jeopardize that, but the Sontaran ship couldn't stay there for ever. And as soon as it moved, he would teach them a thing or two about death. It was Shiva's will, he realized now. That meant nothing could save the Sontarans. Nothing at all.

Turlough and the Kshatriyas had neither seen nor heard any sign of the Sontarans, and had found central control empty, apart from the dead of both species. His heart had sunk at that, but became marginally more buoyant when he saw that none of them were people he recognized. The same was obviously not true of the sergeant, who leant against the door-jamb to steady himself.

There was, however, some sort of internal monitor system on one of the broader consoles. 'Maybe we can find them on this.' The monitor screens flashed from image to image of empty rooms and passages. Suddenly a living face appeared, in a small room packed with shelves. It was Sharma. The sergeant looked at the camera number listed on-screen, and sent one of the Kshatriyas off to find it and release Sharma.

Another few minutes brought up an image of the Doctor and Nur being escorted through a ruined laboratory. A wide airlock was set into one wall, with a dark and metallic corridor on the far side that was quite different in design style to that of the station. Turlough and the sergeant immediately rushed back out of central control, almost bumping into Sharma and the other soldier.

'They took the Doctor to the medical lab,' Sharma told them. 'Their ship's docked on to the emergency airlock in that section.'

'We saw.' Turlough wasn't in the mood for conversation; the Doctor was just about the only person he'd consider a friend, as well as being the only person who could allow him to travel freely. Being trapped in the colony didn't sound too attractive at the best of times, no matter how much it was like a pleasant day on Trion. 'We have to rescue him before they leave.'

'Just the five of us?'

Turlough grimaced; that should have been *his* line. 'Would you rather leave your bride to them? I'll go alone if necessary, but I'm not letting them go without a fight.'

The interior of the Sontaran ship was dim and dank, with solid metal grilles all over the cylindrical corridor. Nur didn't think much of it at all; it had no style whatsoever.

The Doctor seemed admirably calm as he strolled beside her at gunpoint, and she wished she could get some of whatever he must be taking. 'It's quite an antique you've got over there,' he was saying. 'I thought the Veltrochni had reduced every piece of every Tzun ship to molten slag.'

Loxx's strained wheezing had ceased when they entered the ship, and his voice had grown stronger now

214

that he was breathing his native air. 'We found a derelict Stormblade in a trans-solar orbit in the Reticuli system. All of the more . . . interesting, shall we say, systems had been melted into slag, but the engines were operable, and we knew we would find a use for the graviton drive.'

'What happened to the rest of the ship?'

'There was no further information to be gleaned from it, but it made a very impressive impact when we crashed it into the Rutan dry-dock on the moon of Betelgeuse V.'

'Betelgeuse V doesn't have a moon,' Nur said.

'It doesn't . . . now,' Loxx admitted, licking his lips at the thought.

'Enough old reminiscences, Loxx,' a new voice interrupted. Another Sontaran, with greenish-brown skin and some sort of rank shoulderboards, was standing by a junction ahead. 'We are, after all, working to a schedule, and don't want to bore our captives to death with tales of glory.'

'Really?' the Doctor said lightly. 'Your concern for our welfare is touching.'

'Such courage in the face of death. You can only be the Doctor.'

'You have the advantage of me, I think, Major?'

'Major Karne, of the Seventh Army. You have caused us a great deal of trouble.'

The Doctor looked back into Karne's reddish eyes levelly. 'It's a habit, I'm afraid. A bad one, I'm sure, but I don't seem able to break it.'

'In the interests of fostering comradeship between species, I'm certain I can help you in that regard.' Perhaps thinking that that was his cue, Loxx raised a transparent rod, and activated a control that set it flashing with a steady lulling rhythm. Karne waved him back. 'Nothing so mundane for the Doctor.' He gave the Doctor a calculating look, and the Doctor folded his arms with exaggeratedly bored movements. 'The ocular conditioning process will not work on a Time Lord brain.'

'Nothing ventured, nothing gained.'

'Not for you, Doctor, no. But it would hardly do for you to have faked being conditioned and then sabotaged our plans from within.'

The Doctor threw him a mock-reproachful look. 'Would I do that to you?'

'If your file is accurate, you'd do that to your own president.'

'Not necessarily, he's a terribly endearing chap. Perhaps your file is a little outdated?'

'That is not our department. I am a soldier, not a clerk.' He gestured towards a heavy door with the familiar diamond pattern. 'Show the Doctor to his, ah, quarters, then report the drive nacelle.'

Loxx saluted. 'And the female?'

'Comes with me.' Karne shoved her forward as Loxx opened the door for the Doctor. Nur tried to hold back, but Karne was surprisingly strong, and the chokingly thick air wasn't doing her any favours. She caught the Doctor's eye, and he nodded slightly, then stepped through his door.

Unsure how best to proceed, Nur decided to bide her time, and walked ahead of Karne. He shoved her through another door, into a small gunnery booth, and followed her in. She wondered what he wanted, and hoped it wasn't what a human captor might want. Surely this Karne was too alien for that. He glared at her for a long time before speaking. 'Our apologies, but we had to be sure you too were not a Time Lord.'

Nur was confused, to say the least. Obviously this was some sort of act to get her to confess. 'I don't know what you're talking about.' What was a Time Lord? She backed away, and her hands brushed against something metal. Some sort of locking bar by the feel of it. She didn't dare turn round to look, and hoped her expression wouldn't give away what she was thinking.

'Of course. Loxx is irritatingly precise at times, so certain plans have had to be changed. Fortunately for us, the human – Jahangir – was able to identify your form as

216

Raghir from the security monitors. The Tzun nacelle –'

'We know what it's for.' She wrapped her fingers around the metal bar, ensuring that it was loose and could be lifted. She recalled the Doctor's actions with the cricket ball, and hoped she had as good an eye – if Karne would just turn away.

'Excellent. Loxx was always there while we examined it. If you were to escape –'

'We'd love to.' She looked back at the door, eyes widening. Karne turned as instinctively as she'd hoped, and she immediately swung the bar round with all her strength. It slammed into the rim of the socket at the back of Karne's collar with such force that she thought she'd dislocated her shoulder. Karne toppled over like a falling tree.

Not waiting around to see who else would turn up, Nur leapt over him and rushed out the door. The passageway to the Doctor's cell was blocked, however, and she couldn't find the control that opened the bulkhead. Muttering a curse, she scampered deeper into the ship.

Once Nur had slipped out of the room, Karne sprang to his feet, fully alert. An escaped prisoner might do a lot of damage, he knew, especially if she was who he thought she was; namely the same intruder who had been here earlier.

First things first, however. The Doctor would have to be interrogated. He opened the bulkhead and slipped through, entering the impromptu cell which the Doctor had been put in. The Time Lord was now strapped on to a board in the destroyer's sick bay. Since Sontarans rarely accepted treatment, the instruments were surprisingly crude for a spacefaring technological power.

'Short back and sides, please,' the Doctor suggested.

Major Karne strutted in front of the supine Doctor. He had never seen a Time Lord interrogated before, and was curious to see how this one would bear up under the pressure. 'I'm sure you understand our problem, Doctor.

We must know what you have discovered and what you have done with that information, but we cannot delay to find out. We are, as you see, working to a schedule which will not wait.'

'So it's talk or die time, I presume. That is standard Sontaran procedure, isn't it?'

'Of course not. That is propaganda perpetrated by our enemies, Doctor. No one dies until after they have talked. However, as a Time Lord, and one who knows Sontaran ways, I can hardly expect you to respond to such threats, as you are intelligent enough to realize that talking won't save you.'

'Then why all the theatricals?'

'Time is passing us by, so the quicker you realize your situation, the better for all of us.' He tugged the communications box from his belt. 'Route fire control's monitors to the screen here.'

A screen brightened into life, showing the front of the habitat block. It was a huge artificial cliff overhanging the station's wide hangar deck. A targeting grid was superimposed over the image, with vulnerable points already encircled by firing reticules. 'Interested now, Doctor? This colony is about to be destroyed; nothing can stop that now. The transport you have in the hangar deck is quite another matter. The people on board can be saved by making a jump to hyperspace, or I can collapse the station on top of them. Which it is, is up to you.'

Loxx settled into the tiny makeshift cabin atop the Tzun graviton drive nacelle, and plotted a course to descend into the swirling clouds of Indra.

The nacelle would easily withstand the pressures inside, but this made little difference to Loxx. All that mattered was that he survived long enough to press the button that would start the huge gravity field generator that filled the nacelle on its buildup to overload.

He wondered if they would name a new ship class after him, as so many other war heroes had been honoured. He hoped so. Then his honour would be confirmed for all to see, and the other clones from his hatchery would be proud to be of the same genetic lineage.

'Sir! Parvi called out from the *Nandi*'s tactical console. 'That other ship is moving.'

'The Sontarans?'

'No, the new one.' Jahangir was in two minds. Obviously the new arrival had something to do with the Sontarans' plans, but he didn't know what. More importantly, Karne and his cronies were still aboard their own cruiser.

'Leave it. It's the other one we want.'

The Tzun nacelle drifted outward, its shields sparkling as it passed deeper into Indra's dense radiation belts.

Turlough and the others paused momentarily in the main corridor between the habitat block and the control centre, as the nacelle shrank into the distance. 'I hope you're all insured,' he muttered.

'Not against this.' Sharma's energy drained from him, and he slumped visibly, as if deciding that it was already too late. 'If we had another ship . . .'

'That's it!' Turlough could have kicked himself for not realizing it sooner. 'The Sontarans are leaving. That means your ship might be free.'

Sharma had activated his communicator before Turlough had even finished speaking. 'Come in *Nandi*, this is Sharma. Can anyone hear me?'

'We hear you, Captain,' a familiar voice answered. Turlough and Sharma exchanged glances. How had Jahangir got aboard the *Nandi*?

'What's your status, Jahangir?'

'Everyone is free of conditioning. I've got a weapons lock on the Sontaran ship, but —'

'Ignore it.'

'But, sir —'

219

'Ignore it. Do you read the other ship out there?'

'Yes . . .'

'It's been set to turn Indra nova. You have to stop it at all costs, or Raghi is doomed. Do you hear me?'

There was a muffled chatter from the communicator. 'I hear you. We're taking up pursuit. Jahangir out.'

Sharma put the communicator away. 'What gets destroyed is all in Shiva's hands now.' The *Nandi* tilted slightly to starboard, the wide exhausts from her ion drive flaring up, and climbed away from the infernal surface of Agni. Turlough and Sharma paused by the transparent alloy wall to watch as it hurtled away from the hangar level, its gleaming skin losing the reddish tints of fiery reflection with every passing moment as it receded further.

Sharma looked away with a haunted expression and hurried on towards the door to the central hub. Turlough watched for another couple of seconds, until the *Nandi* had shrunk away entirely, before joining him. Sharma's reaction was something of a puzzle to him. 'Aren't you pleased that something's being done to deal with the threat to the system?'

'The *Nandi* doesn't have functional torpedo launchers – Nur saw to that – and I don't see the lasers getting through such thick armour. The only chance they've got to stop the nacelle is to try ramming it. Would you be pleased?'

'Probably not,' Turlough admitted, 'but it does mean we shouldn't let it be in vain. We still have to deal with Sontarans here, or they could just find another way – and that means rescuing the Doctor.' He didn't think it worth mentioning that, without the Doctor, he'd never get off the colony. If he said that, he felt, Sharma might take it the wrong way.

Sharma nodded decisively, and checked that the magazine for his gun was fully loaded. 'All right, let's get to the medical lab. We all go together, or not at all.'

Seventeen

Jahangir wept. He was cheated again, and torn between preserving and destroying. He hoped there were some Sontarans aboard the other ship. 'Parvi, lock main batteries on that vessel.'

'All maser batteries locked on target.'

Technically, there was supposed to be a warning before opening fire. Jahangir was in no mood for such trivialities. Destruction and preservation: those were all that mattered. 'Fire.'

Lances of tight-beam microwave radiation stabbed out at the slab-like nacelle, striking sparks from the shields. The nacelle didn't falter in its course, however, and the *Nandi* swept after it, striking at it repeatedly.

Parvi looked up from her station and shook her head sadly. 'All direct hits, no effect. We just don't have enough fire power to crack their shields. We'd really need the torpedoes to collapse them.' Jahangir glared out at the nacelle. He just knew there were Sontarans on board; they must be doing this deliberately to irritate him.

Through the all-encompassing viewport, he saw the nacelle begin to fade into the clouds. Well, he wasn't going to stand for their baiting any longer. 'Nirad, rig the helm controls for voice control. Parvi, give the order to abandon ship.'

She stared at him dumbly. He smiled weakly. It was personal now, between him and the Sontarans, and he wasn't going to be responsible for anyone else's death.

'Do it. I'll follow them into the atmosphere, and ram them. Without torpedoes, nothing else will work.'

She hesitated, then nodded. Nirad scratched his moustache, and set to work on the helm controls.

Indra's horizon was flat as the *Nandi* swooped towards the cloud-tops. Aurorae glistened across her forward shields as she began to descend towards atmosphere, and smaller pinpoints of light shot away from the rear of the ship as the escape pods and remaining shuttles hurled themselves into the void.

After only a few moments, the first wisps of cloud wreathed themselves around the hull, drawing it softly downward.

The air was cold empty now that no one manned the ship's stations. The only sounds were harsh and mechanical as the ship's systems hummed to themselves, and there was no spark of life anywhere in the cabins or companionways.

Jahangir settled into the *Nandi*'s helm seat, momentarily perplexed by the colour-coded jumble. He was, after all, a healer, and not a pilot. All members of the service had undergone some basic training in such matters, however, and it was only a few seconds before the first faint twinges of familiarity drew Jahangir to the link to the flight computer.

'Scan for metallic mass.'

'Target bearing zero-four-zero mark three-three-two. Distance seven thousand miles,' the computer's inflectionless voice answered.

Jahangir hastily entered the figures into the helm. He couldn't see anything other than smoky clouds out of the viewports, but he didn't need to see. He started increasing engine power, wondering how far he could push it before the heat shields started to show the strain.

He had no idea how long it would be until the Sontarans tried for detonation, but had to assume that it was as soon as possible. That way, his personal hell would be over as soon as possible, too.

The Doctor looked back at Karne. 'All right. I know you've tagged the human population with your own cloning signature in the hope of luring the Rutan into a trap. Why should the Rutan even visit this sector; it can't have any strategic significance?'

Karne tutted softly. 'To a true conqueror, there is no such thing as the insignificant.' He stabbed at a control in front of the screen. A glittering array of stars spread out through the image, a considerable number of them tinted red, with little glyphs beside them. 'As you see, this sector is rich in the mineral terullian; it has many properties which would be of value to us.'

'Yes, of course. It's a very good energy resonator, and can be programmed as software definable. The entire Tzun Confederacy was built on the stuff, figuratively and literally.'

'Precisely; this whole sector was home to the Confederacy, and now is but a wasteland. Ten thousand worlds or more scattered with terullian all there for the taking, both in unused deposits and salvage from ruined Tzun ships and colonies. It would be of inestimable value to the war effort. We, and our enemies, have been seeking a bridgehead in the sector for millennia –'

'But the Tzun threw you out?'

Karne glared at him through slitted eyes. 'We . . . reprioritized. Now, with the Tzun Confederacy gone, the Rutan have set up a headquarters in Antares, and launched thousands of remote probes into the sector.'

'To scan for terullian deposits.'

'Naturally. But they are also searching for Sontarans. They are concerned that a Sontaran force might –'

'Jump their claim?' The Doctor gave him a disbelieving look. 'Is that what all this is about: who gets to some mineral deposits first?' His tone bordered on the incredulous.

Karne didn't care for that attitude at all. 'The addition of the terullian to our technology will give us a vital lead in the arms race that will determine the outcome of the war.'

'Arms race? Really, I thought it was supposed to be Sontaran courage and skill that would do the job. Or perhaps you're not up to that?'

'That's rhetoric, Doctor, the last line of defence for the defeated. I would have thought you were above that. Look at this.' Karne altered the settings on the screen.

An image of Indra and its attendant moons filled the screen, with a small time display at the bottom. The planets were so perfect that looking at them was like stepping outside of reality for a moment and watching from some heavenly otherworld. Myriad tiny ovals representing Rutan ships flashed into place in a complex sequence a short distance from Raghi. As soon as they appeared, a cone-shaped pattern of ripples descended towards a red rectangle at the heart of Indra. As soon as the sensor ripples touched the rectangle, it began to glow, brightening to a blaze in an instant. The tiny pinpoints of the Rutan cruisers wheeled in unison, sweeping past Agni en route for Raghi. Indra was already brightening as well, the cloud-tops swelling outward.

The Rutan cruisers' course faltered as streams of light reached out from the rapidly swelling Indra. Finger-like prominences stabbed between the Rutan ships, which milled around as their computers tried to calculate new hyperspace jump coordinates. Agni had already become a solid mass of glowing red as the searing cloud-tops reached it, and the atmosphere was thinning from around Raghi as the seas boiled and the very atoms of the air molecules were stripped apart.

The first Rutan ships started to vanish into the encroaching corona as Agni finally sprayed apart in a cloud of magma. Raghi itself was engulfed in the spreading light along with the rest of the Rutan ships, the superheated explosion of its disintegrating substance overwhelmed by

224

the brightness of the growing infant star that had been Indra. 'I think you'll agree it will be an impressive spectacle,' Karne suggested blandly. He gave an ironic grunt. 'A lasting testament to Sontaran might.'

The Doctor glared back at him, paling as if the mere simulation was a heinous insult. 'It'll be an obscene spectacle! You'd wipe out the whole population just for a diversion? That's monstrous beyond even Sontaran standards.'

'There are only a hundred million inhabitants.' What was so terrible about that? Karne wondered. Such numbers could be replenished in a day. Then again, for all he knew perhaps humans bred more slowly than true lifeforms. 'And it's not just a diversion, of course. Terullian is formed by the action of solar prominences on certain types of geological structure, so the fires that bathe these moons when Indra explodes should also help create further new deposits right here, where we already have a foothold.'

'And the people on this station?'

'You should be more concerned about your own fate. The humans here will all be destroyed when Indra undergoes nucleosynthesis. You, however, will be taken first to our flagship, and then back home. You, Doctor, will give us mastery over time. Perhaps we shall start with preventing the enemy from evolving, or perhaps we should conquer Gallifrey to begin with.'

'You've tried before.'

'We have?' He frowned, then snorted derisively. 'A mere exploratory expedition.' He waved the thought away dismissively. 'With Gallifrey's own technology at our disposal, there will be no defence. You seem well enough acquainted with diversions yourself, Doctor. I still want to know what you have learnt.'

A loudspeaker chimed, and Karne pressed the intercom switch. 'Yes?'

'The generator nacelle has entered our atmosphere. The colony's ship is in pursuit, but its weapons are having no effect on the shields, and its hull won't withstand the pressure for long. We should leave now if we're not to be detected.'

Karne looked thoughtfully at the Doctor. 'All right, I'm coming up.' He turned to the door, then looked back. 'Rehearse your final speech, Doctor. I won't be long.'

Nur had always prided herself on her sense of direction, so although she couldn't get directly back to the Doctor's cell, she was confident of finding her way back to the airlock by a different route – so long as she wasn't found.

With any luck, she could then find her way to the cell by the original route. Satisfied with this plan, she turned the corner, and almost walked straight into a pair of Sontarans. Heart racing, she turned and took a few running steps, then halted. There was no sound of pursuit.

Cautiously, she crept back to the narrow passageway. Two Sontarans stood there like suits of armour in little niches, their eyes closed. There seemed to be some sort of hose or cable attached to the backs of their necks. So that was what those little sockets were for, she thought. These two must be . . . recharging, or something.

Treading very carefully, she slipped past them and found herself in a corridor she recognized from earlier. If her memory wasn't playing her false, the airlock was to the right, and the cell to the left. She hoped they were still docked at the station; she hadn't felt any sense of movement, but perhaps if their technology was sufficiently advanced, a take-off might be smooth enough that she'd miss it.

Footsteps echoed down the corridor to her right, and she stepped back into the little recharging annexe, hoping it was a long process. The footsteps grew nearer, but she couldn't resist peeking out. Fortunately, it was Turlough and Sharma, with two armed Kshatriyas. She stepped out into the corridor, putting a finger to her lips as they looked as if they were about to make exclamations of surprise. 'There are two Sontarans just back there. I think they're recharging, or sleeping. How did you get in here?'

'Through the airlock from the medical lab. Their sense of security seems a little lacking; even an Earthman knows to close his front door. What about the Doctor?' Turlough asked urgently. 'Isn't he with you?'

'Along this way.' She led them to the door that Loxx had opened. A small keypad was beside it. 'He's in there, or was the last time I saw him.'

'There's bound to be a code for opening the door,' Turlough muttered. 'In for a penny . . .'

Sharma looked around, then glanced sideways at Nur. 'See, I can rescue people without hitting them afterwards.'

Nur smirked slightly. 'You know, for a minute there you seemed even more appealing. Right up until you opened your mouth.'

'Sauce for the goose.'

'So long as it's not cooked.' She let the smirk soften. 'Thanks anyway.'

A small lamp flashed on Major Karne's console. Checking that no one else was watching, he switched on the tiny monitor it was linked to. He watched the monitor screen in surprise, as the Doctor's companion experimented with the keypad to the holding cell. He hadn't expected a mere humanoid to display such courage or loyalty. After all, such facets weren't properly bred into them. On the neighbouring screen, the Doctor was calling instructions out through the door. The humanoid youth was still having no success, however.

Karne began to wonder if perhaps this was exactly the solution to his problem. They were merely a Time Lord and a few humanoids, not Rutan agents, but the potential for trouble was there all the same. Killing them would be contrary to Stentor's orders, and that would be sure to be punished, so perhaps it would be better for him if he found a compromise solution.

'Start the engines, prepare for take-off.' He reassured himself that his officers were busy following the order, and allowed one hand to creep across the console before him.

Turlough thumped the keypad with a groan of frustration at its solid resistance to everything he'd tried. The decking under his feet was already starting to buzz with vibrations from the engines, and he suspected that there wasn't going to be much more of a chance to get away. Nobody could say he hadn't tried his best, he reminded himself. But as someone once said, a good man knows his limitations.

'Come on,' he said stiffly. 'Unless you want a one-way ride to Sontar.'

'The Doctor,' Sharma protested icily.

'It won't work!' Why couldn't humans realize when they were beaten? Turlough wondered. He thumped the keypad again to demonstrate. The door promptly slid open. Turlough blinked in surprise, and dashed in.

The Doctor was strapped to a wide table of some kind, and Turlough immediately started on the straps that held him. 'We must stop meeting like this.'

'Very amusing,' the Doctor replied with an irritated look. Sharma made quicker work of them with his issue knife.

'You're forgetting your manners.' Turlough remembered their predicament. 'Thank me later,' he suggested, and turned to leave.

The Doctor peered at the keypad through his half-moon spectacles. 'Hmm. Well it looks like I ought to thank somebody . . .' He straightened. 'Well? What are you all standing around here for? Come on.' Tucking the spectacles away, he hurried off down the corridor.

'Is he always like this?' Sharma asked, a little flustered.

'Except when he isn't,' Turlough informed him slyly. They followed the Doctor along the corridor to the vestibule area just inside the airlock. Turlough had almost left the ship when he realized that the Doctor was no longer with them. He looked back to see the Doctor, having ignored the airlock, stepping into another corridor opposite the one from which they had emerged. 'Sharma, look.'

'What is he doing?'

'Going the wrong way, obviously.' There was a sudden grinding from under the floor, and the airlock doors started to close. Nur immediately leapt out through the opening. Exchanging a single glance, Turlough and Sharma bolted across the corridor, and grabbed the Doctor by the arms. 'This way!'

'No –' The Doctor's protestation was cut off by the distinctive screech of a Sontaran rheon carbine, and a shower of sparks exploded from the wall. Sharma pushed the time travellers aside and returned fire at the trooper at the far end of the corridor. His shots had no effect, and the trooper lumbered towards them.

The Doctor darted up, slapping a wide green button on the wall with his palm. A thick pressure door immediately slammed across the opening to the corridor. A few muffled bangs indicated that the trooper was still not going to be put off by this barrier. A volley of shots opened up behind them, and Turlough saw that another couple of troopers had finally followed them from the cell bay. The Kshatriya sergeant and soldier who had accompanied Turlough in search of the others took cover in the airlock, returning fire at the Sontarans.

This was going to be fun, he thought sarcastically. Running through a crossfire was just how he liked to spend his days, now, wasn't it? Sharma unhooked an acid grenade from his belt, and tossed it along the corridor. The resulting explosion produced a cloud of vapour in the corridor, which thankfully – as far as Turlough was concerned – hid whatever was causing the troopers to squeal like that.

With the firing stopped, the three of them scuttled past

the corridor opening and out through the airlock. Sharma waved Nur back into the more sheltered cleanroom, and led Turlough out. Ensuring that the two Kshatriyas got clear, the Doctor squeezed through the almost-closed gap between the outer doors, and through the medical lab's airlock. Emerging into the lab, he hit the control to close the lab's airlock, and ran for the cleanroom.

A cloud of frosted air gathered outside the lab's airlock as the Sontaran destroyer disengaged from it, then dissipated as air rushed through the lab with a howl. The screaming wind faded as the lab's airlock door thundered shut. Its twin engines blazed white, and Karne's ship shot away from the station, banking upward until the fiery reflection of the lava pools had faded and only the engines' burning plasma marked out its location among the stars.

Turlough picked himself up, relieved to see that the Doctor was not only all right, but already standing and . . . angry? Turlough couldn't understand the Doctor's furious expression. After the risk he had taken to perform this rescue, he'd have thought a little gratitude was in order.

'Oh, Turlough, what have you done?'

'Rescued you.' Turlough nodded out at the stars.

'Why didn't you just leave me well enough alone?'

Turlough frowned; surely he couldn't have been wrong about this? 'I may be misjudging your taste in resorts, but I assumed you didn't want to spend the rest of your life on Sontar.'

'No, but we might now have to spend it here; and it very likely won't be very long. If you had given me the chance, I would have made my own way out in the TARDIS.'

Turlough's pride and relief drained away with an awful sinking feeling. 'It was on board?'

'Well, of course! If you'd been after one for years, would you leave your prize behind on a planet about to be destroyed?'

* * *

The Valt-class destroyer which Karne commanded swept away from Agni in a long curve, until Agni had been swallowed up by the ruddy reflections from Indra, which itself fell away at a steady pace.

'We are now outwith Indra's warp limit,' a trooper reported.

Karne didn't dare let himself relax, even though they were now far enough out to make the jump into hyperspace without Indra's gravity being strong enough to distort the spatial warp required by the jump. 'Lock jump coordinates into the navigational system.'

'Locked in.'

Karne turned to reassure himself that the TARDIS was still solidly beside him. The Doctor remained on Agni, but that might just be a good thing. At least they had the TARDIS, and Loxx would no longer be around to get in the way if he had to alter his plans in a hurry after this code-breaking development. A more or less good day, in all. 'Make the jump.'

The destroyer's sublight engines flared. It suddenly flickered and vanished, like a flea hopping away from a dog.

Eighteen

The Doctor, Turlough, Nur, Sharma and the two Kshatriyas pelted breathlessly through the corridors of the Agni station. Despite the strict training of the Kshatriyas, it was Nur who pounded into the assault carrier first, though the others were close behind.

Her chest had never felt so sore as it did now, but she was scrabbling at the controls even as she literally bit at the air to try to get her breath back. The toothed cargo doors were slamming together even as the Doctor leapt through them, having made sure that Turlough and Sharma got in.

'Hold tight,' Nur called out. She'd imagined that everybody would have the sense to do so anyway, but you never could tell. The habitat block dropped away as the engines screeched loudly, pushed to their limits.

The force of take-off squashed Nur back into her seat, and purple spots flashed before her eyes. She roared with effort just to reach out for the throttle. She wasn't going to let mere acceleration distract her, though, and kept a tight grip on the controls as the transport hurtled outward.

The *Nandi* rocked violently as it passed through the edge of the storm, slipping to port as the rushing clouds dragged the trailing engines around, while the ship's curved nose remained calm in the eye of the storm.

'Outer hull stress levels at 110 per cent of design limits,' the computer announced blandly. A squealing of tortured metal echoed up from below decks, and several engineering monitors exploded into static.

Jahangir ignored them; he didn't need any machine to tell him he was dead. The Tzun graviton drive nacelle now filled almost all of his forward view, sinking with precisely planned laxity towards the auburn field of Indra's stratopause. Risking movement despite the buffeting, he unclenched his hands from the arms of Sharma's seat, and lunged for the flight engineering console.

The vibrations of the ship's structure sent him tumbling to the floor almost as soon as he parted company with the seat, and his forehead cracked against the engineer's chair. Purple spots flashed before him, but he dug his nails into his palms, sure that the pain would focus his mind. Death didn't matter, but he was not going to die without at least partially repaying the debt he owed for being weak enough to allow the Sontarans to dominate his mind.

Sitting in the tightly cramped cabin with the manual overrides for the graviton nacelle, Loxx had to admire the humans for once. True, they were ineffectual weaklings whose attack now was really little more than a death throe, but at least they had finally mustered some warrior's spirit.

It was difficult to equate their current hopeless but brave effort with their earlier willingness to accept whatever fate Karne decided for them.

The shooting had stopped, and the wide curve of the humans' ship was spreading across Loxx's monitor screen. It coalesced darkly; like a patch of smoke amidst the gauzy clouds that parted around them, like clotting blood.

Loxx checked the strength of his shields, just to be on the safe side. There was nothing to worry about there. He relaxed slightly; the humans could do no better than share his fate.

Agni fell away, shrinking into a more familiarly sized globe that was dark against the face of Indra.

Nur relaxed slightly, though the transport's lack of

manoeuvrability troubled her. At least this should satisfy her father with regard to her attitude to others. What was a civil service visit compared to this? She allowed herself a small smile.

'Hull stress levels 115 per cent of design limits. Structural integrity failure in seventeen seconds.'

Jahangir spat out a gobbet of clotting blood. 'Range to target?'

'Seven miles. Time to impact twenty-nine seconds. Structural integrity failure in thirteen seconds.'

Jahangir tried to sigh, but succeeded only in sparking a lance of pain through his chest. He wasn't sure that they were close enough, but there was no more time to spare before the ship was obliterated more cleanly than he would like. 'Computer, disengage power to the magnetic antimatter storage bottle.' He turned to look at the sparkling nacelle in the forward view. Whatever happened now was very much his responsibility or, he feared, his fault.

Loxx could feel the steel sinews of the graviton nacelle flex around him as the liquefying elements of the atmosphere pressed in upon it.

It didn't bother him in the slightest, since he was confident that Intelligence's report on the remarkable strength of Tzun construction was accurate. He was surprised, however, the humans' ship had survived so long under the phenomenal pressures.

The human ship was no more than a shadowy blur, like an unsettling dark cloud on an X-ray. Loxx began to wonder if it had been a mistake to leave the nacelle unarmed. If the humans had some previously unknown or concealed technology – or perhaps assistance from the Doctor – then maybe they could reach him.

He snarled in frustration, willing the humans' ship to be crushed by the pressure. He refused to allow for the possibility that he might fail Karne. Karne had taken such care with this mission that failure would be an insult such a great Sontaran didn't deserve. A seat on the Grand Strategic Council was more what Karne should have had.

If only the humans would be destroyed . . .

Now that the constantly changing magnetic field that simulated a neutral envelope for the antimatter was gone, the antimatter in the ship's reactor was free to consume itself along with the normal matter around it. The *Nandi* flashed into oblivion some six miles from the mile-long gravity engine.

The clouds lit up, flashing through the whole spectrum in a wink of an eye. Loxx was momentarily reminded of the only other blast of such magnitude he'd seen; a battered and beaten cruiser exploding when rammed by a Rutan corvette.

He'd found Karne in an escape pod all those years ago, and gained a promotion for it. Now he'd gained another promotion, and hoped he'd earn it by saving Karne's mission and honour.

Then the moment ended. And with it, the reminiscence.

Loxx ended.

A shock wave of vaporizing atmospheric particles battered the Tzun nacelle, crumpling and burning through its side. The glowing power flow that had remained so steady beforehand raced across the surface of the collapsing nacelle, and flared into an inferno that entirely consumed the engine.

It didn't stop there, however, but billowed outward, consuming the dense gases and liquid clouds. Herds of airavata flickered into wisps of nothingness like popped bubbles as the shock wave spread.

Indra shuddered.

* * *

The clouds parted across a huge patch on the northern hemisphere, which flickered with enormous releases of energy. Unimaginably huge bolts of lightning glowed beneath the outermost layers of the turbulent clouds. The patch of light spread out like a damp stain across a cloth, until it covered almost a sixth of the visible face of the planet.

Then it stopped growing.

Nur wanted to be sick. It wasn't that the view had been obscene, but it was so unsettling to be at the heart of an event that had millions of people balanced on a knife-edge between life and death.

Sharma squeezed into the cockpit and put an arm around her as they stared numbly out at the seething giant. 'Jahangir always seemed to take things so personally,' he mused. 'We could have flown her by remote . . . I wonder how long that fire will be visible for.'

'Well, it's not exactly fire,' the Doctor said. 'At least not in the way you mean, but it'll probably be visible there for at least a year or two.'

'At least Raghi is safe now.'

'I shouldn't go jumping to conclusions about that if I were you.' The Doctor looked across at them. 'The question now is what the Rutan will do when they arrive. Will they recognize the con trick the Sontarans have worked, or will they just bombard the planet to be on the safe side?'

Turlough thought that it was definitely time to leave the colony. Even a trip on an ordinary hyperspace lane was preferable to waiting to be bombarded by a Rutan fleet. Unfortunately, the Doctor had decided to see Ambika as soon as they had landed back in Kuru's spaceport.

Turlough hoped he wasn't planning some sort of heroic last stand; not that he had anything against heroic stands, but the 'last' part was distinctly uncomfortable. He thought hard as Ambika paced the courtyard. 'How soon can we expect these Rutan to arrive?' the preceptor asked.

'The Sontarans expected a scout to arrive today or tomorrow,' the Doctor told him. He noticed a platter of celery on the buffet table before him, and selected a fresh stick to attach to his lapel.

'The Alliance ships are still four days away. We don't have the fire power to withstand an attack, or enough ships to evacuate the planet. Is there any way we could . . . persuade them to leave us alone?'

'Why not?' Turlough said. Every race wanted something or other; perhaps if they could offer the Rutan something better . . . 'Maybe we could offer them a deal.'

'A deal?' the Doctor exclaimed. 'This is the Rutan Host we're talking about, not a Sicilian family. They aren't going to go away just because we offer them a percentage of the gross planetary product.'

Turlough hated being treated like an Earth youth that way. His people had been colonizing and trading around the galaxy for several centuries, and he knew that if you could just find what your opposite number wanted the most, you had him. 'They're engaged in a blood feud. If we offer them the chance to ambush a Sontaran fleet –'

'They'd probably be able to destroy both.'

Ambika snapped his fingers, then looked a little guilty at bringing attention upon himself. '*Arthashastra*. That's how we can beat these aliens at their own game. If these Sontarans are our neighbours, and natural enemies, and the Rutan beyond them are their enemies –'

'My enemy's enemy is my friend?' Turlough didn't see any problem with that in the short term. 'It's a tradition at home, too.'

'Exactly. The strictures of *Arthashastra* may be our only chance.'

'Do you mean the planet's or the family's?' Nur asked, giving Ambika a hurt look. Turlough looked to the Doctor for encouragement. 'We can't just sit and wait to be destroyed, surely?'

The Doctor looked sceptical. 'There's a saying on Earth: "When you sup with the devil, use a long spoon." '

'We have a saying, too: "Keep your friends close, and keep your enemies closer." Look, I know it's not much of a chance, but it's all we've got.' If religion hadn't been abolished on Trion for centuries, he would have prayed that the Doctor would listen to him on this.

'We'll need a ship,' the Doctor told Ambika. 'It would be better if we met the Rutan before they detected the cloning signatures, so we'll have to go out to them.'

'How do you know where they'll be?' Turlough wondered as well, but knew that the Doctor would have his methods.

'Ruta Three is an icy planet, so they'll come out of hyperspace in as cold a spot as they can. Where would you go?'

'The shelter of the furthermost planet.'

'It does seem a likely candidate.'

'I'll take you,' Nur offered. 'The techs have been working all day and night to combine the workable segments from the *Garuda* and another old Burro-class ship.'

'This will be very dangerous, you know –'

'I know, but look. I owe the Sontarans a bloody nose. Besides, if these Rutan things aren't willing to listen, you might need a really good pilot in rather a hurry.'

The Doctor looked as if he was about to resist further, but then shrugged. 'You're old enough to make your own decisions, I suppose.'

'So am I,' Sharma said from across the courtyard. Turlough hadn't seen him for a while, as he was seeing to the hospitalization of the prisoners recovered from Agni. He stepped fully out from Arjun's office. Turlough began to wonder how big a ship they were going to need, if everyone and his brother wanted to come along. He grinned at Nur from amidst his immaculately trimmed beard. 'I'm not letting you out of my sight again. You might need someone handy with a gun.'

'There doesn't seem anyone around who fits that description,' Nur said wryly, 'but it's my ship, so I'll choose the passengers and I suppose you're as good a choice as any.'

Turlough felt a little more confident, now that they were showing interest in his plan. Now it was just a matter of what precise deal to offer. 'What are we going to bargain for?'

'Whatever we can get. We'll explain what happened here, and ask them to leave the colony alone. In return, we'll give them the copy of the Sontaran files we recovered from Loxx. There is something else, though. We have to get the TARDIS back. It'll be kept on the Sontaran flagship, but they won't be able to get into it without me. If the ship is destroyed, it might survive and be recovered by the Rutan.'

'Not a pleasant prospect.'

'No. So we persuade them to let us steal it off the flagship first.'

That was pushing it, even for the Doctor, Turlough thought. 'And just how do we do that?'

'I haven't the foggiest idea. We will have to visit the ambush, though. Nur, can you have a hyperdrive fitted to your ship while it's being pieced together?'

'If I could afford it.'

'You can now,' Ambika told her. 'It's probably the last order I'll sign in this job, but if it's to save the colony . . .'

'Right.' The Doctor rubbed his hands together. 'Now we just wait.'

Nineteen

The sixth planet in the Unukalhai system was a frigid globe of liquid gases that Turlough thought looked not unlike a gigantic breath mint of some kind. He didn't like being at a loose end; at least not when there was no opportunity for recreation. There were only so many times he could count the weld-spots on the bulkhead wall.

Sharma had allowed himself to doze off in the best military style, while the Doctor and Nur kept watch on the ship's sensors. All Turlough had to do was get increasingly irritated by Sharma's obscene snores. Sometimes – often – he couldn't tell what the Doctor saw in humans.

There was a sudden commotion from the flight deck up ahead, and Turlough hopped up the steps, hoping that the wait was over. Then again, he reminded himself, his life might very well be over with it. 'Is it them?' he asked. He wasn't going to let his worry show in front of a human.

'Hyperspace egress just off the starboard bow,' the Doctor replied.

A pinpoint of light appeared some way from the curve of the frozen planet, growing larger as it hurtled towards them. It slowed as it approached, and was soon drifting inward with a stately grace that had an air of great mass and power.

Turlough was speechless at the sight of the ship. He had never seen a Rutan vessel before, but going by what he had heard about the species, he had expected some sort of slimy and diseased-looking lump of half-molten metal.

Instead, it was a huge glass nest, with delicately stretching crystal spires webbed together with beautiful loops and flying buttresses of gleaming light. 'It's beautiful.' Beside him, he heard Nur gasp in agreement. Watching the Rutan ship approach was like watching a glittering fairytale castle rise up towards oneself, its delicate translucent spires stretching out as if to embrace the small vimana. The after end of the cruiser seemed to be fitted around a silvery meteoroid of some kind into which the main engines were embedded.

Turlough could just make out the vaguely throbbing shapes that were attached to the interior surfaces of the tinted translucent walls like gelid limpets. Filigreed lines of bluish sparks flickered across the crystalline material, as if there were veins of electricity beneath a diamond skin.

'Open a channel,' the Doctor said quietly.

Nur looked surprised at being addressed while still awe-struck, then touched a few controls. 'You're on air.'

'Chance would be a fine thing.' He cleared his throat. 'Rutan vessel. This is the Lord President of the High Council of Time Lords. I come under a flag of truce, and wish to speak with you.'

'Time Lord,' a burbling voice responded after a few moments. 'We are a Rutan scout. Any attempt to obstruct our mission will result in your destruction.'

'I'm not here to obstruct you. I have information to offer, which you may find useful. I wish to strike a bargain.'

'Maintain your position. We will board your craft, to discuss terms of your surrender.'

'Nice work,' Turlough muttered.

The Time Lord's airlock slid open, and the Rutan entered cautiously. They were unsure whether the Time Lord's words were true, but they were aware that the Sontarans had tried to conquer them before. Perhaps their desire for revenge would see them side with the Rutan.

Time Lord arrogance was legendary, however, and the

241

Rutan had no intention of letting themselves fall victim to some sort of plot by them. The Rutan moved into the main hold, which had some sort of passenger section as an annexe. The monochrome heat traces of four lifeforms – the Time Lord, presumably – were watching them carefully.

It was uncomfortably warm in the ship, but the Rutan ignored it. A little discomfort was worth it, if it would lead to a greater victory. The Rutan drew themselves into a stubby column, bifurcating the lower half with only mild discomfort for ease of crossing the obstructions scattered across the floor. They also tensed, building up charge just in case the Time Lord was hostile.

'We will hear your offer,' they said.

One of the heat traces moved forward slightly. 'We wish to make a bargain. When your probes enter orbit around the fourth planet of this system, they will detect Sontaran lifeforms on the sixth moon.'

'Why should we give anything in return for that information?'

'Because there are no Sontarans there. They have infected the indigenous population with a tag to make believe they are there, intending to lure you into a trap. We have destroyed that trap. If you leave that moon alone, we will give you the location and strategy of the Sontaran fleet. Furthermore, if you can get us safely through the battle to the Sontaran flagship, we will lower its shields for you.'

The Rutan considered this. Why should the Time Lord be so accommodating, and why did they wish to board a Sontaran ship? Some part of the truth was being kept from them. 'Why do you wish to board their ship?'

'They have something that belongs to me, and I want it back.'

The Rutan crackled in surprise, though they doubted that the Time Lord understood the significance of the sound. Could they be referring to a TARDIS? Such a machine would enable the Host to do anything. Perhaps even prevent the Sontaran from ever evolving . . . The Rutan tried to spread these thoughts to all of their mind, but received only silence in return. Obviously the Time Lord's atmosphere didn't contain the conductive elements that allowed freedom of thought on the Rutan ship. 'We will consider this.' The Rutan stepped back on their makeshift legs, keeping a few eyes on the Time Lord.

Nur let out a breath once the pulsing gelatinous alien had left. 'You must have been out at noon too often,' Nur was protesting. 'How am I supposed to sneak on board a battlecruiser in the middle of a battle? Even with an escort to keep the fighters off our backs?'

'With this,' the Doctor told her, holding up a small data crystal. 'A copy of the transponder code from those files.' He frowned. 'Karne was really remarkably careless leaving all this stuff lying around in Agni's database with just Loxx to look after it. And that door as well . . . Sontarans normally martyr themselves to caution, and it doesn't help at all.' He shook his head. 'We'll feed this into your transponder system, and the Sontaran sensors will think the *Garuda* is one of theirs. The Rutan will keep a note of the code, so as not to shoot us down themselves, and all you have to do is avoid stray shots.'

'If they go for the deal,' Turlough said doubtfully. Nur thought his tone was somewhat ironic, since this had been his idea.

The Doctor smiled faintly. 'Oh, I think they will. One hint that my TARDIS was on board and it was as excited as a jackpot winner. They won't be able to resist a chance to get their . . . whatever, on it.'

The main hangar bay of the Linx-class Sontaran flagship wasn't large enough to contain the Valt-class destroyer that had so recently arrived, so it had merely docked directly on to one of the hull's airlocks.

Fleet Marshal Stentor was waiting for Major Karne when he crossed through the transfer tube. 'Permission to come aboard, sir,' Karne said. The formalities of the Sontaran army bored him, and he didn't really see the point of them, but he knew how much senior Sontarans liked to stick to them.

'Granted, Major. You have brought the Time Lord's machine?'

'His TARDIS is on board.'

'Excellent. Have it brought aboard this vessel. I want it kept close.'

'Yes, sir.' Karne had expected that. If only he'd been able to open the thing while it was in his care . . . Still, what was past was past.

'I shall also be transferring you to my staff. You have proven your capabilities, despite a few failures.'

Karne was delighted. 'Thank you, sir.'

'You are surprised I accept you, in spite of your failure to capture the Doctor?'

'Yes.'

Stentor grunted. 'Failure is only failure if you don't learn from it. That is why I give second chances.'

Karne thought about this. Perhaps Stentor was going senile, he decided. All the better for our – my – purposes, he reminded himself.

The Rutan consulted among themselves. The thin atmosphere in which they melded together to exchange thoughts with themselves was cold and unbreathable, but they didn't need to breathe. It was much more comfortable, through, and the primordial compounds that drifted though the chilled gas helped carry the thoughts to dissociated parts of the scout in other regions of the ship.

The description of the trap did sound like a Sontaran tactic, they agreed, though others could have discovered this for themselves. No Time Lord or other humanoid could want to protect Sontaran; even they weren't *that* corrupt. It seemed reasonable to assume, therefore, that there were indeed no Sontaran here.

Part of the Rutan dissociated, and arrowed towards the

sixth moon of the fourth planet. They felt the distant confirmation of Sontaran life-signs, and decided to examine more closely. The moon was infested with the Human, but there were no Sontaran.

A Human was sensed to register as a Sontaran clone, and was taken by the scout. It was examined closely, its organ removed, but carefully put back. It died anyway. It didn't matter to the Rutan; if the Human were so fragile, that was their business. The examination showed that the Human had a hatchery tag, but no Sontaran tissue.

The Rutan recalled their scout, and reformed. The fleet at Antares could be called for, but if this was a trap, then the fleet must be the target. The Time Lord's story was true, it seemed.

The Rutan dissociated. A part of them steeled themselves to return to the Time Lord's vessel. The Time Lord was waiting for them. 'Your story is true. We will agree to your terms, but we will accompany you.'

'I thought you might say that,' the Time Lord agreed. One of the heat forms held up something in its hand. 'The Sontarans intend to draw your fleet away from Antares to be destroyed here. Their fleet will then make an attack on your base in Antares.'

'We will notify our fleet –'

'Might I make an alternative suggestion? If your fleet doesn't leave, the Sontarans won't attack. I imagine they have probes watching for its departure. I'd suggest that you have your fleet jump a short distance, just so that the Sontarans see them go. Then, when the Sontarans drop into Antares, you hop back.'

The strategy was obvious, but the Rutan weren't interested in pointing that out. All they were interested in was making it work. 'We agree, but we will travel in this vessel with you. We are in contact with the fleet, and will schedule departure.'

'You're staying with us?'

'Other races are not trustworthy. We will watch for any sign of betrayal.'

'Then what do we call you?' another of the heat forms asked.

'We are Rutan.'

'Our species need something a little more particular,' the first heat form of the Time Lord said. 'I think we'll call you Fred, for ease of reference.'

Twenty

General Skelp was almost ready to plug in for a burn when the probe telemetry from the Antares system suddenly peaked. 'Fleet Marshal, the Rutan sector fleet is moving. Our translations of their communications are reading orders to mobilize for Unukalhai. Our probes are reading energy buildups in their hyperdrives. They're falling for the bait!'

'Switch probe frequencies to scan for gravitational lensing; I don't want to get there just to find that they've only gone into Clear.'

'Switching. Nothing so far.'

Fleet Marshal Stentor leant on the truncated battle standard he carried as a cane, and watched the holotank with a critical eye as his own fleet formed up in a trailing cone abaft of the flagship. He saw that he wouldn't have to issue any reprimands today, as the fleet was forming up with clinical neatness. He took that as a tribute to his imposition of discipline on the individual commanders.

With such unity of purpose, how could they possibly lose? Despite himself, he couldn't help but take a last look at the sector map, thinking of all that vital terullian that he would be able to deliver to the Grand Strategic Council after today. His place in the Ranks of Heroes would be assured through decisive action, not skulking around the fringes of the sector waiting for some vague 'right moment'.

'Sir,' Skelp called up from the starboard blister, 'the commanders all report full readiness. All hyperdrives are functioning strongly, and the commanders await only your signal.'

Stentor's blood had been burning with anticipation for days. 'Transfer engine power from sublight thrusters to hyperdrive and stand by.' He moved away from the command seat, disdaining its promise of rest for his legs, and braced himself against the railing that surrounded the operations ring.

'Power transferred. Hyperdrive operational and ready.'

'Send to all commands: Today we make history, by taking the first step towards total annihilation of the Rutan. We will take no captives, and show no mercy.' He looked towards the helm station. 'Engage.'

The spitted triple-globe of the flagship started forward, then twisted out of realspace and leapt away in a flash. In a matter of milliseconds, the next ship had done likewise. Then another, and another, until the widest section of the cone vanished in a flurry of blazing engines.

'This is not going to work,' Nur told the Doctor with a quiet certainty. It was really the Rutan's plan that she was finding fault with, but she didn't have the nerve to tell it fact to . . . whatever. The Rutan whom the Doctor had christened Fred crackled slightly in the corner. She hoped it wasn't a sound of disapproval. She turned, and gave a sudden start, as she saw that there was now another Rutan with Fred.

As she watched, both Rutan pulsed and swelled, parts of their semi-visible organs breaking up and swirling around. She made a conscious effort to keep her last meal where it was as the two aliens split apart and gathered themselves into slightly smaller forms. Now, however, there were four of them.

'Who are those three?'

'We are Fred,' the three newcomers chorused sneeringly.

'We will ensure that you will lower the Sontaran

248

shields once on board,' the original – and largest – Rutan rasped. It had drawn itself into a stubby column not unlike one of those inflatable clowns that children sometimes had which were designed to be impossible to knock over. 'Your fears are groundless. The Sontaran cruiser's weaponry will not be able to target a vessel so close in as we will require to be. We, however, will kill at the slightest sign of treachery.'

'The transponder code should let us through their shields as well,' the Doctor reminded her.

' "Should" covers a multitude of sins. For example, this hyperdrive should work, but it wasn't designed for this class of ship, so it's just as likely to turn us into a spreading cloud of tachyons.'

'Just think positive.'

'I've been thinking nothing but nice thoughts about the damn piece of junk since we came on board.' With a grimace, she triggered the makeshift hyperdrive, and the ship leapt out of reality.

The greyness of unreality flowed around the observation blisters, and Stentor felt the excitement scurry through him. It was as if they were flying through a universe of smoke, ready to leap at the source and fan the flames.

'Prepare to engage sublight engines,' he announced after a glance at the countdown. Everyone hastily readied their systems for the power transfer, then looked back at Stentor, Skelp and Karne in the operations ring. Stentor felt a pride that was far more invigorating than an energy burn. 'I know you've all been rankled by the long wait for the call to action, but I don't see anyone tired among you. No; here are the warriors who will sweep across all the worlds of the Tzun sector like the unstoppable winds and rain of a storm front.' He lifted his battle standard, holding it high. 'We are riders on the storm, and lords of it. The Rutan are waiting for us. They expect a fight to the death. Let's not disappoint them.' He glanced at the countdown as a throaty murmur of appreciation wound its way through the bridge. 'Engage sublight engines. Divert hyperdrive power to shields and weapons systems.'

As the vibration of the deck plates changed pitch, the grey void outside dissipated as the stars peeked through the dark veil of realspace. A fingernail curve of reflected daylight glowed a few thousand miles ahead, while a baleful red star glimmered far beyond it. Stentor was proud; his warriors had calculated the jump precisely, and brought them almost to within touching distance of their target. Already, signals from the rest of the fleet were hooting and whistling as the other ships confirmed their arrival. 'Scan for energy concentrations on the planet below.'

'Scanning,' Karne reported. 'Heavy communications traffic originating on the southern ice field. No orbital traffic, bar a few fleet auxiliaries and supply vessels.'

'Target the southern communications source. Deploy picket ships to mop up the auxiliaries.'

'All commands acknowledging.'

A blaring chime sheared through the command deck. Stentor looked up irritably, annoyed at having his concentration disrupted by the noise. 'Switch that off –'

'Sir!' Skelp yelled in a shocked tone. 'Sensors report hyperspace egress, bearing two-four-four mark two-one-two!'

Momentarily confused, Stentor glanced at the main tactical display, gauging the number of green icons there. 'Impossible! The fleet is all here.'

'Sensors detect four new cruisers . . . six . . . eleven!' Red spots began swelling like blisters across the tactical display. 'Hyperspace egress, bearing one-six-five mark one-seven-seven. Six cruisers, numerous smaller ships.'

'Battle computer confirms new arrivals are Type 97 Rutan escort cruisers,' Karne reported in a tense voice.

Throughout the system, invisible to the naked eye, but detected by the sensors and overlaid on to the screens and viewports by the computer, the jewel-like and icy Rutan ships were dropping into realspace around the Sontaran vessels. Stentor slammed his battle standard into the deck with frustration. 'It's a trap!'

'The Doctor!'

The tip of Stentor's battle standard again crashed explosively into the decking, silencing the confused babble. He'd had enough surprises for one day. Now it was time to spring a few of his own. 'No more talk! We will adapt, improvise and overcome. Launch all fighters and gunships. Signal the fleet to give covering fire. Set course for that planetary base.'

A two-tone whistle rose and fell from the console. 'We're about to drop out of hyperspace,' Nur informed the others. She swept a hand across the new consoles, powering up the sublight engines preparatory to their return to realspace. 'Hang on to your breakfasts.'

The greyness dissipated, burnt away by searing streams of brightly radiating particles that probed out from a field of neutral iron-colour. Lights were flashing overhead as they streaked past the viewports set into the hull of a bulbous Sontaran cruiser literally only yards away. Energy streams poured out of a bulging weapons pod directly ahead to grapple with the jagged Rutan constructions. The first blasts stabbed around the crystalline ships, like the fingers of wrestlers seeking a firm grip on their opponent.

'Shit!' Nur threw the *Garuda* in a tight bank to the left, barely in time to avoid crashing into the weapons pod as they decelerated. A chorus of surprised yells rose from the hold as she kept an eye on the sensor displays, making sure that nothing else was close enough to detect the *Garuda*'s true nature by the naked eye.

The weapons pod crumpled as one of the *Garuda*'s Rutan fighter escorts ran straight through it, and a cloud of debris and rapidly freezing atmosphere dissipated in a blur. The other fighters spun away in formation to avoid the obstruction. 'This is the last time I let a vindictive jellyfish file my flight plan.'

Stentor consulted the main battle display in the central holotank, noting the positions of the Rutan ships carefully. The Rutan seemed to be forming a line defence across the orbital approach to their headquarters, with lighter ships trying to harry the Sontarans into the line of fire. But if they could smash straight through the centre of the formation, Stentor saw that there would be sufficient time for a barrage on the headquarters before the defenders could regroup. 'General Skelp; send to Colonels Lugg and Vord to run interference on a long orbit towards the headquarters. Have them draw off some of those Rutan corvettes.'

Karne looked up from an internal monitor. 'Gunnery officer requests permission to divert drive power to the main batteries.'

'Granted.' Stentor pressed the intercom for contact with gunnery control. 'Zone black, target that frigate at mark two-seven-one, and fire at will. Zone red, target assault carrier bearing three-three-two mark zero-zero-nine, and fire at will. All other firing zones target those picket corvettes, but hold fire for now.' Stentor didn't like surprises, but with the shock past he was quite enjoying himself. It wouldn't have felt like a real victory without some Rutan to kill anyway. Those on the planet hardly counted, as they couldn't shoot back, but the other ships would give him a good fight, he thought. Just like the old days, before he was forced into a desk job with the Grand Strategic Council. He'd show them that he could still cut it with the best of them.

The tone of the power humming throughout the ship changed distantly, as arrows of energy rained out from weapons ports set into the aftermost globe of the cruiser, peppering the two closest Rutan capital ships. The forward batteries remained dark and cold as the ship tilted to one side.

Stentor thought the damage he could make out on the converted asteroid – the Rutan frigate – off the port bow was satisfactory. It was already withdrawing slightly. 'New course, translunar.'

'Picket corvettes in range and locked into targeting computers,' Skelp called out.

'All firing zones fire at will.'

Throughout the ship, troopers who had been brought along for the anticipated ground assault joined the ship's blue-quilted crew in exchanging cooling pumps to the overheating guns, putting out electrical fires, and general damage control.

Streamers of lethally energetic radiation flashed out from all over the flagship's surface, melting away chunks of Rutan ships on every side until it was surrounded by a nimbus of decaying particles like some giant dandelion puffball in a storm.

Nur was delighted to be seated to fly her ship, since she felt that if she tried to stand, her bowels would simply drain away. She rolled the ship hard to port to get out of the path of a flock of torpedoes which were rushing past all around them, en route for the Sontaran flagship.

One of the escorting fighters flashed into vapour just behind them, as a salvo from a Sontaran gunship bracketed it. A Rutan fighter tracked the gunship with focused solar energy, pouring a steady stream of radiation into it. Nur doubted that these Rutan were any better than the other aliens, but she couldn't complain. After what the Sontarans had done to Sharma and his crew, they deserved some measure of repayment. The solar energy beam was a lance of pure heat and light, causing a patch of the hull several feet wide to melt and slough away in a liquid spray. The gunship crumpled and flew apart due to the resultant catastrophic hull breach.

A pair of torpedoes, locked on to some more distant target, hurtled past the canopy, and Nur let out an involuntary yelp of alarm. Not having so much as a second to regain her breath, she sideslipped to port, making a run for the spitted triple-globe of the Sontaran flagship. She wondered if her current terror was exactly the last thing her mother had felt before her shuttle crashed, and scarcely realized that she was already murmuring a somewhat vague prayer through gritted teeth.

The sensor cloak seemed to be holding so far, but the gunship attack had proven that they were still vulnerable to detection by the naked eye if anyone happened to be looking in the right direction.

The flagship ahead looked as if it was ready to fall and impale Antares VII at any second. More importantly, it was surrounded by a halo of energy discharges, both to and from the ship. This was too much, she decided finally. 'We're never going to manage a docking in the middle of that.'

'Typical humanoid fears,' Fred warbled scathingly. 'Death or victory are the only choices.'

'Yeah, well, if we get killed before we get aboard, you lot won't get that victory.' She heeled the ship over as she spoke. It was the last straw, really. No frothy green blob was going to talk to her like that! 'All right,' Nur said with a deep breath, 'is everybody all right? You've all still got all your fingers and toes or whatever?'

'As far as we can tell,' Turlough said, with a pointed glance at Fred.

'Good. Cross the lot of them.' Ignorant of Turlough's baffled expression, Nur banked the *Garuda* past a pair of Rutan fighters making a strafing run on a Sontaran destroyer, and spun into a fast orbit of the central sphere of the Sontaran flagship's hull. The occupants of the *Garuda* could see the pit-like depression in the hull that sloped down to the atmosphere-shielded docking bay. It rolled towards them as if they were dropping towards a planetary surface.

As the rim of the pit rolled towards them, a trio of gunships hurtled out and away from the bay, narrowly missing the incoming *Garuda*. 'Hold tight,' Nur yelled, diverting power to the retros. Swooping down not so much like a pouncing eagle as a chicken with ideas above its station, the *Garuda* dropped through the atmosphere shield and slammed on to the deck.

Sontarans were pouring from the interior doors even before the engines had been shut down, firing ineffectually at the ship with their sidearms.

Sharma tightened the last cinch on his kevlar body armour, and waved his men to the hatch. 'My department, I think.'

'Wrong.' Nur flipped open the plastic cover over a patch on the console, revealing another set of buttons. Stabbing at them viciously, she paled visibly, perhaps as much at what she was doing as at anything else. 'I salvaged a little something else from the palace.'

The Sontarans were baffled as to how the intruding ship had made it on board, but weren't interested in recriminations yet. All that mattered was to destroy it now that it was here. But rheon carbines seemed to be having little effect.

A cargo-loading hatch on the underside of the intruder's hull slid open, and a cargo pallet dropped out on pneumatic arms. Mounted on the pallet, however, were a pair of rotary cannons.

The cannons opened fire with the screaming roar of an enraged dragon, explosive-tipped shells gouging furrows of charred metal through the walls of the landing bay.

Sontarans leapt for cover as the cannons rotated in a steady circle, ripping their comrades apart in an ochre flurry.

Those troopers who were far enough along the bay rolled into the shelter of a last gunboat still mounted in its launch rack, their heads clouded with the painful screech of the guns which echoed through the bay.

* * *

Karne looked across at Skelp and Stentor blandly. 'Incoming!' A full spread of warheads were hurtling from the Rutan assault cruiser a few miles to starboard, homing directly on the flagship.

Skelp wondered how Karne could remain so calm – wasn't he excited? Stentor's reaction was immediate. 'Manoeuvring thrusters, zero-nine-zero! Transfer aft weapons power to reinforce forward shields.'

'Sir?' Skelp wondered if Stentor was falling prey to battle fatigue. Admittedly a fine death was preferable to a dishonourable life, but surely they should finish off the Rutan headquarters first before turning towards incoming fire?

The planet spun away to port as the flagship pointed itself directly at the Rutan cruiser and its incoming torpedoes. The torpedoes, tinted red for easy identification by the battle computer, swelled alarmingly. There was a blinding flash, and a tremendous shudder that hurled everyone to the deck. Skelp felt himself tugged away from the floor by an invisible hand.

It let him go, and he fell heavily to the deck once again. Most of the screens were flickering and hissing, with sparks crackling around shattered consoles. An emergency shutter had sealed off the entrance to the port-side observation bubble, which meant that there no longer *was* a port-side observation bubble. 'One impact only,' someone reported after a fit of coughing.

Stentor looked down at Skelp impassively. 'The point of a broadside is that it is broad. How do you think I came to reach this rank?' He looked around at the wrecked bridge. 'Gunnery control, all zones open fire on the vessel directly ahead. Arm photonic missiles and fire on my command.'

A monsoon-like shower of meson cannonfire swept out towards the translucent fairytale castle that was the Rutan cruiser. For a few instants, the energy blasts spread out harmlessly across the Rutan shields, but they couldn't hold up for long against such a barrage. A scattering of molten fragments were blasted from the side of the cruiser as the energy blasts drilled through it.

A photonic missile streaked from the Sontaran flagship as soon as the Rutan shields were down, and crashed through the brittle crystalline hull. A second later, the whole side of the hull sheared away, and the rest of the cruiser exploded in a fiery bloom of volatile Rutan atmosphere which had been ignited by the blast of the photonic missile.

Stentor not just smiled, but actually grinned as the milliard fragments of the Rutan cruiser dissipated. The battle was not going as expected, and he was now certain that they would all die here this day, but he could hardly deny that it was exhilarating.

Karne hurried forward, clutching a printout. 'We're sustaining heavy losses, but if we pull back to the system's Oort cloud, we can hold position long enough to –'

'Hold!?' Stentor bellowed, turning on him with a snarl. 'Defenders hold! Every Rutan ship which survives a clash with one of ours is just another Rutan for us to kill. We will win, or we will die. Even death is better than the cowardice of switching to a defensive position.' He controlled himself with visible effort, and looked back out at the planet. As far as he was concerned, there was no such word as impossible, which meant that victory was possible. Survival didn't matter, so the question of its possibility was irrelevant. The problem was how long they could hold out, and how they could cut down the time they needed to finish the job. 'Skelp, can we still tap into their computers?'

'We can interpret the entire Rutan comnet, until they change their codes.'

'Then perhaps we can take them with us; if it comes down to a race for reinforcements, our forces are closer.' He turned to face his command crew, knowing that his confidence would reassure them. 'If we can gain entry to their comnet and enter false signals, perhaps we can start the Rutan cruisers shooting at each other, or at least lower their shields. Have the Intelligence section see to it immediately.'

Skelp saluted in acknowledgement, but Stentor had already turned away, to coordinate an attempt to bring down the planetary shields with sheer fire power. Behind him, back in the operations ring, Major Karne paused in his work, and looked first to Stentor, then below towards Skelp in the observation blister.

Fred and his comrades allowed their skins to harden before rolling themselves down the *Garuda*'s ramp. Their speed was surprising, and the remaining Sontaran troopers had no luck in trying to kill them. The three Rutan lashed out at the gunboat's landing gear as they passed, and scintillating flashes of energy sparked across the metal hull. A couple of the sheltering Sontaran troopers immediately arched and twitched to the ground as their armour conducted the electrical charge from the hull and earthed it through their bodies.

'Come on,' the Doctor urged. 'They'll be too busy to bother with us right now, and we might not get another chance.'

'To do what?' Turlough asked hazily. He had never seen piloting quite like Nur's. It was the best he'd ever seen, all right, but his stomach was wishing that he'd seen it a little more distantly.

'Get away from Fred. The Rutan have always wanted time travel as well, and I'd rather not be the one to give it to them.' He led the trio out of the ship and across the landing bay, keeping low to avoid the crossfire of rheon-fire and electrical discharges that was crisscrossing the far side of the bay.

The doors opened as they approached, and three more Sontarans charged through. Sharma immediately gunned them down, and the travellers ducked through the doors. The Doctor immediately prised off the door control panel with a screwdriver from his pocket, and ripped out the workings. The doors slammed shut. 'It'll take Fred a while to burn through that. Now we need to find a plan of the ship.'

Sharma nodded. 'For the shield generators.'

'For the TARDIS.'

'Somehow,' Turlough told Sharma firmly, 'I doubt the Rutan will hold to their side of the bargain either. After all, we're the trustworthy ones, and look at what we think of it.'

The flagship's command deck rocked slightly as a distant blast slammed into the shields. Everyone ignored it, like the good soldiers Stentor knew they were. 'Sir,' Skelp called excitedly. 'We've found something.'

Stentor lumbered across to the blister, peering over Skelp's shoulder. 'Their targeting codes, I trust?'

'Better, sir. Look.' Skelp's voice was as close to awed as it was possible for a Sontaran to get. Karne looked across at them, wondering what was so distracting that it could entice a Sontaran away from running a battle. Or perhaps the word should be 'important', not 'distracting'. This business of tapping into the Rutan computer and communications network with stolen codes was getting more unnerving by the second. Surely this was supposed to be a combat assault? Shutting down his console, he joined the others at the Intelligence officer's console. A rushing torrent of flickering characters was cascading across the screen. Skelp and Stentor looked almost hypnotized.

Karne could make out the odd phrase here and there, and recognized the wording as following the form of the Rutan central database. If that had been penetrated, the Sontarans might even find that which they'd sought for centuries, he thought. 'Here, sir,' Skelp announced, halting the scrolling, and running one digit through the lines of text. 'We have to get this downloaded to the Grand Strategic Council.' Stentor grimaced, exposing ancient whalebone teeth.

'I'll take it in a fast ship,' Karne offered. 'Then the assault could continue.'

Stentor half-closed his eyes, and for a moment Karne thought he was about to agree. 'No, it's too important. Your offer shows courage, but this is too important to chance to a single small ship. Skelp, download this data into the mainframes of every ship in the fleet large enough to hold it.'

'Every ship? Even the gunships?'

'Even the gunships. The more ships have the data, the better chance that at least one of them will get away. And you must admit that the gunships are the most manoeuvrable, therefore the most likely to evade destruction. After that, transmit to all commands to regroup at two-seven-seven mark three-zero-zero and form a rearguard formation.' He looked back at Karne, his features a mask of bitter disappointment, as Skelp hit the transmission controls. 'I know you'd rather press the attack – so would I – but you'll have your chance. I'm even more disappointed by this turn of luck than you are, Major.'

Karne gripped Stentor's shoulder in a stylized comradely manner. 'I very much doubt that, Fleet Marshal.' Then he loosed five thousand volts into Stentor's armour.

Stentor arched, squealing like a punctured boiler, while Skelp and the Intelligence officer were blasted to either side by the discharge. Angered by the necessity of abandoning his cover, Karne released the slightly steaming Stentor, and thrust his fists into the console. The fists dissolved into squirming tentacles, relieving the constant strain of keeping them in shape, and poured in through the nearest sockets to disrupt the power flow. Karne drew off the power to replenish himself, while at the same time routing it back out in a charge that would blow the circuitry.

A trail of sparking explosions rushed around the bridge's consoles. A flash of heat spread throughout Karne's body as he pulled himself back from the shattered console. A trooper had opened fire on him with his side-arm, but the energy was easily absorbed. There was no time to waste here, he knew; damage to the bridge consoles wouldn't harm the data now fully integrated into the computer core. Not bothering to reshape the tentacle tips into fists again, Karne bolted for the heavy blast doors that separated the bridge from the rest of the ship. A few shots from the more alert guards scorched the closing doors as he leapt through them.

Skelp could feel the towering rage threaten to overwhelm him, but was grateful that at least it drowned out the pain from the secondary burns he'd received. Hitting the intercom switch in the operations ring hard enough to crack the fascia, he sent out an alert signal throughout the ship. 'Intruder alert. Major Karne is a Rutan altered to take Sontaran form, and clearly intends to sabotage the ship. Kill on sight!'

Twenty-One

Alarms thundered through the tubular corridors as the Doctor led his three companions into the launch control cabin overlooking the hangar. Below, they could see that the Sontarans were all lying in charred heaps, while Fred and his three comrades were blazing angrily at the doors with arcing discharges.

Nur looked over at the *Garuda* with a pang of regret. It was one of those strange empty moments, when you realize you're not going to see someone or something dear to you again. She turned back to the Doctor; the *Garuda* had been living on borrowed time anyway, after that Sontaran attack on the palace. It was fitting that it should return the favour.

The Doctor was looking over a plan of the ship on a monitor. 'There we are,' he said finally, pointing at a spot on the plan. 'Turlough, have you still got that TARDIS homing beacon I gave you when we first met?'

'I think so.' He hunted through his pockets, finally coming up with a small device which had a pulsing bulb set into some circuitry. 'Here it is.'

The beacon pulsed softly as the Doctor switched it on. 'Hmm, about eight hundred yards forward . . .' He looked back at the plan of the cruiser, stabbing at a point just forward of the first globe. 'Storage area beside the main lock.'

Sharma looked at the distance between their current location, and the place the Doctor had indicated. 'They're bound to be out looking for us by now. We'll never get through the crew.'

We might not have to. Remember I told you there was a way to deal with them all on Agni if necessary?'

'Except that it wasn't.'

'No. Well, it *is* here.' The Doctor started typing furiously at the control panel in the booth. 'You might have noticed the thick air aboard Sontaran ships – Sontar's heavier gravity makes for a denser atmosphere. If I can just repressurize the sections between here and that forward section to something similar to a mountaintop on Earth, we should still be able to breathe.'

'And the Sontarans?' Turlough asked.

The Doctor paused silently for a moment. 'Will either have to keep out of the way, or be asphyxiated. Fortunately they're as cautious as they're stubborn and brutal. They'll sacrifice themselves willingly, but only for a good reason.'

He – they – had been Karne for a long time. It had been almost 30 years since the staged attack on a Sontaran cruiser in which they had been deposited at the site in a Sontaran escape pod. It was strange to be allowed to think in proper terms again, instead of restrictive individualism. No matter; there would be time enough to resume a normal life later, if he survived. If we survive, he reminded himself – themselves – more forcefully.

The boots of busy troopers clattered across the deck above Karne, hurrying in all directions, depending on which particular alarm was sounding at the time. It was cooler and more comfortable down here in the inspection crawlways, but this was obviously the first place the Sontarans would look for them. They had allowed himself – damn – to dismiss the repulsive form they had taken for so long, so that they could think more clearly without the distraction that the pain of maintaining such an unnatural state caused.

They had been disappointed to discover that the Doctor was a Time Lord. They had hoped that the intruders on Agni were other Rutan, who would have the sense to allow themselves to be ejected into the void in order to return unobserved later to prevent Indra's detonation. A thousand curses on Loxx and his troops for never leaving him alone long enough to try anything themselves!

Still, the Time Lord was notorious for interfering in Sontaran plans, so Karne had been glad that their manoeuvres to ensure his interference in this one – leaving those data chips for him to find, for example – had been so clearly successful. Their own mission was now in doubt, however. True, they had discovered much about Sontaran plans over the last few years, but that was of no importance next to the data the Sontarans had downloaded here.

Karne had to try to stop the data here, and that meant finding a way to destroy the ship. They couldn't take anything for granted, so the Rutan High Command had to be warned of this development as well. But how to do it? The self-destruct system was voice-coded, and they couldn't precisely match the tones of Skelp or Stentor, even though he could take on their faces. Dropping the shields might not necessarily lead to destruction if the ship made a run for it. The torpedo stocks would be too well-guarded . . . The engines, Karne decided. If the safeties could be disabled and the main reactor core overloaded, they would have time to reach a gunship or escape pod and rejoin the main body of the Host. Or better still, they realized, the Time Lord's TARDIS.

They might have smiled at the prospect if he still had a mouth, but instead settled for a tinny electrical purr. All they needed was a form to adopt. Most of the activity on the deck above was the movement of several troopers together, but there had been the occasional one of his own.

A few moments' patience rewarded Karne with the approaching footfalls of a lone trooper in the blue armour of Engineering and Support Services. Karne let him pass over the deck grating unmolested, and then stretched himself upward, growing up through the gaps in the grating. Once through the grating behind the trooper, he lashed several tentacles around the unsuspecting Sontaran, and released just enough charge into him to be fatal.

Steeling themselves against the pain, Karne drew themselves in, forcing the skin to bulge and solidify into the form of the Sontaran's armour, while they forced two of their compound eyes outward and upward to where their skin was clouding towards the grey shade of a Brol clansman. The process was completed in a matter of seconds, and all that remained was to lift up the grate and deposit his unfortunate model into the crawlspace.

Then he set off in search of the source of the constant vibration of the deck.

'That should be long enough,' the Doctor muttered, as he stepped out of the hangar control booth. There were now several angry Freds below, and Turlough was beginning to worry that perhaps they'd devised a defence against the wrong pursuers.

The corridor outside was chilly and the air was thin, but just breathable. Turlough took deep and steady breaths, hoping to get as far as he could as quickly as possible. The Doctor seemed to be experiencing no difficulties whatsoever, while Nur and Sharma looked a little out of puff.

Yellow warning lamps were flashing at every crossroads, while the doors to either side were sealed. Turlough wasn't reassured, though. There were bound to be backups and overrides that would enable the Sontarans to repressurize the passageway and come after them. If they could just hold on for another few minutes, though . . .

'Depressurization alert in the hub corridor,' someone told Skelp.

He was momentarily nonplussed; how was he supposed to take over full command in the middle of a losing battle, with half the command crew dead? 'Are we holed?'

'Negative. The environmental controls have been overridden.'

It must be Karne, Skelp thought. Rutan didn't need to breathe, and depressurizing would trigger the bulkhead doors, to keep pursuers out of the section. That would leave him free to do whatever he wanted. 'Repressurize, and get as many troops in there as you can. Karne must be going after the Time Lord's TARDIS.' It was the only logical target, and keeping time travel out of Sontaran hands would be an important consideration for a Rutan.

Karne stood on the balcony that encircled the midsection of the reactor core. It was a large translucent sphere the size of a small scout ship, with dozens of tubes and pipes festooning the crackling surface.

Several other blue-armoured Sontarans bustled around the metal catwalk, making constant adjustments to the core's controls as its power requirements altered with every passing moment. They would have to be dealt with first, Karne knew – but how?

Many of the cables that formed a canopy between wall and reactor were live, Karne sensed, the tingling of inducted energy stimulating him. If they could reach one . . . It was a risk worth taking. Allowing themselves to revert to a more fluid form, Karne reached upward for the cables, wrapping a whip-like tentacle around one.

A chorus of angry roars from the Sontaran engineers was quickly silenced, as Karne channelled the energy from the cable down and into the catwalk floor. Every blue-armoured figure jerked and twitched, acrid steam rising from their leathery flesh as the energy consumed them.

Karne let go of the cable, and looked for the coolant pumps. If he could shut them down, the reactor would quickly overheat and go critical.

Sharma had found that his breathing got easier as they went on. He hoped this was due to his getting used to the thinner air, rather than the atmosphere being repressur-ized. He took his gun off its safety setting just in case. 'Have we much further to go?'

'Not far,' the Doctor said after consulting the homer. 'Just along here and to the left at the next junction.'

'Right, I –' A shower of searing energy blasts poured through the bulkhead doors as soon as they began to open behind the four humanoids. Everyone flung themselves behind bulky pump covers and lockers as a small knot of Sontaran troopers leapt through.

Sharma opened fire, and they toppled like skittles as the rheon charges seared through them. 'Run, I'll cover you!' Another door was already opening as the other three dashed up the corridor. Sharma started firing through it, then followed the others up the corridor, pausing only to recover another rheon carbine.

Karne strained with all their might, and finally succeeded in tearing free the last of the reactor core's cooling pumps. It would have meant certain death to any other species, but the radioactive energy that flooded through Karne's cells merely invigorated them.

The coolant pumps could still be replaced, of course, but Karne had a solution to that. Gathering all the extra strength the energy had given them, they discharged it into the sockets and mounting set into the outer wall of the reactor itself. The fittings blurred and melted under the blue-white heat of the electrical discharge.

Their work done, Karne hurried from the reactor room. The TARDIS was probably too far to reach right now, so the hangar bay would have to suffice. The data the Sontarans had recovered took precedence over everything.

The others had run on as ordered, and Sharma had held off the pursuit so far, but he had no intention of staying behind to die. He just needed to give the Doctor and Nur enough time to get safely to the Doctor's ship. More troopers appeared at the far end of the corridor, and Sharma fired before they got the chance to do likewise.

A couple went down, but the others took cover. Sharma cursed; they had too good a field of fire for him to risk running.

Fred had been irritated that they had been betrayed, and the energy that surged through their superconducting nerves crackled dangerously. Fred had ignored the depressurization alert, as a mere lack of air meant nothing to them.

They were tired from the effort of burning through the hangar door, but ignored the weariness; the Time Lord had a debt to pay first. The four heat traces of the Time Lord followed this corridor, so Fred made their way along in pursuit.

The corridor was littered with dead Sontaran, and Fred felt cheated. The sound of gunfire came from somewhere ahead, and Fred hurried on, gathering their body up and gelling their tentacles into legs so as to move faster.

Their hopes rose as a group of grey heat traces became visible ahead. One was recognizably part of the Time Lord, and the others were Sontaran. Gathering their strength, Fred lunged forward, lashing out with their crackling cilia.

The Sontarans scattered as Fred and his cronies began discharging sparks into them.

Realizing that he might not get another chance, Sharma leapt through the door into the next section, and hit the emergency button to slam the door shut. Now he just had to follow the Doctor and the others. His confidence was premature, however, as the depressurization alert lights above the doors in this section winked off one by one.

As he feared, the repressurization had overtaken his own progress, and there were now Sontaran troops ahead of him. They'd had their way for too long, he decided, and he wasn't going to let them stop Nur getting to safety. If she didn't make it, he thought, he'd probably be better off staying here than going back to face her father.

What was going to be needed here was speed, he saw. The Sontarans were somewhat restricted by their armour, so if he dodged around fast enough, he might be lucky enough to deal with them in time ... Sharma strode forward, barely twisting himself aside to avoid the shots as they flashed past with screams of disrupted air, firing from both guns.

All around, Sontaran troopers, some armed, most not, jerked and twisted before falling lifelessly as he passed them. Sharma barely even registered the presence of returned fire as he stalked down the main companionway. His mind was completely focused on trying to balance the need to get rid of the enemy while at the same time avoiding getting killed. All he registered were the forcible attempts to change his duty for him. Everyone knew that it was impossible to change what one was meant to be, and the attempts of these aliens to change what he was had proved that.

Even as he tossed a grenade into an opening turbolift, and blasted the door controls so that they trapped the arriving Sontarans inside with the coronic acid, he saw not dying aliens, but the blank features of his crew, blindly accepting deaths that were not fated for them.

Every radiant shot that flashed through the air to make the dying Sontarans jackknife before him. Aside was the arrow fired from Kartikeya's bow. He tried to get a grip on himself; that sort of egotism could lead to mistakes. He reached the airlock storage bay at last, and froze in horror.

The strange blue box which the Doctor had insisted was his TARDIS was still there. There were dozens of troopers both on the wide floor ahead and on several catwalks above.

Skelp clung on to the railing of the operations ring as the

cruiser shook under several impacts. 'Shut down life support to all non-essential areas, and divert the energy to shields.' The troopers in those areas would die, but that couldn't be helped. This was war, after all.

An alarm blared before the engineering officer could reply. 'Intruder alert,' someone called over the intercom. 'The Rutan have boarded. Repeat, the Rutan have boarded.'

A second screech had joined the first, and the engineering officer glared at his console in horror. 'Reactor chamber temperature is now 112 per cent of tolerance limits. Four minutes to meltdown and reactor core breach!'

There was no point in abandoning ship, Skelp knew. The Rutan would pick them all off anyway. 'Send to all commands; disengage and leave the area. The data dump must be returned to the Grand Strategic Council at all costs.' This wasn't an option for himself, of course. The ship would never make it into hyperspace with an imminent core breach. Still, he could at least take the Rutan with him. 'Helm – all power to forward shields. Set course for the centre of the lagoon field, and sound collision!'

Karne staggered slightly as the ship rocked. The core breach couldn't be far off now, and they had already reached the blast doors to the main hangar. They were surprised to see that the doors had been melted through with the familiar sharp edges of concentrated Rutan energy discharges. Evidently there were more of them on board.

Excited, Karne tried to make contact with them, but their mind remained silent. Perhaps the lack of the conductive elements found in the Rutan atmosphere was preventing contact, he thought. He thought . . . Perhaps Karne had been separated from the Host so long that their mind was not the same any more. The thought was like a blow, and Karne wanted to melt away into a pool and forget the world.

No, they thought aloud. It is the lack of Rutan atmosphere; that is simple fact. Nothing else matters, not even personal distress.

This was nothing, however, compared to his surprise on seeing the small light freighter which had caused Loxx's troops such trouble on Agni. Obviously the Doctor had indeed interfered as Karne had hoped.

They tried again to listen for the thoughts of the other Rutan, but with no luck. Perhaps he had been alone too long, after all. Karne crackled slightly with irritation, and moved off.

If Sharma had to die because of these aliens, then at least he would retain the freedom to pick his own individual method of turning the wheel of life. Personally, though, he'd rather kill them than the other way around. Lifting the gun in his left hand, he swept it upward, its constant fire tearing along the catwalk and sweeping the Sontarans from it, while the gun in his right hand swung back and forth across the advancing ranks as he made a run for the TARDIS.

There were far too many for him to overcome by such direct means, but there were other ways to fight, especially when the battleground was in a launch bay protected from space only by an atmosphere shield. A glass-walled booth to his right held the launch controls, and Sharma dived for it, rolling up to hammer the sole occupant with repeated blasts.

Sparks and sprays of superheated metal and glass fanned out through the air. A stray shot from high to the left blew a cloud of steaming blood from the left side of his abdomen, while his cessation of fire gave the Sontarans an opportunity to rush forward, guns blazing. Another shot lanced through his right shoulder, with a crisp scent of roasted flesh that was almost as nauseating as the white-hot pain itself.

The shooting stopped abruptly, and the echoing silence was marred only by the harsh tramp of metallic running and the clatter of the gun falling to the deck from his right hand. They probably thought they'd won, he realized, but he still had a few shots left, and Nur, the Doctor and Turlough would be safe in the Doctor's ship by now. He just had to join them there.

He tried to take a deep breath, but found that he couldn't, and settled for slumping against the wall of the TARDIS with the left-hand gun resting on his knee. The small breaths he could manage tasted sickeningly coppery for some reason, but he ignored it. There should be pain as well as weakness, he thought vaguely, and knew that the absence of it was a bad sign, though he couldn't quite recall why.

He'd heard that when someone died, their life passed before their eyes, but all he could see was the airlock door control panel, somewhere at the centre of a fuzzy darkness. Probably just as well, he thought. It was hard enough to concentrate as it was, and he knew he had to concentrate if he was going to get out of here in one – Too late for that, he thought wryly; just to get out of here at all, then.

A pair of blank masks loomed forward at the edge of the fuzziness, their black eyeholes giving no hint of any life within. What kept you? he tried to say, but no air passed his lips. He tried to push away from the wall, and wondered if his finger was firing the gun as his brain had instructed it to.

Was the brightness the memory of the first sight after birth? Or –

Those Sontarans close enough to the walls grabbed frantically for handholds even as the first of their comrades spun wildly off into the void. Heavy bulkhead doors came together with leaden finality as the remaining Sontarans hammered ever more weakly upon them.

The lamp atop the TARDIS flashed balefully, and the ship faded away silently in the vacuum.

* * *

'I thought I told you to get some practice with that thing.'

Sharma's eyes adjusted to the glare, and he saw that it was coming from some sort of hexagonal light source on the ceiling of a wide, white room. A gentle melodic humming seemed to permeate his body, making it ache some more. Nur was looking down at him with a sad and worn expression. Clearly this was no rebirth so . . . 'What is this place?'

'The Doctor's ship, the TARDIS.'

'Then, we won?'

'We survived,' Turlough corrected him. 'There's no such thing as winning.'

Karne allowed themselves to discorporate with a profound sense of relief, slipping gelatinous tentacles into the burnt-out section of the flight console. The damage didn't bother him particularly; in fact it would make the unfamiliar controls easier to handle since they could guide the currents through themselves to the mechanisms they wanted to use.

Drawing off power from the thoroughly unnecessary life-support system, they routed the current through his tingling body, saving some for themselves before discharging the rest into the flight-control system. The *Garuda* lifted from the buckling deck just as a cluster of helmeted troopers blew open the door to the landing bay.

Karne purred happily with static charge, and kept a couple of eyes on the engine power buildup. A furious rain of shots thudded into the rear of the hull, but Karne ignored it; they'd lived with Sontaran equipment long enough to know that the side-arms weren't powerful enough to do serious damage to the ship.

A satisfied glow spread through them as the engine-ready signal came back through the system. It was time to show the troopers what real power was. They triggered the engine start.

* * *

The threatening glow from the stern of the *Garuda* suddenly flared into full life, slamming back towards the rear wall with a heat beyond mere brightness or intensity.

The triangular ship shot from the hangar bay like a cannonball, leaving behind only melted fixtures and a number of scorched shadows that steamed on the rear wall.

The Linx-class cruiser was already listing and covered in a rash of flares from atmospheric friction as Karne poured everything the ship had into gaining more speed. Distance would be the prime factor when the reactor core blew. Once they were safe, they could make sure whether or not any Sontaran ships made the jump to hyperspace. If even one got away, the most sensitive files could become common knowledge . . .

Behind the speeding *Garuda*, the cruiser shook, the central globe starting to collapse while still in the upper atmosphere of Antares VII. A flash of light briefly split the forward globe and pointed nose from the central globe, and the forward section began to twist away from the rest of the ship. Then the rearmost globe vanished in a blaze of dissipating burning gas, which consumed the rest of the cruiser in an instant and sent a wall of minuscule particles of wreckage hurtling into space ahead of the first wave of radiation.

The blast also travelled downward through the atmosphere, the ice field flashing into steam as the remaining sections of the flagship vaporized on impact.

The *Garuda* snapped forward abruptly, and Karne briefly had to tighten themselves to avoid being wrapped around the console. Something small and glowing – a piece of shrapnel from the cruiser, Karne supposed – burst through the cabin and out through the canopy. He immediately felt a tugging sensation as the air tried to drag them out through the new puncture with it. They forced himself to coagulate somewhat in response. Since they had no lungs, a lack of air wasn't going to pose much of a problem, and they could always hibernate until they reached orbit. Before they could lay in the course, however, an alarm squealed briefly in the last remaining air from somewhere behind them, and the engines roared with a rising howl. Karne tried to work out where the power was moving through the system, and realized that everything felt as if it were rushing into the hyperdrive.

Another piece of shrapnel must have become lodged in the hyperdrive, they realized, short-circuiting it and starting an energy buildup for one last jump using every erg on the ship – and with the planet's warp limit at that. If he couldn't shut it down, there was no telling what might happen. They tried to alter the charge in each tentacle, to route the power away from the drive, but to no avail. In fact, they couldn't even feel the change in polarity. With a shock of – could this be what humans called fear? – Karne realized that the short-circuit wasn't just taking power from other ship's systems, but from them as well. Hastily, they tried to withdraw their tentacles from the connections in the console.

Nothing happened. Their outer skin was already solid and glassy from exposure to vacuum. They tried to force himself to move, unwilling to succumb until he saw every Sontaran ship destroyed, but had no idea whether they were succeeding. All they could feel was a falling sensation.

Could one or more of them have already gone? They hoped not. If only Karne could tell –

Everything went grey.

The *Garuda*'s engines flared more brightly than ever before, and when the glare died, the ship had flickered into infinity.

The Doctor and Turlough finished tying off a bandage around Sharma's shoulder. Nur stood in front of the scanner, watching with horrified fascination.

She wondered what the point was, as a Rutan battle-cruiser flared brightly as it streaked across the surface of one of the system's planets. Its run ended abruptly, with a flash that scored a layer of the crust away from the surface, leaving lava to ooze out over hundreds of square miles. 'Does anyone live there?'

'Not likely,' Turlough said dryly.

'Not yet, anyway,' the Doctor said. 'There was no life here, but there could have been, given time.'

Sontaran cruisers spun slowly before erupting into huge fireballs that turned a world's polar caps to steam, while the black field of space was peppered everywhere with sparks and dying flashes. 'What now?'

'Now,' the Doctor said, turning the scanner off, 'I imagine we'd better get you home.' He turned back to the console, and started manipulating the controls.

'I meant, will they come back to Raghi?'

'No, they're both cautious, you see. Each will think that the other has too strong an advantage in this region. They will be back eventually, and the Sontarans will get their terullian, but not until around the time of the Solar flares. About thirteen thousand years in the future.'

The last Rutan assault carrier – a carved and filigreed asteroid wrapped in a glass cocoon – held off a swarm of Sontaran gunships as its daggers of solar radiation stabbed repeatedly at a bulbous Sontaran destroyer.

The destroyer's hull began to collapse in places. The Rutan concentrated their fire on these spots, and burnt a hole clean through the destroyer. The destroyer exploded, a wall of particles expanding outward to the Rutan.

The shock wave shook the Rutan ship, and shattered its outer crystalline hull. Taking advantage of the opportunity thus offered, the Sontaran gunships descended upon the weakened assault carrier like carrion birds, wheeling around in tight turns to deliver rapid and repeated blasts to the Rutan superstructure.

Since it was already weakened, the Rutan ship couldn't hold out for long, and finally ripped itself apart under the strain of bombardment.

Weaving their way through the continually spreading cloud of debris from the battle, the gunships swept away above the plane of the ecliptic, and vanished into hyper-space in search of the nearest Sontaran base.

Raghi nestled like a glimmering jewel against the ethereal veil of Indra's distant rings. The brighter patch of clouds on the face of Indra was clearly visible from Raghi's surface, giving the diaphanous curve the appearance of a huge eye peering over the horizon.

Ambika stood on the warm and smooth steps of the preceptor's palace's northern ghat, and watched the boat that would shortly pull up at the bottom of the steps for him. The ascetic life didn't hold much attraction for him, but then he was supposed to be unegoistic. Perhaps his karma had become somewhat tarnished after all, despite his determination only to do things that were for the good of all.

He'd always thought that only selfishness led to cor-ruption, but it seemed otherwise. Detachment had its advantages as well, as he now found. He heard some delicate footfalls behind him, and turned to see who had come to see him off.

Nur stopped a few feet away, while Sharma waited above, on the plaza between the steps of the ghat and the warm, baked tones of the palace wall. Ambika nodded, as much to hide the tears in his eyes as to acknowledge her presence. 'It seems that you are now the head of the household.'

'A household of one isn't much of a household to be head of. You don't really want to do this, surely?'

'What I want doesn't matter. Perhaps as a renouncer I will be of better use.' He shrugged. 'Or perhaps not. I don't suppose it matters. After what I've done to the people, it's only fair that I choose to depend on their

277

mercy. They used to say on Earth that "By teaching, so we learn." Perhaps the reverse is true as well.' He thought for a moment. 'Who did the central computer pick as my replacement?'

'It hasn't yet.'

'What about you? What are you going to do?'

Nur looked back at Sharma, and smiled faintly. 'I need a regular copilot.'

The Doctor and Turlough watched from the delicate swan-neck of the marble bridge between the city and the palace as Ambika stepped into his boat. Turlough couldn't believe what he was seeing. 'He's going to *what*?'

The Doctor unlocked the door of the TARDIS, which had materialized on the bridge. 'He'll become a traveller, depending on what handouts he gets. As a renouncer he'll be a sort of mirror of what he was before.'

'I could think of better descriptions.' There were always jobs around for leaders, if he'd only look. 'You sound as if you approve.'

'Of his leaving his people to become a wanderer on the edge of life? Who am I to cast stones?' They stepped back into the TARDIS and, after a few moments, it paled into incorporeality. The TARDIS slipped away altogether, its pachydermic bellows sending clouds of kalkalachi into the blue skies that veiled Indra and the distant stars.

Off in the depths of space, lit only by coldly distant stars, a tiny triangular chunk of metal, perhaps the size of a medium transport aircraft, sailed gently across the galaxy's barely perceptible gravitational tides.

Its hull was frosted with the last breaths of a long-vanished air supply, and pitted with the melted craters of some sort of heated impacts. The twin exhaust ports at the stern were dark and cold, and no running lights broke up the field of reflected starlight. Above the pointed prow, a dark canopy was cracked, but no instrumentation gleamed within.

Instead, frost rimed the steps down into the empty cargo bay, sealing in the darkness that cloaked the walls. There was a tiny flicker from the flight deck, nonetheless – a dull and dim luminescence not unlike the glow of certain rotting fungi.

It glimmered on the edge of visibility, at the heart of a mound of what seemed to be sculpted glass, immobile and unaware. The flicker at its heart, dulled further by strange clusters of darkness within, was not regular. Nor was it irregular enough to be called truly random. Rather it was slight yet rapid, reminiscent of the movements showing through a human eyelid while dreaming.

Everyone dreams, but every dream is eventually shattered by waking.

But that is another story . . .

Well, not exactly mind-expanding, but at least this has been more upbeat and fun than *Sanctuary*, and a change is as good as a rest, and I prefer the change! I shall go now, but with any luck I'll pop up again. Before I go, however, I'd better not forget this bit, which Rebecca has asked for – and who am I to refuse a lady's request?

Glossary

Agni: Hindu god of fire.

Agneya: Legendary weapon of the Mahabharata, which some hacks with a fondness for Von Daniken like to equate with nuclear missiles.

Airavata: Celestial four-tusked albino elephant on which the god Indra rode.

Arthashastra: Sanskrit book of the fourth century BC. It was later adapted as a mandala for political gaming to show that neighbours are natural enemies, while the neighbours' neighbours are friends by virtue of being the neighbours' enemies.

Atcha: OK.

Brahmin: The most spiritual of what most people recognize as the four main Hindu castes, though in fact subgroupings mean there are really many more than four.

Brol: Sontaran clan from temperate regions of Sontar (originally), with deep-set eyes and grey skin.

Garuda: Giant eagle of legend on which the god Vishnu rode.

Ghat: Terraced array of steps on a waterfront.

Goban-class gunship: Single-seat Sontaran heavy assault craft. As with all Sontaran ship classes here, the type is named after an old Sontaran war hero.

Gunar: Sontaran clan from desert regions of Sontar, with mottled ochre and olive skin.

Indra: God of thunder and rain.

Jingo: Sontaran clan from the arctic regions of Sontar, with brownish skin.

Johar: Suicide by fire, which used to be practised by women seeking to avoid being raped by conquerors.

Kartikeya: God of war.

Kshatriya: Warrior caste.

Koda: Elite military security branch of the Sontaran military, their SS, as it were.

Linx-class cruiser: Heavily armed Sontaran capital ship carrying troop transports, gunships and fighters.

Meson cannons: Standard Sontaran ship-mounted weapons, essentially like an open-ended particle accelerator using mesons.

Namaste: A respectful greeting along the lines of 'Good morning'.

Nandi: Giant bull ridden by the god Shiva.

Nimbu pani: Lime juice and soda.

Niwas: House, with a capital H.

Rheon carbines: Sontaran side arm of choice, firing pockets of charged particles.

Rudra: God of disease, but also of healing.

Rutan: The plural of Rutan (see below).

Rutan: The singular of Rutan (see above).

Sabha: Council formed of the leaders of a local social group.

Shikara: A gondola-type boat, or beehive-shaped tower.

Strag-class frigate: Midsized line Sontaran warship carrying gunships and fighters.

Sudra: Menial caste.

Vaisya: Mercantile caste.

Valt-class destroyer: Smaller and faster line warship carrying fighters.

Vimana: In modern times the central shrine of a Hindu temple, but in legend a flying vessel beloved of Von Daniken-ites, hence the usage here.